REVENGE

VOLUME 11

I0706111

THE CASTLE OF HORROR ANTHOLOGY

CASTLE BRIDGE MEDIA
DENVER, COLORADO, USA

CASTLE BRIDGE MEDIA
Denver, Colorado
Edited by Jason Henderson and In Churl Yo
Designed by In Churl Yo
Cover Photos by Alexander Krivitskiy/Unsplash,
Josep Martins/Unsplash

This book is a work of fiction. Names, characters, business, events,
and incidents are the products of the authors' imaginations.
Any resemblance to actual persons, living or dead (or undead),
or actual events is purely coincidental.

"First Impression" first appeared in *Clothes Make the Man
and Other Crimes: Four Short Crime Stories*
by Scott Pearson, Stuck in the Middle Press, 2016.

ISBN: 979-8-9895934-6-0

TABLE OF CONTENTS

INTRODUCTION

HISTORY HAS SHOWN THERE IS nothing as primal or instinctual as the need for revenge. When we are harmed, we long to harm the harmers back. Whether the act is instantaneous in the heat of the moment or occurs many years later after much cooling off is beside the point. The satisfaction derived from the act of revenge is the same. Delicious. Filling. With all due respect to Klingon proverbs, revenge as a dish can be served either hot or cold.

As a theme, revenge has long been plumbed as a narrative device for just this reason. It allows us as storytellers the ability to explore the complexities of human emotion and relationships, the gray edges of morality, and the often times double-edged sword of what we perceive to be justice. We are flawed people. Our characters are flawed. And so, their actions and motivations are suspect, even within the context of vengeance. Especially so. The darkness within our frail human psyches feeds into our stories of betrayal, lust, and retribution. That's manna for authors. That's the stuff of intrigue and titillation, and it makes for great writing.

Shakespeare knew this. Homer did as well. So did Dumas. Revenge is a powerful drug, and like any drug, it can destroy the lives of users and the innocents around them alike, of both protagonists and antagonists alike.

You don't have to be Hamlet or Odysseus or Edmond Dantes to know that the path of vengeance is more often than not lined with tragedy, chaos, and destruction. That's the compelling nature of revenge stories. The idea that good people are forced to do bad things, paying a high moral cost for their obsessive pursuits in the name of justice and revenge, is a basic tenet here, as is the notion that violence begets violence. This circular nature of vengeance provides the perfect backdrop to explore not only themes of morality and duality, but of redemption and catharsis, and compassion and empathy as well.

We here in the Castle of Horror have assembled a mighty team of literary avengers to offer you their own dark tales of retaliation and retribution for your reading pleasure.

Enter the world of a female ghostly pirate's life in *Die Ravanche* by Leanna Renee Hieber. Claire Low's *I Hope the Night is Quiet* is a deeply unsettling tale of disappearances in a town that revolves around pork. *I'll Never Understand Ghosts* by Dotti Enderle is a Christmas tale of gifts and hauntings. Jeremiah Dylan Cook's *The Monster in the Mine* asks where the edges of trust lie when it comes to hauntings. *Hard Sell* by Will McDermott shows us a curiously demonic curio shop. A woman's revenge takes on a cyberspace edge in *Unauthorized Access* by Sara Martinez. Scott Pearson's *First Impression* explores the world of a dangerous assassin and a woman who joins him one night. Rob Nisbet gives us a pitch-perfect pastiche of HG Wells in *Return of the Invisible Man*. Serena Jayne shows us a conniving world of VR vacations in *Future Perfect*. A group of women plot their escape from the machinations of a wealthy narcissist in *To Die Like a Pharaoh* by Katya de Becerra. Carmen Gray's *The Suicide Tree* looks at the plight of an immigrant worker and a talented woman who comes to her aid. Michael Joseph Tharnish Roby gives us a grisly faerie tale of multiple revenges in *Small Retributions*. Charles R. Rutledge returns to the world of his immortal hero Kharm in *The Terrors of the Grave*. *Severed Cape* by Melanie Schubert gives us a dark variant on Wonder Woman. Heath W. Shelby's *The Clowning* goes whole-hog into small-town-American circus horror. Bryan Young contemplates the morality of taking the law into one's own hands in *Justified*. Alethea Kontis brings us a tale of a brilliant woman getting even at her high school reunion in *Pocket Full of Posey*. And *Another Day* by Liz Holliday brings the Groundhog Day effect to a harrowing moment in a woman's life.

Jason and I are once again humbled by the writing collected within this volume and the amazing authors who have graced us with their talent, all of them unique voices from the genre's top writers. As always, thank you for supporting independent publishing, and please consider checking out the other volumes available from the *Castle of Horror Anthology* series for even more horrifying, spooky stories that may inspire you to go out and settle a few scores of your own.

And remember, payback's a bitch! You have been warned.

—In Churl Yo, publisher, Castle Bridge Media

DIE RAVANCHE

By Leanna Renee Hieber

SHE CARRIED THE SOULS OF the dead, and she would come for those who had wronged them.

At least that's what Greta had always been told. So, with that sweet promise in mind, the young woman had cried out for *Die Ravanche* with her dying breath.

Now, Greta's spirit waited for her ship to come in. It was just a matter of the right weather.

Tonight, the conditions were *perfect*. What would grow to a blinding white fog began accumulating, spreading its blanket thickly over dense forests and unforgiving layers of craggy rock; shredded fingernails of land reaching out towards the unknown.

"*The Revenge* is coming!" whispered nervous townsfolk. As misty tendrils crept close, women lifted their skirts, scurrying back from the shoreline like rats clearing rising water. As residents retreated to higher ground in panic, Greta wafted towards the incoming haze.

It was all the tricks of sound that made this part of the northeast coast particularly uncanny. Murmurs were uttered far from Greta's ear and yet they carried as if they were right upon her. The eerie acoustics along these fangs of rock meant that every sound was a ghost; a disembodied voice in the immediate while no silhouette was visible.

As the fog thickened, those whispers grew into cries.

It was no wonder people thought this coast was haunted; the sounds bouncing off ragged environs to land against the ear; fully disorienting the living and calling forth the dead.

Floating at the end of a wooden pier along a jagged patch of northern coastline that really ought not to have had a pier at all, Greta waited for the foretold. Her phantom pulse pounded in the memory of a heartbeat, out of a fond habit of rhythm. In her corporeal days, her heart used to race like the thunder of a thoroughbred's hooves. A passionate creature on her best days, a fury on her worst, she was insatiable always. If there was a mandate for her soul to pass on somewhere sweet or someplace acherontic, no one had led her onwards to any such eternal notion. All she knew now was that she waited. And ravened.

Nothing but fog in any direction. If the living were to take one step too far forward, they'd find themselves cast into a watery depth impossible to gauge, or one step back could cast them off a precipice to dash against sharp rocks.

This was the kind of weather where it was only safe to be still.

That's when the ghost ship docked.

A long black prow split through white, gauzy vapor.

Gasps surrounded Greta. The tricks of sound along these gashes of land meant she heard those who had gathered by the paltry whitewashed lighthouse and its clapboard cottage right at her ear. They all drew in their breath.

Everyone seemed eager to see a haunting until they actually did. Then they'd find reasons why they didn't see what they saw, the way the cruel excused their actions within a victim's flaws. Greta had appeared to her killer before, refusing to be forgotten. He had dismissed her floating form as a mere nightmare. Perhaps he'd think twice about that tonight.

When the onyx prow pierced the fog like a lance, Greta found herself gasping too. The schooner drifted silently into view and the lovingly painted letters noting *Die Ravanche* made their way across Greta's vision; the German word for revenge passed mere inches from her face as she hovered at the edge of the pier in anticipation.

Die Ravanche's figurehead had once been a beautiful siren of a woman, but half of her was shorn off. Still, even below the top wooden layer, an artisan had taken the time to craft her bones and viscera. Her masthead mortality now laid bare, half torn, with a ribcage held just as proudly upright as her bosom, a grinning skull on the other side of her lovely face.

The ship's grey sails were trimmed and slightly transparent. Her black hull, directly below her name, bore a wide gash. But it too shifted between solid and shade, as if the entire ship were a trick of the light and a sound that shouldn't have carried.

With a grunt and a splash, an unfurling metal chain clattered down towards the water, carrying half the volume of what once would have roared.

"The Revenge has dropped anchor!" came a terrified whisper beside her. Greta turned and saw no one. The living villagers, huddled around the lighthouse's base, must have heard the echoes of the ship's routine, their horrified exclamations sounding as though they were the ghost right in front of her.

"Ah, so we're picking up today, not just dropping off?" boomed the tall, greyscale woman in boots, breeches, a brocade waistcoat, and a voluminous greatcoat. Long dark hair cascaded out from beneath an embroidered kerchief, waves of locks gathered into a loose braid over her shoulder, the tail of which was knotted around a shard of sharpened bone. She was luminous and floating, much like Greta, but her boldness gave her an opacity the other spirits on board lacked.

There were many souls aboard. Passengers had come to crowd the deck; a range of charcoal-colored bodies in an assortment of dress. Their silvery faces stared down at Greta impassively. None of them bore the signs of various violences done to them; just as Greta wore the simple linen dress she'd died in, her wounds long ago wicked off of her spectral form. Her memories, however, remained fresh.

"Yes... yes ma'am," Greta answered. "Permission to come aboard... Captain?"

"Captain Lorelei Albtraum at your service." The captain reached out and grabbed Greta by the forearm, pulling her up and over the rail and onto the deck before releasing her.

"Albtraum... *nightmare*?" Greta quietly posited the translation. The name *Lorelei* went without saying; Greta's grandmother was from the Rhineland and told stories of the siren along that great river, luring sailors and ships to their destruction beneath a castle outpost. As told by her family, the story was a metaphor for women's inherent wickedness. Greta had always admired the creature.

The captain only grinned, black eyes glinting in delight. Greta took that as proudly affirming tortured dreams. "You are welcome aboard, Miss..."

"Greta Knott." She rubbed her arm at the forceful pull, relishing the feeling. It was the first time she'd been touched since she was pushed to her death. The captain's grip was a welcome contrast.

"Welcome to *Die Ravanche*, Greta. May your peace begin here."

If the townsfolk saw or heard any of this exchange, they didn't clamor about it. Perhaps this was business reserved only for the dead.

"How long have you been our avenging angel?" Greta asked.

The captain laughed– a mirthless, harrowing sound. "Avenging angel? Is that what you heard from the living?"

"No. The living remain terrified."

"Still? Oh, it's been what, two, three generations to them? *Ach*. How good of them to keep me fresh as a daisy in their tiny little minds!"

"I cried out for you with my dying breath and here you are. Isn't that what angels do; come at your time of need?"

"I suppose so," the captain mused. "Avenging angel. We'll add it to our list of monikers. The ghost ships all get conflated out here, you know, there's the *Sarah* and the doomed *Isadore* and more, but I'd like to think that *Die Ravanche* stands out among them all."

"Oh, you do. I want to know your ways. I yearn for justice."

The captain clapped her hands, a thundercrack. "And you will have it, lovely girl. Where did it happen?"

Greta nodded ahead. "Down the coast a mile. There is no landing. Only a terrible drop."

"Indeed. Next on the docket. *First*, we've an appointment right here on this very pier." The captain stated. She turned to the crowd. "John Good? Come, it's time."

The spirit of a man in tattered deckhand's clothes stepped up from within the clustered throng and floated to the opening along the ship rail. His form sunk to the pier below, waiting. The spirits of the wronged gathered along the edge of the deck, a silent audience.

"Do you know everyone's stories?" Greta whispered, watching the man intently.

"Generally I ask, sometimes they tell. But the fog remembers. You'll see it all play out, all over again. But I've got to call the players to the stage!"

The captain held out her hands and floated up to the crow's nest and opened her mouth. A glorious, keening, intoxicating melody issued forth. There was instant commotion from the cluster around the lighthouse. *That*, the villagers heard. Benedictions and pleas for God's mercy were uttered and wept. Greta could see none of the living come into view, but she did begin to see forms and actions lit against the fog like shadow puppets.

The mist indeed played out John's story: he'd taken a respite along this pier after loading cargo. He clutched at his stomach, clearly ill, and sat back against a post to recover. He'd just drifted off against a hoist, his arm around a mooring rope, when two carousing men, wearing immaculate clothes and smelling of the finest tobacco, stumbled onto the pier. Seeing John, one spat at him and hurled insults, assuming him a shiftless tramp. In a moment of pure cruelty aided by inebriation, the other kicked John into the water and the deckhand hit his head on a beam going over. The rope kept John's body near the surface, but not above the water. Once the laughing offenders realized they'd actually hurt him, rather than lifting him out of the water, they quieted. Silently, they let loose the rope. They watched as the water became still once more while John's body slipped to the depths. A simple murder of a man they seemed sure no one would miss.

And as the scene faded, a new corporeal reality took the place of the shadows. The two offenders appeared out of the fog, standing along the edge of the pier, seemingly baffled as to how they'd gotten there. Years had passed, the cruel boys were now mean-faced adults, reeking still of liquor and smoke.

John floated around them. They turned, as if trying to focus on the spirit, but losing track of the figure. The spirit's form created a whirling circle of clearance in the fog.

"Remember me?" John asked in a whisper of a voice. Greta couldn't be sure if the men heard him or not. But they certainly saw something, as their eyes would land in horror for a moment upon the man's greyscale form before losing it again as they whipped their heads around, now standing back-to-back. "My ship moved on, thinking I'd abandoned my post. No one knew. No one mourned me. But *Die Ravanche* knows. *This* crew mourned me. And they bear witness to my vengeance."

John moved to the side of the pier, and it was only then that Greta saw that as he had encircled his quarry, he'd managed to slip a mooring hawser around the men's necks like a noose and had joined it to another hoisting rope. With a scream of righteous fury, the spirit used the momentum solely of his own rage to shift a counterweight at the base of the pulley mechanism and the men lifted into the air, heads cracking against the thick wooden post at the side of the pier, necks snapping from the angle, weight, and swiftness of the action. John looked up at his grim work, bodies dangling like pelts from a trapper's haul, and nodded.

The man turned to Captain Albtraum who had, during the events, come down from the crow's nest to the ship's rail again. John saluted her. "Much obliged, Captain. I'll be on my way, now. Do take care."

Albtraum returned the man's salute. "Be at peace, John Good," she announced with all the confidence and solemnity of a clergy blessing. The silent passengers held hands to their chests, over hearts stilled too soon.

With a brightening then a fading, the man's form vanished into the mist. The captain signaled to her crew to pull up anchor. They did.

The fog gathered close to the ship, retreating from the pier like a lace curtain drawn aside. Greta heard the murmuring voices close around her ears once more, the living venturing away from the meager lighthouse whose lantern cast the dimmest of rays in a slow circle. As the light swept onto the end of the pier, the limp, hanging bodies of the murderers were revealed. A shriek rang out into the night, the angle of the inlet making the sound batter every ear.

Albtraum stepped up to her helm, took hold of her ship's wheel, and turned her vessel away from the pier, maintaining course south.

Die Ravanche floated on as the villagers kept screaming.

Greta turned and focused on the dark outcropping ahead, joining the captain at the ship's wheel. "I've heard five accounts of how this ship came to do what it does, and I know from personal experience no one ever tells the whole truth. But what is *your* truth, captain?"

The captain stared ahead at the black water as she spoke, hands firm on the great wheel. "I grew up in my father's shipyard in Bremerhaven. He built *Die Ravanche* for me; naming it for everyone who said I'd never make it out of port. That a woman couldn't captain a ship. He demanded success would prove revenge. I traded the North Sea for the Atlantic Ocean and maintained brisk trade between Northeastern states at an unrivaled pace. While I anticipated trouble, I didn't bargain for the end I was given. But you know the *wonderful* thing about where a person comes from? You can take it with you. All the folklore. All the magic. All the legends. They're there for you if you know how to invoke them. To call for and then *become* them."

"Like the Lorelei."

"Precisely. The Flying Dutchman and *his* cursed ship. Every silly New Englander who assumed every German was a Hessian. You can use fear to advantage. Every legend and cautionary tale can become a template. A weapon. A tool of justice. If you're determined enough to wield it."

This thrilled Greta to the core.

"What about you, lovely?" the captain prompted.

"I was taught that women's sole purpose was to serve; to be secondary. Never my own body. I chafed against this and was forever punished for it. I was born hungry. No experience has been enough. I have wanted everything life could offer, every person, every material thing, every thought, every sensation. When I tried to run away with a secret lover I thought adored me, it became clear at our rendezvous point that he only valued jewels I'd brought with me. As if I were ballast to jettison, he tossed me in the sea instead. I don't know if my body ever surfaced or if I merely became one with the water. I am still listed as 'missing'; an unfortunate girl who didn't know her place and suffered the consequences. Weaponized as a warning to disobedient girls, I suppose. No one has looked for me. Except for you."

"And what do you want to happen now?"

"I want to matter. Just like John's life mattered. He was discarded. I was *discarded*. I am so much more than dead weight. I slipped below the waves, no one the wiser. But I have more to see, feel, and do. I am not *done*. I am *ravenous*."

The captain nodded slowly.

A stab of agony, mirroring her impact against the rocks, bloomed in Greta's body before heat lit up her luminous form instead, trading pain for fury. Her form grew more solid.

"I didn't choose this cycle," the captain declared, shifting the wheel subtly, the sails softly rustling agreement. "It chose me. And I, too, want it to matter. For this ship to not just matter but to *transform*. What good is evoking the great legends if we cannot use them? *The Revenge* is a cautionary tale. As you said."

The captain turned back to the pitch-black waters the same color as her dead eyes, shaking her head, her voice rumbling like a distant peal of thunder.

"When I went under, struck and sent overboard by a violent man who simply could not *fathom* that a woman owned and captained this ship– he sent me into the depths just before I could turn starboard to avoid a jagged stretch of rocks. He didn't hear the warning. My last mortal sensation was the dash of my head against the same rocks that would soon tear my ship's hull open. A curse on my lips as the sea stole my breath. But the water did not steal my spirit any more than it did yours."

The captain ran her incorporeal hand lovingly across the port rail. "I awoke as this shade, here on this beloved deck. She and I floated soundlessly; resurrected from those dark waters just as I was. She must have made the same bargain I did."

Turning back to Greta again, the endless pools of her inky eyes drew Greta forward. An apt name. Lorelei could drown a soul, just by staring. Invoking the legend indeed.

"The power of the name, Greta. Every deepest magic comes back to that transformative capacity. Names can become verbs. *Die Ravanche* does what she was born to do."

"Yes..."

"Now go on ahead to the site while I summon the devil."

Greta nodded. This was the way of it. The cycle was not her own.

As the captain climbed the crow's nest once more to sing, to draw out quarry from sleep, to demand a man confront his sins, Greta stared ahead as the rocky outcropping her body had been thrown from came into view.

The fog rolled in accordingly. Greta moved with it, one with its cloudy murk, slowly floating towards the cliff-line as the boat remained on the water behind her.

"Mr. Bledsoe..." Greta whispered on the wind, hoping it would sound upon her former lover's ear as if she were right beside him, lying folded against his shoulder like she used to do. She watched as the fog replayed their last moments; a passionate clutch, his securing the jewels she'd brought for their supposed elopement, a final kiss, then a shove. No ground beneath her. She watched it all. Her stomach growled.

A silhouette appeared at the center of a path worn between the trees that led direct to the dangerous precipice. A handsome man with disheveled hair, Mr. Bledsoe wore only his trousers, shirt, and open waistcoat, as if he'd been getting ready to rest when he was lured from his home across the wood.

"What is this... why am I here..." Bledsoe asked in a croaking whisper. "Who was singing..." Greta stepped into his view, and he cried out in dismay, shaking his head. "You! What is this nightmare?"

"You once *loved* to see me, Arthur," Greta said, drawing close, hearing the hammering of his heart, seeing the pulse against his throat, "Nightmare again, is it? How can you say such a thing when your wickedness brought you here? Here where *Die Ravanche* may deliver you. This is the way of it."

"*Die Ravanche*..." Bledsoe murmured, dread realization setting over him.

"See her there, in the distance? She carries the souls of the dead and she comes for those who have been wronged." Greta pointed a bony finger out towards the barely visible masts below.

Her prow could be seen jutting out of the mist. Her sails rustled in an eerie beat that matched the crash and withdrawal of the waves.

"You always told me I was impossible, *insatiable*. You're right. And now, I *always* will be..." Greta brought her face close to his, as if she were about to kiss him. Instead, she remembered what it had been like to touch and grasp him; pull him close and taste him. And from this recollection, she managed a forceful shove.

As he fell from the cliff, he looked up at her, eyes widening, scream cut short by the sharp rocks.

His broken, bloodied wreckage slipped down into the black depths, no one the wiser.

Greta returned to the boat, the fog moving with her. As the murk retreated, Greta's stomach stopped roaring the moment she saw the bloodstained rocks.

The captain turned *Die Ravanche* out towards open sea.

"Onto the next pier, the next outcropping, the next scene of unfinished business," the captain murmured. "Along these jagged shores the tides prove a dirge." She tapped her boot at the base of the ship's wheel in the same slow thrum of the lapping waves. "Tides breathe in. But what they have drawn in they may not exhale. The sea isn't a lung. It is a mouth."

"And like me, it hungers..." Greta whispered, looking down into the darkness of the water below and recognizing her own bottomless abyss.

The captain turned to Greta, and she gasped– in fascination rather than shock. Lorelei's face was merely a skull, her grin bare teeth. A face had been an illusion; now the other half of the masthead was laid bare.

"Are you at peace, Greta Knott? Will you find your rest?"

Greta thought of John the deckhand brightening then winking out. Pain shot across her again and she clenched her incorporeal fists. "No. Not yet. I need more. So much more."

"Well then. It would seem I've earned *myself* a little rest!"

The captain walked away, skeletal form fading against the night sky. Her coat just a length of hanging sail, her kerchief just a knotted rag on the mast. Greta was at a loss.

"Wait... what..." Greta called after the retreating form.

"You're the nightmare now, Greta Knott," came a voice along the cove, glancing off her ear. "Just keep your hand on the wheel. Trust her. *Die Ravanche* knows how to sail herself."

Die Ravanche does what she was born to do.

Her new captain, hoping to slake her endless thirst, placed her hands on the wheel as an alluring siren call reverberated around the rocks before it slipped below the waves. She donned a greatcoat made of cautionary tales.

If the coast is foggy, best be sure your heart is pure.

All those secrets you thought you'd take to the grave? She'll bring that watery grave to you. The dark abyss yawns open, not just hungry for justice, but starving.♜

I HOPE THE NIGHT IS QUIET

By Claire Low

EAST ARCADIA DOWNS IS A pork town. There are towns known for tulip festivals. Towns known for fleece. For us, it's pork. We're fed it almost from birth. That advertisement on television around Australia, it sticks in your head like the Vegemite jingle—and it comes from our town. A blond kid pops a piece of pork crackling into his mouth like honeycomb, and a golden smile spreads across his angel face like God himself peeking out from behind the clouds and he says, "That's what I'm talking about."

When the drought came, we all got nervous. It was a deep drought, a down-to-your-bones drought. One of the cattlemen Dad knew, his friend from a nearby town, shot his five hundred head of cattle, one by one, instead of watching them die of thirst. The cattleman's name was Roger, and he was sixty-seven, and no one ever saw him cry, but once he'd shot the cattle, he sort of shrank up into himself and the big blackness of his house swallowed him up.

He told Dad the worst part was how the nights went quiet. He used to dislike the sound of the herd vocalizing in the dark as it usually meant distress. Now, the nights were big and empty. Vast, black sky, a million stars over the yellow, cracked ground, every bit of grass turning to dust and crickets shrilling. Dad said Roger, something changed within him; he wasn't so sure about Roger anymore.

Dad hoped our nights were quiet. Sometimes the pigs screamed, without any obvious cause for their agitation. I hated the sound, how it was so human-like. I found it hard to shake the feeling that pigs were so very like us: how inside, their meat was like our meat; and ours was like theirs. I once dreamed that one of East Arcadia Downs' children was stretched out over Dad's butcher block and Dad calmly filleted him alive. The boy screamed until he couldn't, and Dad said, "I hope the night is quiet."

The endless drought was a disaster for the pig farmers. You can't just kill them and drag them off to market before they're ready and full-grown. Pigs dying of thirst meant no money and East Arcadia Downs is a pork town. When I say that, I mean it. No one goes to school much beyond age seventeen and you either raise and slaughter pigs or butcher them, or both, or you export pork or create recipes involving thick, glossy slabs of it or you write crisp slogans to help sell pork, or you somehow otherwise spend your waking hours on pork. We don't count sheep here, not even to get to sleep.

Even though the news said this was the worst drought Australia had ever seen, and livestock was better off dead than alive, I don't know how we did it, but we managed it, we got by, pork scratching by pork scratching. There was just enough meat in East Arcadia Downs.

Unfortunately, that terrible year found another way to be cruel to us: cot deaths. So many babies, well, they died. Some tiny angels stopped breathing in the night, or their blankets smothered them, or they choked on their spit.

Dad had Roger around for tea one afternoon. They stood in the shed, looked at tools, talked about tractors and ate the little sultana cakes that had won Mum a blue ribbon at the agricultural fair eight years in a row. I heard a snippet of conversation. First, it was Roger.

"… know it's strange, Joseph?"

My dad's voice had some muffled reply.

"Cot deaths are rare… I mean, it happened once to my aunt's sister-in-law but it's only because…"

"…strange, but in any case, like I was just saying, if you go to the same supplier as me, he'll give you a discount…"

Dad didn't invite Roger around much after that. And awfully, the littlest children kept on dying. So many tiny caskets sold that year, all of them displayed closed, with a little spray of baby's breath on top, and a photo of a miniature human who had barely begun to live, and a hushed rendition of Amazing Grace.

Mrs. Gross' boy, he wasn't a baby or even particularly little, he was eight, going on nine. We all knew Kevin Gross—when he was three, he had been the blond kid in the TV advertisements—you know: "That's what I'm talking about."

He disappeared. They said he'd gone out to the creek to search for lizards or something and got lost. This happens sometimes. It's usually flash flooding trapping them on a ledge somewhere and they have a big adventure and come back begging for more.

Mrs. Gross said she saw something in the weeks before Kevin disappeared. Someone—a man, she thinks—had been standing by the edge of the bushland. He wore flannels, jeans, and steel-capped work boots, the same as every other man in East Arcadia Downs. But he had one thing that every other man didn't: a pig mask. And he stood there. And she could feel somehow, that inside the pig mask—a boar mask, really, with tusks, wrinkles and this terrible fleshy color, the shade of an old piece of pork, left out too long, uncooked and starting to rot—he was smiling.

When the weather man finally predicted rain, good rain, a steady downpour, several families came together at Mr. and Mrs. Peterson's house to eat dinner together after Sunday mass. We had roasts, buttered peas, and Brussels sprouts, we had golden crackling as good as any Kevin ever bit with his shiny young teeth. And Mrs. Gross didn't touch a thing. She kept her head down and I realized after a moment—she was crying.

The pork was good that year, it had a sweetness, freshness, and creaminess that wasn't common, and Mrs. Gross cried, oh she cried and cried over her lost son; her heartbreak was as big as the sky. Vanessa Knox, who was Mrs. Gross' great-niece, told me that instead of counting pigs to get to sleep, Mrs. Gross' mind was crowded with all the cot-death babies, who gasped one last breath, then breathed no more.

The window was dark, showing thirsty trees and a gloomy sky, all shadowy silhouettes. The wind was blowing, a storm was coming and there was a squeaking sound, a creaking sound at the window where the branches rubbed glass. And when thunder rumbled and lightning lit up the sky for a moment, I saw something rather like a pig mask looking in through the window.

But the men kept eating and drinking. Their big, tobacco-stained teeth kept grinding up that pink-and-white meat and yellow crackling. There was a bit of drool at the edge of Mr. Peterson's mouth and that mouth was a big black hole from which light would never escape.

A phone rang in the room next door and Dad motioned to me to go answer it. As I picked up the receiver, thunder and lightning rolled through, and the sound crackled through the receiver.

I saw green eyes in the dark—only the Petersons' cat, Effie.

"Hello?"

The study had wide windows, like wide grey eyes. I felt exposed. I could hear laughter and talking from the dining room.

Muffled sounds. Then a voice I could just make out, distorted as though spoken through a mask: "I hope the night is quiet." The line went dead and somewhere not too far away, a pig screamed.

#   #   #

I remember when my dad first approached me with a knife. He called out to me. "Sean? Sean?" The mother-of-pearl inlay handle of his best knife was snug in his fist, a shiny blade jutted downwards, and his other hand was wrapped around a whetstone.

"Joseph, he's only eight," my mother chided.

"Exactly, and if he doesn't learn to use one of these, he'll starve. Is that what you want, Meredith?"

"Boys around here learn when they're thirteen," Mum pointed out, her voice a little soft.

"You're talking about slaughter. This is completely different," Dad retorted. To me, he said, "come."

For the first hour, he only let me watch. Then he guided my hands as though I were a marionette. Finally, I was made to gash meat from the bone, fat from muscle, bristly hair from skin. Dad was very exacting; it took all afternoon. Once I was covered in sweat and had seen so much flesh-pink that

I could only imagine I would dream about it, he allowed me a glass of water. "I suppose this will do," Dad said.

He took the knife and whetstone away with him, leaving me with books on animal husbandry, books on anatomy, books on carving. And after that, I had to help him with this task and that, heavy with the understanding that apprentice butchery would be my fate, it was carved into me deeply, it was written inside my bones.

The details of what awaited me on my thirteen birthday I knew from Kai at school, who had a brother, Tristan, now eighteen. The basics went like this: you kneel, speak briefly to God in your mind, then swiftly draw the razor over the major artery in the neck. You must do it quickly, you must do it fearlessly, you must not cut yourself in the process.

It's so much harder if you can't, or won't, Tristan told Kai. Don't spend too much time in there, don't listen to the sound of the pig breathing, don't smell the straw in the pen, for heaven's sake, don't look the creature in the eye.

"They're just meat, it doesn't matter. There's not much to them; they're not complicated animals, see," Kai said.

I would be thirteen in just under a year, and I wondered what it would be like for me. I had to do it well; I was Joseph's son. Couldn't be like Soren Winchester. When he turned thirteen, he walked to the barn like it was the gallows. Afterwards, Soren became sort of colorless, as if all the hues in his hair and skin had leached out of him like blood out of a body. He was the sort of boy who painted like Edgar Degas, and he didn't want to slaughter anything, but he had to.

#   #   #

I had this feeling, somehow, that the drought and the dying babies and Kevin's disappearance were linked. So surely, now that the rains had come, there would be no more cot deaths, and Kevin would reappear somewhere, whole. When Bailey Gunderson failed to come home after school on a Thursday, the wrongness of this flared bright and red in my brain. Bailey was pretty and brown-skinned, and I had walked behind her on the way to assembly at least a dozen times. Each time, I'd stared at the bright pink pom-

pom keychain on her backpack, bobbing along with each step she took. I was sure if I kept staring at the pom pom, maybe Bailey would psychically understand that I liked her a whole lot.

That afternoon, watching a black and white movie on television, I noticed a milk carton on the screen. The cartoon had a small girl's face printed on it under the word MISSING. We didn't have milk cartons in East Arcadia Downs, only glass bottles delivered by the truckload from a neighboring town, the cattle town. Since other cattle farmers had destroyed their stock like Roger, the milk was coming from further afield, at least, I think it did.

"Dad?" I ventured. He was in the kitchen, scoring and salting a magnificent pork skin stretching high and pink over a hunk of meat. Once cooked, the skin would be a heavenly bliss of melt-in-your mouth crackling, it would shatter like Violet Crumble and taste richer than God's own butter.

"What is it, boy? Why don't you come over here and help me?"

I came over, washed my hands, and began to slice carrots. "Dad? Could we put up signs about the missing kids? Like, not on milk cartons, but on lamp posts or something?"

"Hmm," he replied, distracted. "S'pose so. S'pose we could. No harm in it. Maybe you could get that started."

After dinner, the phone rang. I paused before picking up the receiver, remembering the muffled voice from the other evening. It was Kai. "It doesn't feel like anyone's searching," he said. "Why aren't they searching for Kevin and Bailey?"

"We'll do it," I said. "We'll search." We talked about skipping after-school cricket lessons to have a spare hour before we were expected home. Then we talked about homework for a moment. Kai was stuck as usual and since there was no hope there, I hung up.

Pretty much straight after, the phone rang again. "Kai? I told you. I can't do your algebraic equations."

Crackling, static. Then the voice, that same voice I'd heard at the Petersons' place. As I heard it, a feeling crept over me, like I was being watched. But the window was dark, there was no one there. The voice said, "The largest meat locker."

I said, "What?"

There was no answer.

#   #   #

The largest meat locker in town belongs to Mr. Bennington. We are not friends with his son, Nigel. It's not possible to be friends with Nigel Bennington. The only exception is Christian Lacey who is so kind and so religious that he's friends with absolutely everyone.

I approached Nigel and this wasn't the best. I still remembered when he flipped his eyelids inside out and laughed. The meat colors of those eyelids were way too much like the colors of the day when I began to learn knife skills.

"Hullo," Nigel said, the vowel in this word being wrong and everything.

"Listen, Nigel, does your dad need a helper?"

Nigel squeezed the crackers he was holding, which had Vegemite and butter spread between them, and this made little worms ooze out, like thin little maggots, like the ooze of blackheads being scraped. "Naw. He's got me."

"Yes, but it's a pretty big meat locker."

"The biggest," Nigel agreed, with pride. He licked at the 'worms' that had oozed out of his crackers, then set the licked crackers down and grabbed a stack of prosciutto, which he picked apart like—ugh, why is my brain making this comparison—like layers of healing sunburned skin. He chewed with his mouth open and began to talk with the meat on full display. "You wanna see it?"

I glanced to the side, then back to Nigel. "Yeah, show me. I bet it isn't even that big, not half as big as you say."

Nigel kicked at the ground, hands in pockets. He took an almighty sniff that rattled the snot in his nostrils. "Yeah, well, you'll see."

After school, he brought me over, just me. We didn't have much to talk about. What could I have asked Nigel: how did you get head lice three times in one term? Why do you smell like feet?

"Ummm, your dad won't mind us visiting the meat locker, will he?"

"Naw, he's away."

The meat locker was vast. It was unbelievably cold and full of bodies. I mean, meat. It was full of carcasses, hanging up on hooks or stored on racks.

It stretched on forever, seemingly with enough pork to fill an Olympic-sized swimming pool and it smelled OK, fresh, even. I guess I was used to it. Honestly, it was all fine in there. Not a thing out of order.

"So? Like I said?" Nigel's nostrils flared and his chin jutted out. I nodded and tried to make an impressed sort of sound, but I was awfully disappointed. The tip was worthless.

I rubbed my hands together to try and bring the feeling back into them. "Can we get out of here?"

Outside of the meat locker, Nigel and I regarded each other. "Still hoping for a job?" He picked at his teeth, at the yellow substance between them.

I shook my head.

"Ah, well. I gotta take a piss."

He ambled off somewhere. Near the meat locker, there was a closed door marked Employees Only. It took all the strength I had to push my way in.

When I saw it, I felt sure I was seeing what the voice over the telephone wanted me to see: a mountain of clothes: baby clothes, lacy Christening gowns, fancy bibs, knitted booties, and onesies, little hats, on and on. Just the largest number of baby clothes I'd ever seen. The bright red feeling of awfulness flared inside me again. Along with the clothes, all of them unbearably small, there was something even worse: a school bag. Not a nappy bag or anything to do with babies at all. It was a kid-sized bag, big enough to fit a biology textbook, and it was used. I stepped forward and picked it up, feeling all prickly and ice-cold. It had a certain smell, the sweet rot of a bag in which there has been at least a few forgotten apples and bananas left to form a mulch. I shifted the bag in my hands, hoping to see a name. And a bright pink pom-pom keychain swung into view. "Bailey?" I said, my voice barely above a whisper. Nausea rose up from my stomach.

I snatched the pom pom from the bag, stuffed it in my pocket, and left the room, the big heavy door swinging behind me.

Nigel looked surprised to see me emerge from the staff room. "Hey? You're not supposed to be in there." His expression was bland, mild, even. I met his gaze for about a second.

"I guess I should be going."

"No, wait," Nigel said.

I left as fast as I could, at one point dipping my hand into my pocket. The furry pink pom pom was in there, and it was much too cold for a fluffy object, like it was slightly wet.

When I got home, my parents were watching television, glassy-eyed. "Hi, kiddo," Dad said.

The 5 o'clock news was playing. A stern-faced young woman with dirty-blonde hair was holding a sign that said: *Dina barn har ingen framtid.* I wasn't sure what this meant but a number of other young activists had similar signs: School Strike for Climate. The stern woman brandished her sign a few times, then, seemingly sure her message wasn't getting through, held up a picture: a monstrous, naked giant with grey hair, his mouth gaping open, had bitten the head off a smaller, also naked body, which was bloodied. "You!" she roared, tapping the old, hungry giant. "Your children's future!" she added, tapping the tiny, ruined corpse. "The time for change is now!"

Dad muttered, "I thought Swedish girls were supposed to be pretty."

"Oh hush, Joseph," Mum lightly scolded.

The news report cut to a commercial break soon afterwards. My parents, their tasks for the day all done, kept watching docilely. A woman in a red leotard was exercising, stepped off a treadmill, wiped the non-existent sweat off her forehead and bit into an enormous piece of pork. "Bourbon glaze," she exclaimed. "That's what I'm talking about!" My parents' eyes tracked her movements across the screen as though hypnotized. A timer dinged and broke the spell. "Dinner's ready," Mum said.

It was triple-layered pork, Chinese style, with rice and dark leafy greens. A dish I usually loved. This time, I ate the rice and the greens and nibbled at the pork, only a little.

"You're not hungry?" Mum said.

"After all we've been through," Dad said, shaking his head. "You won't even eat it? Eat, boy."

The pink pom pom was still in my pocket. The feeling of nausea rose again.

"Eat, you must eat."

I put the meat in my mouth, I had to. It was delicious. I felt like crying.

\#　　\#　　\#

At bedtime, Dad came into my room to say goodnight, as usual. "Sean? I noticed you came home late today. Is there something you want to tell me?"

"No."

He regarded me in the dim light, the only illumination coming from the full moon peeking through the curtains.

I said, "What about you? Is there something you want to tell me?"

Dad was quiet for a moment. Since I had grown to at least my father's shoulder height, he hadn't seemed all that big like he had when I was in kindergarten, and he could hoist me onto his shoulders. But tonight he seemed vast, blocking all the light of the moon through the window. He put a ham-sized fist on my shoulder and his incisors were bright and beautiful somehow; they gleamed.

"Did I tell you about the man with the hook?"

"Mr. Frederickson?" Johan Frederickson had a face like a glazed doughnut and owned the largest meat hook in town. He often boasted about this. Sometimes when he bragged, Mrs. Petit would giggle, which gave me a tiny feeling of awfulness. It told me that grown-ups could be things to each other, things they maybe weren't supposed to be, and that life as we knew it could split wide open if everyone started saying everything they were thinking.

"No, not him, a different man," my father said. His voice, a sound I had heard since birth, was a bit wrong. Like it was him, but not him. I pulled my blanket up under my chin and anchored it under me on either side of my body. "This man, they say he's looking for children, and that's why you should stay here, with your mother and me."

My mind conjured up an image, a child my age trussed up and hanging from a meat hook, among the carcasses of pigs, inside Mr. Bennington's vast meat locker. I was so frightened the marrow in my bones shifted. Perhaps there had been one, who was to say—there were so many rows of carcasses, there's no way I had looked at everything.

"Why? Why is he looking for children?"

"Revenge, he's out for revenge. He's jealous of everything we have, our wives, our beautiful meats, and he will stop at nothing."

Dad knelt down and gave me a whiskery goodnight kiss. In this moment, my brain conjured up a miniature version of my father, a thirteen-year-old version of him, kneeling beside a pig. A quick hand, a straight razor drawn across the animal's throat. Would he have cried for hours afterwards, or accepted his fate with the same stoicism he applied to everything?

As he turned to leave, the full moon was visible again and when he stood, it aligned with his mouth, it was like he swallowed it whole in the manner of a holy communion wafer. I shivered in the dark until I fell asleep.

#   #   #

At lunchtime in the school quadrangle, I showed Kai the pink pom-pom keyring I'd snatched off the backpack in the staff room near the meat locker.

"Sorry," he said, shaking his head. "Doesn't prove anything. There's, like, a lot of those keychain things in the world. I think my sister has one."

I gave him a half nod, a little disappointed. I didn't want to insist that it was absolutely Bailey's because I would have to admit how much time I'd spent walking behind her.

"Look, it was something, OK. All the baby clothes and stuff—definitely something. It's what the caller wanted me to see."

"The pig man? I've seen him too."

I stopped, cold. "You did?" If Kai could see what Mrs. Gross had seen, what I had seen, it meant it was real, not some shared delusion that had sprung up because of all the stress of the drought.

Kai scrunched up his face. "Yeah, one time. I was walking by myself, just me and Pie (this was Kai's dog). He was holding something out to me, he was signaling for me to get closer. I didn't."

"No? Why not?"

"He's scary, Sean. I… couldn't. My parents warned me…"

"About a guy with a hook?"

Kai thought about it. "No, no hook. I saw him; he didn't have one. My parents warned me about a kidnapper, someone out for revenge, like someone married his ex and had a baby and now they want to steal children, all the kids, until they find that specific kid."

As we walked, we went past the school noticeboard. A flyer said:

Charity clothing drive

WANTED—baby clothes

There were details about rounding up donations and sending used baby items that were in good condition to Third World countries.

Kai nudged me. "There you go. Does that explain the clothes pile?"

I felt skeptical. "I'm telling you, dude, something's up. The pig man wanted me to see the clothes. The pom-pom keychain is definitely Bailey's."

Kai stared. "Nah, it could be any girl's, like any girl's in the world."

I stared back. "I know I'm right. I'm going to ask the pig man myself."

"How?"

"Well," I said, puffing myself up a bit. "I'm not like you. If I see him and he waves me over, I'll go to him."

Kai hissed, "Are you insane?"

"Kai, you said he doesn't have a hook. The story about some crazed man looking for his ex's baby, that doesn't make sense. The pig man, I think he's trying to help us.

"And you go to him, and then what?"

"I ask him some questions."

#   #   #

To increase the chances the pig man would find me, I went wandering alone after school. No pig man. I sat on the swings in the park, by myself. No pig man. I cycled over to the nature reserve where after the drought, trees sprang back thick and wild, kind of around where Mrs. Gross said she spotted him.

I knew he was out there. I knew he was watching me. I knew he wanted to tell me something. I left my bike in the car park and wandered around the thickest, darkest part of the bush, eventually making my way back out towards the clearing near the car park where my bicycle was. Then I saw someone—a man. No pig mask. It was my dad. He hadn't spotted me, and I darted behind a tree—but before I did, I saw his hands, I saw what was in them. Just like when I was eight, he had that bright blade and that whetstone.

"Sean? Sean?" My skin prickled all over with sure and deep knowledge. It was not my thirteenth birthday. The wrongness of this, of Dad, of everything, flared up in my heart like a distress signal over the ocean.

Someone seized me from behind and my heart rattled inside my chest, so hard it was like the Grim Reaper himself had reached out and shook it. It was the pig man. His mask was detailed beyond belief: every bristly hair, every yellowed tooth, with red veins shot through the eyes. It was far from the rubbery gag masks they sold at the costume shop in the nearest big city.

He clamped a bony hand over my mouth and, with his other hand, tore off his mask. Even though his cheeks were sunken and his eyes were wild, I recognized him. "Roger?" It was the cattleman, the one who hated the quiet nights after he shot his entire herd dead.

I heard my father again: "Sean! I know you're out here. Get over here, Sean."

In response to my question, Roger nodded once. He pointed a thin finger towards a car. Its passenger side door opened, and a woman's face looked out. It was Mrs. Gross, Kevin's mother, the one who cried at the drought-breaking feast.

My father called out again. "SEAN! Boy, come here."

Roger cocked his head in the direction of my father's voice, dragged his finger across his throat in a slitting action that every boy over the age of thirteen knows in East Arcadia Downs, and then pointed over to Mrs. Gross again, to the waiting car.

He whispered in my ear, "Run."

I'LL NEVER UNDERSTAND GHOSTS

By Dotti Enderle

AIN'T NOBODY IN THE BONEYARD on Christmas Eve. No worries about being seen. All decent folk were at church, or gathered around their tree, eating sugar plums and telling stories. And bright-eyed tykes were all wrought up, waiting for Father Christmas to bring them some treats. But out here, it's just me. Me, the north wind, and the Lord's own dead. It was safe to light the lantern.

I planned this to be like no other Christmas. So here I was, fetching a special gift for my lovely wife, Beth. After five years of putting up with me, she deserved more than a new hankie or a trinket box I'd whittled out of wood. *So* much more. I'd have given that woman the world if it were mine to give. But it wasn't mine. And neither was the ruby necklace I was there to steal.

The necklace belonged to one Mrs. Hazel Godfrey. She and her husband Horace rested in a crypt on the south side of St. John's cemetery. I'd been their gardener. His death was no surprise. He was a ripe old sixty-eight. People couldn't wrap their heads around why a sweet, young thing like Hazel had tied the knot with the likes of him. It was for his money, to be sure. I remember watching Mrs. Godfrey run her delicate fingers across that necklace, it circling her lily-white neck. Her eyes would be all a sparkle as a gentle smile played on her face. She prized that thing. When she passed, they buried her in a cherry satin frock matching those bloodred gems to a T. She was laid out all pretty. Shame she died so young. She couldn't take them jewels to Heaven, but I could give them to an angel.

The Godfrey mausoleum was a simple structure, enclosed by an iron fence. No pointy spirals or arched windows. Just a couple of naked cherubs laughing down at me. I paid them no mind. The rusted door had a knob on it, sticking out of a lion's roaring mouth. I rattled the knob. While it wouldn't turn, it did feel loose in my hand. It'd be easy enough to unlock. I grabbed my tool bag. A hand drill and a screwdriver did the trick. I opened the tomb to a gust of stale air. I returned the tools to the bag, lifted the lantern, and entered.

Four coffins sat inside. Mr. and Mrs. Godfrey's, along with two littler ones for the babes they lost. Hers was mahogany, trimmed with brass handles. The lid creaked as I raised it, and I held the lantern high.

There she lay, her brown-splotchy face shriveled like a prune. One eyelid stood at half-mast, exposing dark caverns beneath. Her mouth was as black as this December night. And I couldn't help but think she'd been robbed twice. First, by death. Then by me, taking the last lovely thing she possessed.

The necklace hung lopsided on her withered throat. "Pardon me, Hazel," I said, setting the lantern down. Then, spinning the chain around, I unclasped it, freed the necklace from the corpse, and dropped it into my pocket—the one without the hole. Wasting no time, I closed her back up and hightailed it out of there.

The streets were empty, just me, a lamplighter, and a string of shuttered shops. The air bit at me, but I felt no pain. I kept imagining Beth's face all lit up when she saw her gift. As I rounded the corner a snowflake fell on my cheek. Then two. Then more. A light dusting of snow escorted me. But I got this odd feeling in my gut, like someone was following me. I glanced over my shoulder. Just a dead street. Still, that sense of someone there remained. I picked up my step.

About halfway home, the hairs on the nape of my neck stood up. But not from the cold. It was like someone had run their finger along it. I shivered and spun. Nobody in sight. I tightened my scarf and continued, dread not far behind. I pictured Beth's face again and told myself it was nothing. Just a little guilt, maybe, for what I'd done.

As I reached our lodgings, I felt a blow to the front of my ankles. Something kicked my feet straight out from under me. I hit the pavement hard, busting my chin good. I saw stars for a second, but quickly sprang up and looked around. Nothing. Only darkness and shadows among the gas lamps. A lone dog barking in the distance.

Me, being clumsy is all, I told myself. But *was* someone watching? I dipped my hand in my pocket and touched the necklace. It was still tucked in place just fine. I dusted myself off and took the steps up to the door.

Inside, the lodgings were dark and cold. I dropped my tool bag and lit a lamp. "Beth!" I called out. Such a dumb thing to do. Why would she be here, sitting around in the dark? Beth worked in service for the Ashforths. Normally, she'd be home by now, but I suspected they were having some festivities to celebrate the season. She'd be home late. I wasn't happy about it. Not tonight. Not when I was still feeling shook from that walk home.

I shed my scarf, hat, and gloves, then hurried over to get a fire started. Kneeling, I placed some kindling under the logs and lit a match. But as I leaned forward, a breathy *woosh* put the match out. I held my hand under the chimney, feeling for a rush of air. It was as still as the corpse I'd just robbed. I tossed the burnt match in the fireplace and lit another. Same thing. *What the devil?* On the third try, the flame held. In no time I had a roaring fire warming up the room.

I checked the kitchen, though I don't know what for. The tiny little nook was empty and quiet. Next, I went into the bedroom and got some light going in there, needing to chase away the dark. I caught a glance of myself in the mirror. *Lord have mercy!* I'd skinned my chin but good. It looked like someone took a grater to it. The livid wound still bled in spots, and dead flesh curled within the scrapes. I turned my head this way and that. *You dang fool.* What was Beth going to think of her man now?

I dipped my hand in my pants pocket and removed the necklace, then spread it out on our tiny dresser. Such a beauty! I'd go find some paper and string and wrap it up real pretty. I turned and *Bloody Hell!* Hazel Godfrey stood just outside the doorway, her half-lidded socket fixed on me, her black lips twisted into a snarl. She let out a low growl.

Jesus, help me!

I slammed the door shut and pressed against it, my breath sawing in and out, keeping rhythm with my hammering heart.

What do I do now?

I glanced to the small window over the bed. I could make it. I shot out and over to it and flung open the curtains. *Ahhhh!* There stood Hazel, her face practically touching the pane.

"Go away!"

I dashed back to the door, flung it open, and there she was again, standing in that same spot.

Lord have mercy!

Instinctively, I punched her in the jaw. Her head turned slightly with the blow, then she backhanded me so hard I hit the floor. Scooting back, I kicked the door shut again. That time, I braced a chair under the knob.

Trapped! Trapped! Trapped! And now with a red-hot cheek that burned hotter than my chin.

This can't be happening.

I looked around for a weapon—anything I could use to fight back. The fireplace poker leaned against the hearth. I bolted for it. Clutching it like a bat, I stood ready, watching that door like it might explode. But there was only silence. Except for my ragged breath. In the front room I heard the ticking of the mantle clock. I stood soldier-still, poised for action. When nothing happened, I wondered, *Is Hazel waiting me out?*

That's when something occurred to me. What if Beth comes home? Walks right in, Hazel there to claw her to shreds. I couldn't let this spook hurt my Beth.

I tiptoed over and eased the chair from under the knob. I'd go out there. And when I did, I'd go out swinging. But, right then, a sucking noise swelled to my left. Hazel. She was wafting through the damn wall!

I'll never understand ghosts. How they can be corporeal one second and walk through barriers the next. Always leaving huge stains of spirit goo when they passed. That goo was some nasty business, I'll tell ya.

I raised the poker over my head, ready to bring it down on hers. But once she slinked her way in, she simply stood there, her bony hands hanging at her sides.

"Get on outta here, Hazel!" I yelled. But her focus wasn't on me. That one black socket eyed the necklace, still spread out in view.

"No," I said. I waved the poker as a threat. I wasn't fooling around, and she'd learn that if she made a move. "It's for my Beth. You ain't got use for it anymore."

She turned her head my way, and in a split second she was on me, going for my throat. I whacked her with the poker a bunch, but she circled her hands on my neck and squeezed. I kept batting, doing no good. That ghost was one tough spirit. I couldn't help but think how ironic, her now robbing me. First, it'd be my breath, then my heart, and then my life. I wasn't having it though. I gripped that poker like a sword and rammed it hard, straight through the thinning bodice of her red dress.

She dropped her hands and stepped back, looking down at her breast. An expression of disappointment crossed her decayed face. She uttered a mewling sound. But she didn't drop over dead. Why would she? She was dead to begin with. Instead, she gripped the poker in her chest and pulled. Regardless of that spiked curve on the end, it slid out as pretty as you please. And there was no question what she aimed to do with it once it was freed. I made haste, snatching up the necklace, flinging open the door, and rushing away.

I raced across the front room, only to find Hazel blocking my way out. As she raised the poker, I stumbled back. "Hazel, get out of here. Go rest in peace." When she started forward, I snatched up the first thing I could find, a small cushion on the sofa. Like an idiot, I threw it at her. "Go on, now!"

I kept backing up, tucking that necklace in my trouser pocket as I went. If she wanted it back, it'd be over my dead body. Which would've suited her fine.

She cornered me in the kitchen, and that's when she charged, poker raised high. I grabbed the flour sack and smashed it against her head. Flour flew in all directions. When the cloud settled, there stood Hazel, dusted with white powder. But my blow hit so hard, it knocked her head crooked. Her face was looking off, straight over her shoulder. It was a ghastly sight.

Only for a moment though. With an eerie cracking of bones, she righted her head to where it belonged. She appraised me with that slitted eye. My blood ran colder than her tomb.

She came at me, step by step, backing me against the counter. I eased my hand out and grabbed the salt box, hiding it behind me. Just as she was on me, she raised the poker up. But before she could split my skull, I kicked her straight in the gut, hard enough to double her over. Grabbing a hank of her hair, I jerked her head back.

"Begone, you wicked wraith!"

With that, I poured every grain of salt down her gullet.

Both her eyelids popped open; those black holes impossibly wide. She swatted at me with the poker, but her strength had depleted. She collapsed, flailed, then melted into the floor, leaving a dark puddle of spirit goo.

I dropped to my knees, catching my breath.

It's done. It's over.

And the necklace was secure in my pocket.

I didn't rest long. I had to clean up this mess and wrap Beth's present before she got home. I grabbed the broom and got to work.

About a quarter to midnight, Beth came in through the kitchen door. I heard her wiping her feet on the mat.

"Beth?"

No answer. Next came the rattling of her chatelaine.

"Beth?"

Still nothing.

My heart kicked up. But then she appeared, her coat draped over her arm.

"Sorry, I'm late, darling." She made use of the coatrack. "The Ashforths had a gathering." She removed her chatelaine and pinafore, too.

I rose from the sofa, slicking my hands against my trousers. "Happy Christmas, sweetheart."

"Happy Chris—" She stared a second and said, "Darling, what happened to your chin?"

That seemed so long ago, I'd forgotten. I touched the scrape. "I took a tumble on the wet pavement. It's nothing."

She tilted her head in pity. "Oh, honey." She came over, wrapped her arms around my neck and placed the lightest of kisses on the graze. "I love you."

"I love you, too." A proper kiss followed that. I craned my head back and gave her a mischievous look. "I have something for you."

"Do you now?"

I led her over to the tree, and we sat down beside it. I retrieved the gift—the only one there—and held it close. "It'll cost you another kiss."

She giggled then leaned in, touching her tender lips to mine.

"Here." I handed it to her.

She quickly unwrapped it, her brows knit in wonder. The moment she saw that ruby necklace her eyes grew, reflecting the firelight from our hearth. She appeared speechless then uttered a quiet, "Oh my."

"Do you like it?"

"Like it? Darling, I love it." She brought it up to her neck.

"Let me," I said. She turned around long enough for me to fasten the clasp.

"Well?" she asked.

"I've never seen anything more beautiful. And I ain't talking about the necklace."

She blushed and smiled. Then she brought her hand up and rubbed at it. "It's a beautiful gift, darling, but may I take it off? It's a bit tight."

"It shouldn't be."

She pinched at it. "It is. Really tight."

I didn't understand. There was plenty of slack when I fastened it. "Let's get it off you, then."

"Oh my," she said again, this time with urgency. I could see it making red marks on her skin. She tried clawing her fingers underneath, never getting purchase. "I can't breathe." I then saw the thing tighten.

"Hold still, I've got it." But when I reached for the clasp, it was knotted, like someone had gripped the back of the necklace, twisted, and pulled. That's when I realized, I hadn't destroyed Hazel at all. I'd only made her invisible again.

Oh God!

I'll never understand ghosts.

Beth kept pawing at the wretched thing, which was now cutting into her. "I can't breathe! I can't breathe!" And it was true. She gasped and gasped, her face turning blue.

"I'll get it," I assured her, but my efforts at grabbing and ripping it off were as fruitless as hers.

Her voice grew weaker. "I can't… I can't…"

I quickly opened a cabinet and took out a small knife. "I'll get it," I said again.

Her gaze dimmed. "I…ca. I…"

"Hold on!" I pulled Beth into my arms and tried sliding the knife under the chain. But I only succeeded in slicing her skin.

Tears sprang to my eyes. "Hazel, stop! Stop this! You hear me! Stop!"

Blood ringed Beth's beautiful neck as she slumped back, her head resting on my arm. Her dull eyes stared at nothing on the ceiling. Suddenly, the necklace loosened, slid to the floor, and was whisked away.

I shook Beth. "You can breathe now, sweetheart. It's gone. You can breathe."

She didn't.

I softly slapped at her cheeks. "Breathe. Breathe, Beth. Breathe!"

Her head lolled back and forth, but she never stirred.

"Beth." I brought her into a tight embrace, weeping into her shoulder. "Beth. What have I done? What have I done?"

I sobbed and sobbed for I don't know how long. But it was the dark of Christmas morning when I stopped. I gently laid her down on the floor.

Oh, Lord in Heaven, what do I do now?

That's when my gaze caught on a small parcel, peeking out of her skirt pocket. It was wrapped in white butcher paper and adorned with green ribbon. I slid it out. A note, written in her small script, was tucked under the bindings.

My Darling,
Happy Christmas. Think of me every time you check this.
I love you now and always.

Your beloved, Beth

That sent me into another bout of sobs. "I'll love you always, too." Once I took control of my faculties, I untied the ribbon. *Holy smokes!* Inside was a magnificent gold pocket watch. I held it up by its chain. It's gilded casing glinted in the lamp light.

"Oh, Beth. Oh, my darling. It's splendid!"

"And it belonged to me," a voice said.

Old man Godfrey stood beside me, going for my throat. ♜

THE MONSTER IN THE MINE

By Jeremiah Dylan Cook

"WHY DO YOU THINK THIS town has experienced so much tragedy?" My brother asks.

"Well, that's kind of a complicated question. Isn't it?"

"No. It's not. There's a monster that lives under the town. It fuels the cycles of violence here."

"A monster?"

"You're talking to a ghost, and the idea of a monster is unbelievable?"

I glance down to see where my brother's waist tapers into a misty cloud. Bits of ectoplasm drip off him and dissolve on contact with the floor. His upper half is how I remember it, sans clothing, but I can see through him to my closed bedroom door.

He floats to the window. "It lives in the abandoned mine underneath the town, inside the Gates of Hell. If you end its life, the spirits who've suffered from the violence it inspired will be able to rest. You can get revenge for me."

I sit up in bed. "How would I even kill a monster?"

"With a gun."

The door opens. My mom, dressed in her floral, green pajamas, stands in the doorway. Dark shadows color the skin under her eyes. My brother vanishes as she flicks on my bedroom light.

"Who are you talking to, Nate?" She asks.

"No one," I lie.

"You know it's okay if you're talking to Evan. I talk to him sometimes too." Mom walks to the edge of my bed and sits. "No one blames you for what happened."

I let out a frustrated sigh, lie back down, and turn away from her.

"It was cold that day, and your brother shouldn't have let you drive that route with only your learner's permit. Everyone knew how dangerous that hill could be in the winter, and we both know it's my fault for sending him to pick you up instead of doing it myself. I'm who you should blame."

I smell the alcohol on her breath, and I just want her to leave. "It's nobody's fault. The brake lines snapped in the cold. No one could've known what was going to happen."

Mom remains sitting on the bed, but I don't turn back to face her. I stare at the wall. Finally, she shuffles to the door, turns the light off, and leaves.

Evan reappears. "It's been a year, and she's still not back to normal?"

I keep my response low so that Mom doesn't pop back in. "You think losing your firstborn is easy to handle?"

"No, but she still has you to take care of. She can't afford to drown her sorrows at the bar every night."

"Why can't you appear to her? Knowing you still exist would help."

"Don't you think I've tried? She doesn't see me. You're the only one who can. I think it's because you watched me die."

My mind flashes back to Evan sitting next to me in the car. His head hangs limply from his body, and his last breaths come out in ragged, choking gasps. I'd reversed our vehicle into a snowbank when the brake lines snapped on the hill. If I hadn't steered us into the snow, our car would've crashed into the houses at the bottom of the incline. The impact crumpled his side of the vehicle while I only sustained minor scrapes and bruises.

"You were killed in a car accident. How was the monster responsible for that?"

"Didn't you ever wonder why the mechanic who inspected our car failed to notice the faulty brake line? He was old Hazel Peak stock, and he hated us because we weren't. The monster's influence ensures people give in to their worst instincts. This place is rotten to the core because of that thing's psychic emanations. Why don't you check out a history book if you don't believe me?"

I open my mouth to respond, but Evan vanishes.

#   #   #

The next day I am standing in the Hazel Peak Library. I haven't been here since a field trip in the fourth grade. A musty smell lingers in the air. There are countless books, but I have no idea which to review. I crouch down while trying to read some titles related to history.

"Need help?" A middle-aged woman with graying hair and a stack of books stands in the aisle. The t-shirt under her navy blazer displays a book cover for Aldous Huxley's *Brave New World*. The badge hanging from her hip displays her name, Carolyn.

"Yes, but I don't know what I'm looking for. I guess I need historical examples of bad things that happened in Hazel Peak?" I think about how odd that sounds and add, "It's for a history assignment."

Carolyn shelves one of the books from her stack. "Well, I've read a fair bit of Hazel Peak history. I can give you some examples, and maybe they can point you in the right direction?"

"That would be amazing."

"Do you mind following me as I work?"

"Not at all."

Carolyn moves down the aisle, putting books away. "Here's the first historical event I learned about Hazel Peak, and I think it sets the tone for all the rest. Soldiers under the command of George Washington came to the area to scout for Native Americans who'd allied with the British during the Revolutionary War. Unfortunately for the soldiers, the Native Americans knew the area far better than they did. When the soldiers made camp one evening, the Native Americans struck and killed everyone they could find. When families arrived to bury their dead, they discovered that the area was rather beautiful, aside from the blood-soaked soil. They were Hazel Peak's first settlers, and they proceeded to retaliate against every Native American to come through the area, regardless of whether they'd contributed to the initial attack. So, you can see the town began with violence."

"But we haven't had any major issues since then, right?" I ask, following her as she works.

"Unfortunately, we have." Carolyn frowns. "An influx of immigrant miners caused the town to swell in the late 1800s, but the newcomers suffered through horrible working conditions. They were underground all day and in debt to the mine companies for their supplies and homes. You can see why they unionized and went on strike." Carolyn moves to a new aisle, where a new stack of books waits to be put away. "When the workers finally marched for better conditions, the mine owners hired Pinkertons, essentially rent-a-cops, to put a stop to it. They went after the marchers and unloaded on them with rifles. Eleven people were killed, and several were wounded. The newspapers called it the Mine March Massacre. Afterward, the Pinkertons wore disguises to their court date. As ridiculous as it sounds, the tactic worked because the witnesses who were shot at couldn't positively identify any of the shooters."

"That's insane. But nothing recent, right?" I ask.

"Last big tragedy was in the 1970s. The Mafia firebombed a family by mistake when they were trying to intimidate a Sheriff who lived next door. Since then, it's been relatively quiet. Although I've been told our crime statistics are higher than most towns."

I assist the librarian by handing her books from the nearest stack. "I have one last question, but it's going to be a weird one."

"What's that?" Carolyn stops shelving and stares at me.

"Have you ever heard about any monsters, like non-human ones, in Hazel Peak?"

I expect her to laugh, walk away, or sneer.

"A few rumblings. There was a gentleman in here a few years back saying he'd seen something he couldn't explain and asking about the town's history, kind of like you. I filled him in on the Night Terrors of 1792, when several local farmers mysteriously died in the area. Some blamed Native Americans, and some thought bright lights in the sky were to blame."

I felt hope surge through me. "Can you give me that guy's phone number?"

"I'm afraid I don't have any contact details for him, he wasn't a regular member of the library, and I haven't seen him since."

"Well, thanks for all the information."

Carolyn smiles and nods. "I love getting to help people learn. It's one of the perks of being a librarian. Follow me. I'll write down some titles for you to check out on the subjects we discussed."

I walk with her to the front desk.

She jots down several book names on a sticky note and hands it to me. "If you need anything else, come find me."

"Thanks. I really appreciate it." I take the list and head back to the history section to find the recommended books.

#   #   #

After three hours of skimming at the library, I've confirmed everything Carolyn told me, and I've discovered a few extra tragedies she hadn't mentioned. The only topic I haven't found more information about is the monster itself. Aside from mentions of missing farmers in 1792, that subject is a dead end.

I'm sitting on my bed at home when Evan reappears.

"Where do I get a gun?" I ask.

"Mom keeps one in a safe under her bed. The key is in her nightstand drawer." Evan floats near the window.

"I never knew she had a gun."

"It was Dad's before he left. She just never got rid of it. You remember how to shoot from those times I took you out with my friends, right?"

"Yes. You made me go eight times the summer before… "I can't finish the statement, so I pivot to a new one. "Okay, I grab the gun, our butcher knife, some other supplies, and I head for the Gates of Hell. What then?"

Evan mimes shooting a gun. "It won't take you long to find the creature. It stays close to the exit to come out and eat its victims."

"And you're sure a seventeen-year-old with a gun is going to be able to kill it?"

"It's not a physically strong creature. If you don't do this, the spirits who've died in Hazel Peak because of its cycles of violence will continue to suffer spiritual torment. Don't you want us to be able to rest in peace?"

"Yes. I've just never done anything like this." I stand up. "What if you're just in my head? How do I know you're not some manifestation of my grief?" I push my fist into Evan's chest. My fingers are cold, and the hairs on my arm stick up.

"I can prove it without you needing to catch a chill." Evan floats over to my desk. He reaches down to a pencil I'd left out after doing my math homework. His hand becomes more substantial for a moment, and he picks the item up. The writing utensil hovers in the air. Evan's form shimmers in and out of existence before fading to the barest hint of an outline as the pencil drops to the floor. "Interacting with the world is possible for me, but it drains my essence to the point where you won't be able to see me again until I recover. I'll still be here watching you, though." Evan vanishes.

I walk over to my desk, bend over, and pick up the pencil. It feels like I'm clutching an icicle. The thought of my brother watching me while I can't perceive him gives me a shiver, but my doubts are gone.

I leave my bedroom and head to my mom's room. It's a mess inside, with clothes piled along her dresser. Two stale beers sit on her nightstand. I open the top drawer and sort through takeout menus, makeup items, and cigarettes. The key Evan told me about sits at the bottom. I take it and drop to the floor. There's a small, gray safe, one step up from a lockbox, pushed to the furthest point under the mattress. Evan is right again. I haul it out, unlock it, and find a gun that looks like it's been tossed out of a Western. It's a black revolver with a wood grip. I take the weapon and the small box of ammo. The gun's metal is cold to the touch, reminding me of my disembodied brother. I restore things to how they were before my intrusion and return to my bedroom.

After hiding the gun, I venture around the house, stuffing my backpack with everything I think I'll need: Duct tape, just in case, Granola bars, for energy, and my water bottle, for hydration. In the kitchen, I slide a drawer open and remove our largest knife. It's a white ceramic blade that Evan got my mom for Christmas three years ago. He'd broken her best knife trying to pry apart an old television with his friends, and this had been his apology. I put the knife in the bag. Lastly, I dig out my old flashlight and find working batteries for it in our junk cabinet.

When I'm satisfied with my supplies, I sit down at my computer and look up videos about improving my target accuracy, operating a revolver, and navigating old mines.

#   #   #

It's noon on Sunday when I arrive at the Gates of Hell.

The mine entrance is a dark maw carved out of the side of a mountain. A torn-down chain-link fence lies before it. Mom had told me the location got its name when the remains of a chicken set inside a chalk-drawn pentagram were found outside the tunnel in the eighties. The resulting Satanic panic led to the town erecting a fence, which teenagers quickly destroyed. Autumn's winds have removed leaves from most of the surrounding trees.

I swing my backpack down, pull out my flashlight, the gun, the knife, and my ammo. Muscle memory comes back quickly, and I pop the revolver's chamber and load six shells. I store the left-over bullets in the bag, and I slide the knife into my front pocket for easy reach. Prepped, I return the bag to my back and start forward with a gun in my right hand and a switched-on flashlight in my left.

With a deep breath, I scramble over the downed fence and proceed into the darkness ahead. The walls are smoothly tunneled out, and I have plenty of room to walk. At my feet are the remnants of an old cart track. My hope is that there's nothing in here to find, and my ghostly brother was mistaken about the monster.

The air is warm at first, but when I can no longer see the sun behind me, a cool breeze from within the mine starts to give me goosebumps. I look for signs of any living thing in the flashlight's beams. Every step I take echoes through the tunnel, and there's a steady drip of water coming from somewhere. A rancid, rotten smell slithers its way into my nostrils, but I continue forward. Ahead, the path splits. Something out of place in the tunnel to the left catches my attention.

I move that direction, and the light reveals a pile of bones.

A shudder runs through my body. There aren't enough recognizable pieces to identify the supplying creature. More skeletal parts lead deeper into the mine. It's practically a trail of breadcrumbs. I keep the gun held tight and aimed forward as I advance.

It's hard not to step on the bones as they start to clutter the entire path. The horrid stench grows stronger. There's a loud crunch as I shatter old bones beneath my feet. A solitary light, in the shape of a triangle, comes to life in the distance. My heart's beating turns frantic. Something knows I'm here.

I continue forward, ready to face the monster. The wealth of bones grows to ridiculous proportions around my feet. I spot several human skulls amongst the macabre debris.

The tunnel's walls cease abruptly as I enter a cavernous space. As I step closer, I realize the triangular light ahead is a teepee radiating luminosity from within. The pale pigmentation of the teepee's material reminds me of human skin, and a thin figure is silhouetted inside. Whatever is in there has an elongated cranium and two spindly arms.

The head swivels in my direction. "I caught a whiff of your blood as soon as you entered the mine. I'd hoped the skeletons would dissuade you, but you kept coming." The voice emanating from the darkened profile is cold and raspy. "You must have a purpose here. What is it?"

I raise my weapon and aim at the teepee.

"Is that gun oil I smell? You're here for me?"

My finger starts squeezing the trigger back to fire.

"Please, don't."

The plea startles me into halting my shot.

"Why do you want to kill me? Can we talk first?"

My mouth is as dry as sandpaper, but I manage a reply. "Yes."

"What harm have I done you?"

"You killed my brother."

The shadowy figure adjusts its position inside the teepee. "I've never killed a living thing."

I almost laugh. "How do you explain all these bones?"

"All these organisms were dead before I consumed their flesh for sustenance and used what I needed to make this home."

"My brother told me you fuel the cycles of violence in Hazel Peak. You keep people's spirits in agony."

"I thought you said your brother was dead?"

The gun feels heavy in my hand from holding it up for so long. "He is, but his ghost told me everything I needed to know."

"Ghost? There is no such thing." The teepee's illumination fades to nothing.

"What're you doing? Why'd you put the light out?"

The only answer is a tearing sound, and I realize the speaker is trying to escape out the back of the dwelling. Adrenaline surges through me, and I circumvent the teepee. As I reach the other side, my flashlight reveals a hole in the lining at eye level. The noxious scent from earlier oozes out of the opening. Two hands, with six long, boney protrusions, retract back into the teepee's darkness. My light reflects off something scarlet within.

"Human, I've done you no harm. Let me go."

"Even if you only eat the dead, that doesn't mean you aren't causing this town's violence."

The monster cackles. "A series of complex human interactions, beliefs, and goals mix to create violent results throughout your history, and you think a single being is responsible? Your species needs a group or person to persecute at all times, and when you don't have one, you'll find a scapegoat, like me."

Evan appears in a burst of radiant azure. "Don't believe its lies. The monster is to blame for the evil in Hazel Peak."

I jump in shock, but I'm happy to see my brother.

The monster whispers through the torn hole, "I can hear that ghost too, you know, and while I've never found evidence of human souls living after death, there are other beings, hungry things, that live in the dark. They want into this world. I keep some at bay, and they fear me. They want me gone. I've never known them to take human guise before, but there's a first time for everything. You're being used."

Evan floats to my side. "More lies. It's not even human. You've got to kill it and end the violence. Free our souls!"

The gun trembles in my grasp. All the words I've heard swim through my mind. Evan smiles and nods for me to get on with the shooting. I picture his head hanging limply in the passenger seat again. I owe him for taking his life with my stupid driving. Tears well up in my eyes. I fire.

The first shot pierces the teepee, and the monster lets out an agonized wail. The structure rips apart as I fire again. The creature is cloaked by shadows and tatters, but I catch a glimpse of a gray, worm-like lower body slithering inside. I pull the trigger a third time. The shot ricochets off some rocks and bounces around the space, making it impossible to hear anything else. Two boney claws slash toward me as the monster frees itself of its shredded living area and charges.

Atop its head is a single, crimson eye, and its mouth is open wide, revealing rows of vicious, jagged teeth. I pull the trigger as fast as I can, firing my final bullets in rapid succession. Black ichor spills out from its midsection as two holes appear in its flesh. The monster is still coming, and its claws connect with my hands, sending my gun flying into the darkness and my flashlight skittering to the ground.

I scramble to pull my knife out while backing away from the monster. The flashlight spins where it landed nearby. I get a grip on my weapon. One second, the approaching form is illuminated, and in the next, we're both in darkness. I hear the monster sliding over the rocky floor and my breath coming in quick bursts. The light swivels around again to reveal the creature within arm's reach. I see the wormy lower body, the spindly arms, and the freakish head. The alienness disgusts me. I pull back my knife and prepare to strike.

"Please," it says. "Don't. I want to liv—"

My knife plunges through the monster's eye.

Regret surges through me as the thing slides back off my blade and collapses to the ground, dead. Its blood flows out to form a pool around its foreign form. My knife drips with its vital fluids. Mercifully, the light stops spinning and keeps the creature's corpse shrouded in darkness. I look for my brother, but he's gone. The monster's last words echo in my head.

I collect my flashlight and search for my gun. As I explore the area, I'm careful to avoid the spot where the monster fell. I don't want another glimpse of what I did to it. The pistol lies at the edge of the ruined teepee. Inside the dwelling, there is an extinguished lantern and some half-eaten rabbits. My gun is scuffed from the ruckus, but I suspect my mom won't ever notice the mark.

As I turn to leave, I realize the monster's black blood has stained my white, ceramic knife. I'll have to buy a new one for the house and get rid of this one. I look back at the teepee in disbelief as I tuck the gun and ammo into my bag. If only Evan could appear again and tell me it had worked, and he was free, my actions would feel justified.

#   #   #

I add a newly purchased ceramic knife to our kitchen a week later. I'd also cleaned the gun before successfully returning it to my mom's safe. I'm still hoping she'll never notice the six missing bullets. I've struggled with nightmares of the mine every night since coming back. The last words of the monster continue to repeat in my brain, but I try to keep Evan's words there too. He'd said the thing lied.

Mom walks into the kitchen with a grim look on her face. "Oh, God. Did you hear the news?"

"What's up?"

"Some psychos just shot up a diner downtown. It's horrible. They live-streamed the whole thing, and it's all over social media. The cops got them, thank God, but I can't believe people would do something so sick." She goes to the fridge and pulls out a beer.

My body trembles. "But I stopped the monster."

Mom continues to search for a beer in the fridge. "What's that, Nate?"

Evan's ghost appears behind Mom. He smiles and winks at me. His spectral form begins to change. The upper body vanishes, and dozens of spidery appendages erupt from his elongating head as his eyes burst. His nostrils expand into cavernous holes, which consume most of Evan's remaining flesh. In their depths, legions of squirming, insectile figures scuttle for escape. Before the millions of carapaces erupt from the face, the apparition vanishes. There's a moment of relief before a thought shatters my mind.

I killed the monster that was keeping the hungry things at bay. ♛

HARD SELL

By Will McDermott

LA'NAT HEARD THE TINY BELL above the shop's outer door jingle as he sat in the back room nursing a cup of tea laced with just a bit of vodka. His evening meal, a generous portion of goat and carrot pilaf, sat half-eaten in a wide bowl on the table.

"A customer?" La'nat said to no one. "I was not expecting any business tonight."

The shop owner stood, straightened his waistcoat, and tightened his cravat before calling out to the unexpected patron.

"Be right there," he said in a sing-song voice toward the curtain. Before leaving the back room, La'nat carried his cup and bowl to the sink. It often took quite some time to convince customers that his unique wares were exactly what they needed. Else, why would they have entered his shop in the first place?

As La'nat turned toward the curtain, he realized he had received no response from his earlier call.

"Curious," La'nat exclaimed as he bustled toward the front room. "An unexpected and rudely silent guest. What is this world coming to?"

But when La'nat pushed his way through the curtain, the word "Hello" hanging on the tip of his tongue, he found no one in the store at all.

"Well, now. That is most odd," La'nat said as he gazed around his tiny shop. The old, oaken door with its devilishly ornate cut-glass window remained shut. The tiny bell hanging above the entrance stood perfectly still, mocking him with its silence.

No light penetrated the shop through the large windows to either side of the door. So, either the streetlamps had not yet been lit outside or they had already been extinguished for the night. It was impossible to tell from inside.

La'nat fought the urge to open the door to see if anyone lurked on his stoop. He wasn't expecting any customers and unexpected customers were often the hardest sells. He was never keen to invite anyone inside without first knowing them and their business. Plus, there was the distinct chance that nothing lay outside that door, that the world did not exist past the door frame—at least not at this moment in time.

He actually quite enjoyed standing at the open door while the shop was between customers and staring into the turbulent maelstrom—the swirling clouds of gray, black, purple, and yellow filled with blue lightning and screaming red streamers—that existed between worlds.

The sight had frightened him the first time he'd witnessed what he came to call "The Eternal Vortex." Over the decades, however, the shopkeeper had become almost obsessed with the power that lay within that storm. It was always right at hand but forever out of reach, for there was no turning back if he should succumb to his fixation and step past his front stoop.

"Not today," La'nat said, as he forced the vision of the Eternal Vortex back down into his subconscious and tore his gaze away from the door.

And yet, he couldn't simply return to his pilaf and tea. In all the years of being the proprietor of this shop, La'nat had never heard the bell ring without a customer coming through. And if the door had hit the bell as it opened, how did it not ring again upon closing?

Curious and more curious.

La'nat decided to walk the aisles to determine if anything had gone missing. The close-set tables were packed with dozens of rare oddities, novelties, and curios that La'nat had collected across the decades, but he knew exactly where each item sat, whom he had acquired it from, and the price that had been paid.

He kept no ledgers, though. The entire inventory and every item's provenance lived only inside his mind, like lifelong friends who gathered on occasion to reminisce about old times together. That thought alone made La'nat chuckle as it brought the look on the faces of particular past customers rushing to the front of his mind to remind him of hard-earned sales.

The nearest table contained nothing but jars. He had quite the collection, from several as small as test tubes, each of which contained a single octopus tentacle greatly magnified by the curvature of the glass, all the way up to a particularly massive jar that held what appeared to be the emaciated remains of a lynx or bobcat.

In between were jars filled with the skeletons of rats and small birds, one holding a perfectly preserved giant hornet, another with a praying mantis poised to strike, and several with what customers always assumed were shrunken heads, if such things truly existed (which La'nat knew they did).

In the middle of the table sat La'nat's prized jar, which held what only could be described as the mummified corpse of a fairy. Its wide eyes stared dead ahead in shock or horror above a gaping mouth. Its lithe body looked wrenched and twisted, as if in pain, as long, gray, brittle tresses fell over its bony shoulders and down across the delicate wings that spread around the back of the jar.

"Beautiful," La'nat whispered as he reached out to caress the fairy jar. "Someday, my sweet. Someday we will find you a home."

The curio shop owner continued checking his stock, moving from table to table and case to case, making sure everything was in its place. He passed by an open coffin that held a large bat, its wings splayed wide and held in place by pins. He checked the cracked and broken oaken wine cabinet to ensure the rusty corkscrew and tarnished jigger remained inside. He glanced at the yellowing and maroon-stained wedding dress that hung on the wall above the ancient rotary phone with the number eight etched onto every spot on the dial.

La'nat turned to head down the last aisle, which would take him past the door. As he scanned the front table, something odd caught his eye just past his lone remaining Monkey's Paw and the Hand of Glory he had purchased long ago from the estate of an accomplished alchemist who had come to an unfortunate end.

It might seem odd to customers that the shopkeeper kept his two most prized items so near the door, but La'nat enjoyed showing them off to everyone who crossed his threshold. The two macabre items were instantly recognizable and ensured that customers knew exactly what type of shop they had entered. What was a curio shop without a Monkey's Paw and a Hand of Glory?

And, of course, the shop was protected from theft. No one could remove any item from the store without paying its cost. Some desperate souls had tried over the years, but none had gotten away with any merchandise, and all had paid the price, in the end.

La'nat moved down the aisle toward the two infamous items to get a closer look at what seemed out of place, but then a sudden chill washed over him as the bell jingled again. The door slammed open, bringing with it a gust of cold, moist air.

Through the door stepped a young lady dressed from head to toe in black. She wore a simple small-brimmed hat adorned with black silk flowers and charcoal-colored ribbons. Ebon lace draped across her face, covering her delicate, pale features in a deep shadow, while a jet-black, tailored jacket covered a dark, high-necked blouse clasped at the top by an onyx stone. Completing her mourning outfit, the young woman wore black gloves and a flowing sable skirt that brushed the top of her buckled black-leather boots.

For a brief moment, before the young widow closed the door, La'nat spied a billowing mist outside, which could have been a morning fog rolling off some nearby wharf, the first whisps of the cold, wet air of a burgeoning twilight, or the remnants of the Eternal Vortex through which his shop traveled when not moored to the real world.

Shrugging off the enticing memory of those turbulent eddies once again, La'nat rallied and plastered his eternal smile across his face.

"Good day, madam," he said, hedging his bets on the local time outside his door. "What brings you to my fine establishment?"

"What brings anyone to Sotuvchi's Emporium?" asked the widow, her voice oddly light despite the tinge of sorrow La'nat detected underneath. "Revenge."

A mixture of emotions swept through La'nat at the mention of that word. Vengeance was indeed his bread and butter, but he seldom encountered customers who were so open about their quest for retribution upon those whom they felt had wronged them.

On top of that, La'nat rarely, if ever, entertained a client whom he had not felt coming from leagues away, whose vengeful passion had not blazed like a beacon in the night, drawing him and his Emporium to their hamlet or village square.

"You are La'nat Sotuvchi, are you not?" the widow asked. "The proprietor of this establishment?"

La'nat's smile faded at the mention of his name. Yes, it was etched in a brass plaque attached to the door along with a date of incorporation, but no one as far as he could remember had ever said his full name out loud inside his shop. It made him feel small, as if reduced to a mere collection of letters instead of the great collector of the magical and macabre and the supreme supplier of supernatural justice, which was how he saw himself.

The shopkeeper tried to cover his sudden diminishment by bowing low and spreading his arms wide in a grand gesture.

"That I am," he replied after straightening. "But I must confess you have me at a disadvantage. What may I call you, Madam…"

"Miss, I'm afraid," the widow replied. "My husband passed recently, and I have no surviving children."

La'nat waited for the young widow to continue but, for a moment so long it seemed to stretch on forever, she did not.

"You may call me Cassandra," the young widow finally added in a breezy and off-hand manner that was certainly out of place from someone in mourning. "Cassandra Nikovna."

Curiouser and curiouser, he thought. A widow who refuses to be referred to as "madam" and requests the use of her first name from a stranger while in mourning. This Cassandra Nikovna was quite an enigma. La'nat needed to find out more about this mystery woman. Otherwise, how could he find the right item to sell to her to enact her revenge, and thus irrevocably ensnare her soul to the power of the dark one whom La'nat served.

"Well, Miss Nikovna, please feel free to browse my wares," he said, deciding to retreat and regroup.

La'nat felt exposed standing in the middle of his shop speaking with a customer who knew more about him than he did about her. He gestured at the tables in the shop as he strode back to the security and power of his counter.

"I am sure you will find the right item to aid in your quest for justice," La'nat said after taking up his normal spot behind the brass register. He could feel his confidence returning. "Perhaps if you told me who wronged you, I might be able to guide your choice."

Lady Cassandra had begun moving away from the door, seemingly unmoved by the power of the Monkey's Paw or Hand of Glory, and glanced here and there at some lesser macabre items along the first aisle. She raised her veil and tucked it into the brim of her hat before giving La'nat a wan smile.

"I am seeking to avenge the death of my late husband," she said. "He did not die of natural causes."

La'nat tried to read the widow's face but could detect little emotion behind her words or eyes. She had a round, almost cherubic face that was bereft of color except for full, red lips that drew one's gaze away from her haunted, hazel eyes. Despite the evident loss reflected behind the eyes of the widow, La'nat detected no bitterness there. Her eyes somehow still sparkled with kindness—or rather the faint afterglow of a once intense kindness now lost to the world.

Although La'nat saw no evidence of a vengeful fire burning in Cassandra's heart, she seemed an ideal candidate for the shop's particular wares. The young widow was little more than a babe lost in the woods of remorse. Easy pickings for Sotuvchi's Emporium, and a tasty morsel for La'nat's master. All he need do was lead this little lamb to slaughter.

And yet, something about her features gnawed at the back of La'nat's brain. He had never seen her before, of that he was certain. Who could forget such a perfect, angelic face? But there was something there, something familiar. It would come to him eventually. Perhaps this customer wasn't a complete mystery, which was something anyway.

"A slain spouse, you say," La'nat said, rallying to try to regain control of the situation. "I am certain to have the perfect item to sate your desire for revenge."

"I'm sure you do," Cassandra replied with an odd certainty, before quickly adding: "What would you suggest?"

Despite the strange tenor of her response, the fact that the widow was now soliciting his advice made La'nat relax a bit. It seemed the power in this conversation was returning to him. He decided to press on, to elicit the information he needed to ensnare this lovely young lady in a web of spite and corruption from which she would never escape.

"Tell me, Miss Cassandra, if it is not too painful for you, how did your husband die? Who was to blame for his untimely demise?"

Cassandra picked up a ragdoll from the table in front of her and held it in a tender, almost motherly fashion despite the black, button eyes on the face of the doll, the tattered dress stained in multiple places, and the blackened hands and feet where the doll had obviously been held to a fire.

To La'nat the widow seemed to be locked in an almost dreamlike state. Perhaps her husband's death had been quite recent, and she was still in shock. Perhaps her need for vengeance had already numbed her other senses. If so, she should be easy to manipulate, if only he could get her to open up about her pain.

"He was consumed by hatred," Cassandra replied after setting the ragged doom-doll back on the table. "It all began when his business partner turned against him."

La'nat watched as Cassandra continued to stare at the doll with a mixture of sadness and longing in her eyes. Again, there was something there that gnawed at the back of his memory.

"Well," he said after a moment, "I have several items that can turn the tables in a business dealing. The wine cabinet against the far wall is one of my particular favorites. It can..."

"Oh! You misunderstand me," Lady Cassandra said, cutting La'nat off mid-sales pitch. "I am not seeking vengeance against my husband's former partner. That chapter of the story has long since run its course."

"I see," La'nat replied, although this customer's story was far from clear. In fact, it seemed to become more muddled every time she spoke. Cassandra lingered around the doll, seemingly unable to break away from its button-eyed stare.

"Does your vengeance have something to do with a child?" he asked. "Your child, perhaps? Forgive me for my impertinence, but I can't help but notice your preoccupation with the Raggedy Tugmasi doll."

Cassandra managed a wan, lopsided smile at the mention of the doll's name.

"It does remind me of a doll my husband bought for our daughter," she said. She reached out to caress the face of the doll. "It too is gone, along with my husband and my child. I have nothing left you see."

Nothing but your vengeance, thought La'nat. And I shall be all too happy to feed that, if only you would let me peek inside your heart to see what dark desires lie there.

"Perhaps if you unburden yourself of all these past memories, you may open your heart to new opportunities," he said. "Confession is good for the soul...or so they say."

"Confession is nothing more than a tool for powerful men to control the lives of the weak-minded," Cassandra said, her demeanor suddenly hard. Her cold eyes bore into La'nat's own from beneath deeply furrowed brows.

A moment later, the widow Nikovna's face returned to the somewhat vacant, slightly bemused naivety it had born before her retort.

"That is what my father used to say on his darkest days when he could feel the black wolf calling from outside his door," she said. "He succumbed to the wolf not long after."

La'nat stared at the mysterious Lady Nikovna, not for the first time befuddled by the enigma of her presence in his shop. Here she was, a husband seemingly slain, a daughter taken from her as well, and a father who had faced his own demons before likely taking his own life. How much death had this young widow witnessed in her short life? And yet, her aura was as muted as that of a young child who had not a care in the world.

Cassandra turned and continued meandering down the aisle. She reached the table filled with glass jars and fingered one of the octopus tentacle vials, twisting it about in its stand as she leaned down to stare at the writhing limb inside.

"Those tentacles are used to curse a body with ghastly skin lesions that never heal," he said as she lifted the vial up to her eye. He, of course, left out the part where the vengeful soul who performs the curse turns into a tentacled monster, and that the vial she held actually contained a remnant of the previous purchaser.

"How intriguing," she replied. "Although not exactly the impact I am seeking with my vengeance."

Some part of La'nat might have felt pity, or at least compassion, for the poor woman, but as she just reminded him, lady Nikovna had entered his shop with vengeance in her heart. She was, despite her young age, her waiflike appearance, and her apparent innocence, nothing more than a client—a lost soul to be guided away from the light and into the darkness.

Before he could lead Cassandra Nikovna into the belly of the beast he served, however, La'nat must first deduce her intent. He must lay her heart bare and divine her story so that he might ensnare her upon the sharpened tines of her deepest wounds.

He had just the thing for the task.

"If you will allow some impertinence on my part, my lady," he said, "I believe you are holding back. You say you wish to enact vengeance upon the person or persons you blame for the death of your husband, but your attention to this task seems out of focus. May I attempt to help you see the goal you seek more clearly?"

Cassandra replaced the tentacle vial in its stand and nodded her assent, although La'nat detected a hint of concern behind her eyes. This was understandable under the circumstances, though, so he returned the smile, cocked his head, and gave her his most reassuring look.

La'nat gestured for the young widow to follow him to a small table in the corner of the shop. Upon this table sat several bizarre pieces of taxidermy, including a two-headed baby chick, a three-eyed fish, and a quite large rabbit with a full, ten-point rack of antlers.

"Quite fanciful aren't they," he said, looking down at the macabre animals. Each, he knew, were completely real, and not just imagined by a deranged taxidermist. And each delivered a quite devastating curse, but that was not why he had brought Cassandra to the table.

Reaching out, La'nat grasped a short brass spyglass that lay, somewhat hidden, on a stand behind the trio of unnatural nightmares. He telescoped the metal tube to its full length and held it out before him. The brass had dulled over the years and was badly pitted in spots from corrosion, but he could still feel the power emanating from inside the object as it lay in the palms of his hands.

"This is the Eye of Qaroqchi," he said. "It is said that any who peer through the lens will see their heart's desire in the distance."

La'nat offered the scope to the widow.

"Take it," he said. "Look through it and describe what you see."

Cassandra reached toward the spyglass but then held back, her fingers curling in on themselves as her eyes furrowed in doubt.

"There is no charge, and no hidden fees or provisos," La'nat said. "I am gifting you this opportunity to help you focus your desire for vengeance so I may better guide you in your purchase today. Believe me, this is a once-in-a-lifetime offer that I have never made to any other customer."

Cassandra grabbed the spyglass quite suddenly, snatching it from La'nat's hands and raising it to her eye in one smooth motion. For some time, she looked through the eyepiece, spinning slowly as she scanned the room.

After a minute, Cassandra stopped turning and peered intently in a single direction. La'nat noticed she was looking toward the front of the shop, although he knew that whatever Miss Nikovna saw through the eyepiece, it was most likely someplace other than this shop.

As he mused on this point, Cassandra gasped and lost her grip. The spyglass toppled from her hands and slid down between her blouse and jacket. The widow clasped her arms around her midriff, stopping the spyglass's descent before it clattered to the floor. After securing it tightly once more in her fists, she held it out to the shopkeeper, a sheepish look on her face.

La'nat took the spyglass, compacted it to its original size and replaced it on the stand behind the Jackalope. He did this all deliberately and slowly to give the widow time to recover her composure and process what she had seen.

"So, what did you see?" he asked finally.

"At first all I saw were swirling mists of colored clouds," she started. "I'm not entirely sure where I was. Lightning streaked through the clouds. It felt like I was floating inside a storm. I was terrified. Then, in the distance, I saw your shop. I tried to push through the swirling vortex to reach your front door, but something held me back."

"What held you back?" La'nat asked. His eagerness to delve into the depths of the widow's distracted psyche overrode his shock that she had seen the Eternal Vortex. "What was behind you?"

"Behind me, I saw my husband and daughter and father," she replied. "My father and husband held me by the shoulders, while my daughter clasped me around the waist."

It seemed obvious to La'nat that the widow Nikovna's conscience was attempting to keep her from taking the final step toward the abyss that lay ahead of her. He needed to break the hold that love had on her heart so she could fully embrace the hate that vengeance brought.

"Your loved ones are gone," he said. "Nothing can bring them back. You need to let go of the past and concentrate on moving forward."

"Perhaps you are right, Mr. Sotuvchi," she said, but she began backing away from him toward the front of the shop. "I don't believe my family would want me to continue down the path I am on."

La'nat raised his hands, palms forward as Cassandra turned at the corner and crept toward the door.

"You misunderstand me," he said. "Only vengeance can truly free you from the guilt of outliving a spouse, a child, or even a parent who were wrongly stolen from you. Let me help you unburden your soul so you may find a new path in this life and the next."

Cassandra Nikovna—bereaved widow, grieving mother and child— stopped beside the shop's two prized possessions and glared at La'nat Sotuvchi. Gone was the innocence and naivety behind her eyes. Those qualities had been replaced by a quiet fire brought only through certainty of purpose.

"No. You misunderstand me, Mr. Sotuvchi," she stated. "I know full well where your path leads. I saw that road laid bare ahead of me after you stole my husband from me with the same smooth lies and counterfeit promises."

"I...I don't understand," La'nat stammered. "What did I ever do to you? I don't even know who you are."

"I am Madam Cassandra Nikovna Qurbon," she stated with a strength and pride in her voice that La'nat had not seen earlier. "You sold an item to my husband some months back to wreak vengeance upon his business partner after that cruel man ruined us for a pound of silver while our daughter lay on her deathbed."

All the sordid details of Nikolas Qurbon's story and purchase rushed into the shopkeeper's mind at the mention of Miss Nikovna's married name. He finally realized what had seemed out of place earlier beside the Monkey's Paw and the Hand of Glory.

"This item, actually," Madam Qurbon continued, as she lifted a tattered deck of playing cards from the table. The backs bore a set of scales that held a human heart on one side and a feather on the other.

"You told my husband he could use these cards to take everything from his business partner in a game of chance."

"That was true," La'nat protested, but he could hear the desperation in his voice. "All of my wares function exactly as advertised."

"Only you never advertise the drawbacks, do you?" she asked. "My husband won our fortune back, and more. He drove his partner into destitution and a despair so deep the man took his own life. But as soon as that wicked man died, so did my husband."

"I am not responsible for the pain inflicted on my patrons due to the evil in their hearts," La'nat said indignantly. "Your husband signed a contract. The price for his vengeance had to be paid. You cannot blame me for his death."

"You still fail to understand my intentions," Madam Qurbon stated as she held the deck in front of her. "I do not blame you. There is no vengeance in my heart. I seek justice and the only peace of mind left to one who has nothing left to lose on this mortal coil."

"What...what are you doing?" La'nat asked, finally realizing why he had not felt the widow Qurbon coming before she entered his shop—twice. She had not come for revenge. She came here to die.

"I plan to free my husband from his hellish prison," she said. With that, she picked up the Monkey's Paw and raised it toward the deck in her other hand.

The deck she had deposited the first time she entered. The deck that La'nat had failed to collect after her husband's demise despite repeated attempts. The deck that now held the souls of nearly three score seekers of vengeance. A very dangerous object indeed.

"I wish for a flame," she commanded the Monkey's Paw.

The third digit of the monkey's paw curled into its palm as a bright, red-and-yellow flame erupted from its index finger. Cassandra pointed the flame at the deck. As the corners of the cards began to char, the air filled with the screams of the damned.

"You'll kill us both!" La'nat screamed. "If you free the souls trapped in that deck, they will tear us apart in a mindless rage!"

"Why do you think I brought this here?" she asked. "These souls will have their justice for your part in their fate. My husband will be free. And no one else will ever pay for the crimes you commit from the safety of this shop."

"But you'll die too, "La'nat replied as he frantically searched for anything at hand that could stop the determined widow. He spied one option.

"If that is my fate, I will spend eternity with my husband, my child, and my father," she said as the flames engulfed the deck. "I will go to my eternal rest knowing you will never harm another soul on Earth."

La'nat lunged for the jar holding his precious fairy. He bashed the jar on the table, freeing the emaciated, winged girl inside.

"Stop her!" he yelled at the tiny creature, which fluttered into the air from the shards of glass.

The naked, nearly mummified fairy rose into the air, its wings fluttering so quickly they seemed to disappear. It opened its mouth and screamed.

The air erupted in sound. Wave after wave of high-pitched wailing emanated from the fairy's mouth. The screams buffeted the widow and the burning deck in her hand, forcing her back toward the door and nearly extinguishing the flames consuming the cards.

Cassandra spoke to the Monkey's Paw again: "I wish Sotuvchi to be the fairy's target."

As the second finger curled in next to the third in the palm, the fairy pivoted in mid-air and wailed at the shopkeeper, driving him past his counter and through the curtains into his kitchen.

La'nat did not see what happened next, but when the screams of dozens of trapped souls erupted from behind the curtain, drowning out the wailing of his precious banshee, he knew that Madam Qurbon had succeeded in destroying the Deck of Maat's Justice and dooming them both to a grisly death at the hands of the ghastly souls trapped inside.

The curtains flapped and tore as wispy shapes blew through them to envelop La'nat. He felt himself grasped from all sides as the formless souls sought purchase of his arms, legs, neck, and head. They tugged and wrenched at his body until his joints gave, his skin ripped in twain, and his bones snapped.

One thought buoyed La'nat Sutovchi during the brief time he had left. At least he would take another soul with him to whatever lay on the other side.

Just then, however, La'nat spied Madam Cassandra Nikovna Qurbon through the tattered curtains. She remained alive and whole, a single ghastly presence interceding between her and the doomed spirits flailing vainly before her.

Just before the ghasts plucked his eyeballs from their sockets, La'nat saw the door to his shop open behind the widow. There, he could see the Eternal Vortex swirling behind Cassandra as she stepped through, the ghost of her husband enveloping her in an eternal embrace.

UNAUTHORIZED ACCESS

By Sara Martinez

SHE HAD ALMOST MADE IT too easy.

Hugh licked his lips under his mask in anticipation. He watched the woman from the shadows. She was swaying slightly as she walked, fumbling about in her purse, paying no attention to her surroundings. The dull streetlight nearby flickered and went out entirely as she stepped up to a door and eventually pulled a set of mag keys out. As she bent over slightly to try to find the right one in the dark, Hugh made his move. He padded up, swiftly but silently and, as soon as he heard the lock click open, grabbed her left wrist, pulling it sharply across her back. He leaned in close, his weight pinning her to the door as his left hand snaked into her hair, jerking her head to the side, and exposing her pale neck.

The woman barely had time to gasp in shock before he whispered in her bared ear "No noise darlin'; I have a knife. I don't want to use it, but I will if you make a fuss." Hugh inhaled the scent of her neck while trailing his masked mouth lightly from her ear down to her shoulder.

Abruptly, he released her hair, pulled the keys away from the knob with practiced ease and pushed the door open. He shoved the woman inside, then shut the door behind them. She stumbled to her knees, pulled off balance by his grip on her wrist and the sudden swinging of the door. Just where he wanted her. "You and I are going to have some fun" Hugh drawled, as he opened his fly.

"Simulation Ended" chimed a pleasant and vaguely feminine robotic voice some time later.

Hugh relaxed in the VR chair and sighed contentedly as he put the headset back on its stand. This lounge straddled the line between seedy and expensive, just the way he liked it. It featured high-end equipment but also had one of the more lenient policies toward extreme virtual behavior, which was essential. He had just finished his favorite program, which let players stalk and attack virtual victims played by other users who were into that sort of thing. It was almost as good as real life. Almost. Hugh stroked his chin thoughtfully as he swiped through the system's menus, contemplating if he wanted another go. No, best to end on a high note. He saved the video feed of the game to his personal account and logged off the lounge's system. Stretching slowly as he stood up, Hugh waved to the holographic attendant on his way out.

It was a short walk back home from the lounge, and Hugh whistled absentmindedly while replaying the game in his head. It had been almost a perfect recreation of his last attack. Now that he thought about it, the other player's avatar even looked kind of like that girl. He chuckled at the coincidence as he let himself into his tiny basement apartment and locked the door behind him. Hugh was sadly getting too old and slow to carry on his little 'hobby' out in the physical world; too much risk of getting caught if something went wrong. The virtual games mostly satisfied the urges, and he tried to be content with that.

\#   \#   \#

Claire pulled off the headset and rubbed her eyes with the heels of her hands before groping around for her glasses.

Was this really it?

Had she finally found him?

She had spent months running algorithms to narrow down a behavior profile and weeks trolling the VR lobbies to meet players and try to find a matching modus operandi. You could never be sure a person's avatar resembled them in real life, but mannerisms were much harder to conceal or alter. After this latest encounter, she was almost certain: this was the man who raped her two years ago.

A shiver went down her spine, but she wasn't entirely sure if it was fear or the anticipation of what she was about to do to him. The wall of monitors surrounded her in a horseshoe, casting their blue light across her face as she pulled up a tracer program. The player she had just interacted with had logged in from a lounge. That meant he probably couldn't afford a rig at home capable of running the VR program -- or maybe he just didn't care enough to be that discreet. He had paid with cryptocurrency bought through a shell corporation to try to disguise his identity, but Claire knew how to run through the layers to find the original account and the name associated with it. From there, it was simple enough to locate his government database profile and address. She had the son of a bitch.

When she'd first been attacked, Claire cried for days. It was weeks before anyone could touch her without her flinching. She couldn't stand to leave the house for a long time and lost her job at the cyber security firm she'd worked at for years. The police had tried to investigate, but they didn't have much to go on. Her attacker wore a masked and gloved bodysuit made of DNA dissolving material as well as a condom so there was no physical evidence. None of the cameras near her old apartment (the ones that actually worked) had recorded anything actionable. Clearly, he'd known how to be careful not to get caught and it almost certainly hadn't been his first attack. She could never forget his voice, though; its soft, almost lilting tone that mocked as he assaulted her.

That voice haunted her dreams for months. Eventually, the fear and loathing gave way to white-hot rage. She wanted to find the bastard and make him pay. The Victim's Assistance stipend she'd been granted wasn't a lot, but it was enough to move to a more secure apartment as well as cover courses to get her private investigator's license. Claire threw herself into her studies, constantly learning new ways to identify and track people. Before long, she knew enough to take on small jobs to pay the bills and start saving for better equipment. In the free time between classes and clients, she pored over psychology handbooks to build a profile for her attacker. That, combined with the PI classes and her skills from her old job meant she soon had what she needed to start searching for her rapist. Over time, her rage smoldered instead of flashed, but it never went away. It was always there in the back of her mind, driving her and infusing her with a never-ending drive for revenge.

She'd turned off the VR inputs as much as possible, but it was still hard every time she let herself be attacked virtually. While her naturally timid personality seemed to attract plenty of predators, it was hard work to fight the panic the 'game' induced in her. Now, that work had paid off. Claire pulled up the picture from the man's official profile and studied it closely. Were those the eyes that had bored into her from behind the mask? Yes, she was sure now; this was her attacker. She leaned back in her chair and took in a deep breath, letting it out slowly. In truth, finding him had been the easy part. Now, the hard part would begin.

#   #   #

"WE KNOW WHAT YOU DID" headlined the top of Hugh's email feed.

The message had no listed sender and no body, just the subject line. Hugh's brow furrowed for a moment, then he rolled his eyes and deleted it. "Spammers are getting weird," he muttered under his breath. No sooner had he deleted it when another one popped in. Then another and another until his inbox was nearly full. The messages blared an accusation at him, but he wasn't sure exactly what it meant. Grumbling, Hugh tried to clear out the messages, but he couldn't keep up with their arrival. Abruptly, his screen flashed almost blindingly bright before going black.

"WE KNOW WHAT YOU DID" now took up his entire screen, stark white against the black. Hugh's panic rose, twisting his guts in knots. What the hell is this? None of the inputs were responding to him.

The message changed ominously. "WE ARE WATCHING YOU." Hugh gave up on the keyboard and started looking desperately for the power line under the desk. Coughing from the accumulated dust that was suddenly disturbed, he finally grasped the plug and pulled, looking back at the screen to make sure it went off.

"WE WILL MAKE YOU PAY," a final message promised before the screen went completely dark. Hugh sunk back to sit on the floor as the weight of that message bore down on him.

Letting out a shuddering breath, Hugh tried to force his racing mind to settle. Who could be doing this? Maybe a prank from one of the boys at his old shop? Even now, there were still some tasks that were cheaper to pay a person to do rather than buy a specialty robot. He'd only been retired a few months, so maybe they missed using him as a verbal punching bag?

Yeah, that must be it. Davey or Frank probably hired some punk hacker to mess with his rig. Just to be safe, he disconnected the network link until he could run a diagnostic on the machine and assess if anything had been taken. Hugh's collection of digital trophies from the lounge (the recordings of his game sessions) were not technically illegal, but in the wrong hands it could cause problems for him. He'd have to find a more secure place to back them up before re-linking to the network.

Crossing his fingers, Hugh replaced the power plug and tried to boot the unconnected rig back up. Everything seemed fine now. The diagnostic program couldn't find any record of a transfer that would suggest someone took any of his files. Definitely must have been some old work 'buddy' playing him for a chump.

\#   \#   \#

Claire's wristband buzzed for attention in the middle of a match; her sparring partner nearly connected a jab to the temple in her split-second of distraction. After clumsily batting the blow away, she asked for a break to go check her tablet.

The gym was a twice-weekly ritual she'd done her utmost to maintain over the years since the attack. She mainly focused on a fusion martial arts class, a style combining savate and aikido which was particularly effective for her small stature. The class was largely made up of other sexual assault survivors and was a great source of comfort and support to Claire.

Digging her tablet out of her gym bag, Claire pulled up the alert and read the full text. She smiled wolfishly. Things were coming together nicely.

One encrypted reply later, Claire started a countdown timer and resisted the urge to simply sit and watch it by putting the tablet back in her bag. She stepped on to the mat again, adopting a defensive stance for the next round. Anticipation of what was about to happen made it difficult to concentrate on her form, but she did her best.

\#   \#   \#

Hugh struggled to consciousness; something felt wrong, but he couldn't quite figure out what. As he opened his eyes, he recognized why he felt so strange: he lay on a bed in a VR simulation. Glancing around the room, he recognized the type of program. He'd only logged on to one once or twice as they lacked any element of the chase he craved, but it was unmistakable—the place where the truly sadistic came to fulfill illicit desires.

No safety protocols were instilled in this type of sim and the players couldn't get out unless someone disconnected them manually from the outside. It was the kind of room used by a new breed of human traffickers; they'd hook a victim up to the VR and let the clients have their way with them without any physical proof of an attack. Perpetrator and victim would feel every stimulus from the rig in a nearly identical way to it physically happening. The program had so many firewalls and redirects, it was almost impossible to trace its source. The law hadn't entirely caught up to this new form of assault to punish the perpetrators legally…if they could even be found.

How did he get here? Last he knew, he was in his bed, falling asleep for the night. Hugh tried to sit up, only to realize that his avatar was cuffed to the bed. Instead of his normal avatar, he'd been downloaded into a naked female body. He thrashed against his restraints, but they held fast like they were programmed to do.

The door opposite from the bed opened and a fat bald man wearing a sweat-stained tank top and gray sweatpants strode in with a leering grin on his face. Behind him, Hugh caught a glimpse of a queue of least a dozen men waiting in the hall before the door swung shut.

"Wait, you don't understand!" Hugh exclaimed as the man approached him. The voice wasn't his, but that of a young woman laced with shrill terror.

"There's been some kind of mis-" The backhand —hard, unforgiving—across the mouth shut him up. His eyes watered and his voice caught in his throat.

"No talking," growled the fat man. "I don't like it when they beg." He shoved a gag in Hugh's mouth. "The screams are so much more exciting when they're muffled."

#   #   #

Claire sat on a stool in front of the window bar at the cafe across the street from the VR lounge. From there, she had the perfect view of the lounge door, and she watched intently while sipping her boba. Hugh had been strapped into one of the VR chairs for about 10 minutes according to the timer she had set, so she pulled up her tablet and executed the command she had programmed to make an anonymous police report. Something serious enough to warrant a quick response, but not so dire that they'd come in gun blazing. She'd given detailed instructions for the thugs she'd hired to kidnap Hugh on how to arrange the scene at the lounge. When the police arrived, they'd disconnect him from the machine and find all the evidence they'd need to convict him of multiple rapes waiting on a data stick in his lap.

Seven minutes later, two hover cruisers swiftly glided into view, coming to a halt in front of the lounge. Two officers exited each cruiser and conferred briefly before walking inside. Claire pulled up the surveillance feed for the lounge and watched the four officers approach the rig where Hugh sat. The lounge owner had been too cheap to equip cameras that recorded sound, but she could read the officers' body language easily enough. Confusion gave way to annoyance as they quickly verified that no one else was in the lounge. They seemed on the verge of leaving when one of them gestured at the paper sign taped to Hugh's chest, blazoned with a single word: Rapist. They leaned in to study the scene, while one picked up his radio to report something. Another donned his gloves and carefully removed the sign then picked up the data stick attached to it. He plugged the stick into his handheld rig, presumably running the necessary security scans.

After a few minutes, his eyes widened at the evidence in front of him, and he hurriedly showed his fellow officers. They all huddled around the screen to watch, periodically glancing over at Hugh. When the playback finished, the office disconnected the data stick and put it and the sign in an evidence bag. A debate seemed to ensue whether they should unplug Hugh from the rig and after a few moments they did so. Hugh's body spasmed when he was disconnected, and he immediately curled up, weeping. At first, he did not even seem aware of the officers standing over him.

One of the officers took Hugh by the arm, pulling him to his feet. His eyes were wild for a moment, but when he realized what was happening his body sagged, and he let himself be led outside. Claire looked up from her tablet to watch the policewoman maneuver Hugh to the rear door of her cruiser and settle him in the backseat. Shortly after, a forensics van pulled alongside the cruisers and several techs stepped out to put on their clean suits before carrying their gear in. Claire didn't envy them trying to extract anything useful from the scene given that the lounge looked as though it was cleaned less than once a month. She had provided the hired muscle with the same type of DNA dissolving jumpsuits Hugh had worn to commit his crimes so they couldn't be tied to the scene.

The responding officers had all returned to their cruisers and were preparing to leave. Claire stepped outside the cafe to watch them pull away. Hugh was staring blankly out the window as it passed when he suddenly seemed to notice her. His eyes grew wide with recognition and all remaining color drained from his face. Claire couldn't help a small smirk creeping onto her lips. Hugh began to yell at the officers, but she could tell they dismissed him. The evidence on the data stick she had left was more than enough to ensure a decades-long sentence for Hugh. Even if he now realized that Claire was behind the entire setup, he would never be able to prove it. She'd made sure of that.

As the cruiser silently skimmed away, Claire felt an intense weight lift off her chest, one she hadn't even realized had been there. It was finally over. The man who had taken so much from her was about to have everything taken from him. The moment she had devoted her life to for the last two years had come and... now what? For a brief moment, Claire felt completely lost as to what to do. But in the next moment, the answer came to her, and it had been obvious all along. It was time to take the skills she learned and the passion behind them and use them to help other women like herself. Women who had been violated but left behind by the system. She would give them a measure of the justice they had been denied. With the decision made, Claire turned to walk home. This was going to be fun.

#   #   #

Six months had flown by since Hugh's arraignment. The amount of evidence Claire had gathered was damning and he'd made a plea deal rather than risk a greater sentence at trial. Though she'd set up alerts to keep her apprised of the proceedings, Claire had been so busy she'd only had time to briefly make sure the case was moving along as it should.

When she had first started seeking out other women like herself who had been denied redress, she wanted to be surprised at how many she found, but she sadly wasn't. Some weren't interested in her services, but plenty were eager for a chance to punish their attackers. While gathering evidence and setting up the operation, Claire liberated enough funds from each bad guy to not have to charge her clients anything. She was careful to avoid patterns; never hiring the same mercs twice and changing up the locations and method of discovery every time. Some of the assaulters even had private rigs at their home which made her work easier. By now, she was closing in on her seventh rapist getting a taste of his own medicine. It felt damn good each time one of those bastards got what was coming to him.

Claire was setting up the final details for the latest job when her screens blanked out. She frowned, checking the cables and input. Everything looked fine. Damnit, this shouldn't be happening with what she paid for this equipment. She was on the verge of checking the outlet when the central screen filled with white words:

WE KNOW WHAT YOU DID ♜

FIRST IMPRESSION

By Scott Pearson

PAUL STOPPED IN THE HOTEL bar for a cocktail just after killing a man a few floors up. He knew it was an indulgence, but he'd done it before when there was the perfect place to sit. A table out of the way, but not too out of the way as if he had something to hide.

He appraised the dry gin martini before him with the same cool stare he'd directed around room 514 before he'd left, opening the door with the handkerchief that was now back in his pants pocket. Only when perfectly satisfied did Paul move on.

Upstairs, that meant leaving the room and walking down the corridor, glancing around as if impressed by the pattern in the carpet, the delicate sconces lighting his way, the tasteful wallpaper border near the ceiling, but, in reality, the casual movements of his head were timed to keep his face away from a security camera.

In the bar, it meant eating the single olive he'd requested then taking his first sip. He generally preferred a martini with a twist but felt that order was more memorable. It was not in his nature to do anything memorable. When he left a public space, he liked to think that people didn't forget he'd been there, but rather that they'd never noticed him in the first place. This was the driving force behind almost everything Paul did.

He always ripped the paper off the pad, moving it to a hard surface before writing, no matter what the note was going to say: *milk, bread, eggs,* or *It's done—you'll never have trouble with your husband again.* It was true, what they showed on cop shows, that if you left it on the pad, you could leave a readable impression on the paper underneath. And electronic messaging left too many traces, copies on servers, on phones.

No, he preferred the old ways. Transitory ways. Never be careless, never press too hard, never leave anything behind—never make an impression. It made him almost invisible on those few occasions when witnesses had been unavoidable.

"I guess there might have been someone there in the dark."

"Average height. Brownish hair. Maybe."

"What's that word? Nondescript. Yeah."

His first kill had been an accident—or, rather, an unplanned necessity. He'd thought the house empty, but he'd been mistaken. After, as he stared down at the woman lying on the terracotta tiles—blue eyes still open as if staring at that one thin red line reaching out across the kitchen floor from her head—he realized how efficient his solution had been. How final, how precise. How revelatory. He'd been buried in thought as he carried out a coin collection which had proven quite valuable, leaving behind the woman's comparatively pedestrian jewelry.

He'd always felt like there'd been something missing, that there was a dark space in himself. Here, he realized, was what he needed to fill that emptiness. This still life without life, an unmoving look on a face in eternal repose. Some with surprise, some with fear, some with rage, some with all that and more. And they would be curated in this cold internal repository that he, unknowingly, had been saving his entire life until this moment of clarity. This, he suddenly knew, was his calling. And he was certain he could also make it his profession. Those coins had turned out to be the last things he'd ever stolen. The woman in the kitchen the last person he'd killed for free.

A dozen years later and he was still at the top of his game. Every assignment was carried out in a different fashion so that he had no discernible modus operandi. If you developed a trademark style, that was just another way of being memorable, of making an impression. That's what earned you a nickname among the police and in the press, and that drew attention. That was not how he worked. He was not some backwoods serial killer. He was a professional.

Just an hour ago he had gotten into the shower with his assignment, that was a first. He'd also never had sex with a man before, but the lathering on of soap had turned out to be pleasant enough, even if outside his usual sexuality. After his assignment had ejaculated via manual stimulation—he had held back to minimize trace DNA—he stepped out, claiming the need to urinate.

The assignment called after him, "That's going to be *hard*."

"Maybe you could help me with that," he had said. He stepped back into the shower with a straight razor he used to slice the assignment's femoral artery. It had worked well, the bleeding out right into the drain. It made cleaning up quick and easy.

"Is this seat taken?"

Paul looked up at a young woman whose left hand—there was no sign of a wedding ring—rested on the empty chair across the small table from him. She looked about twenty years old, almost young enough to be his daughter, not that he'd ever had children. Her brown hair, cut in a fashionable bob, appeared to be her natural color. Her black cocktail dress and an understated silver serpentine necklace indicated she was here for a date or perhaps a formal business dinner. A black clutch was in her right hand. As he noted her bright blue eyes, he made sure to blink his own eyes. He was aware that his focused assessment of his surroundings tended to make him blink less than the average person, which could be off-putting, and therefore memorable.

"No, feel free." He watched as she pulled the chair away from the table, but instead of dragging it away somewhere, she sat down. He furrowed his brow in thought. Had he misunderstood her intentions, or she his? Surely, she wasn't making a romantic overture to a man of his age. Although he dressed well, it was always off the rack, nothing ostentatious enough to attract the attention that wealth brought. He did nothing to accentuate his looks; he was just an average man with an average haircut in an average suit. Could she be a prostitute? He would not have expected such in this establishment, but, obviously, if anyone were to work this bar, they would want to project the youthful class that this woman did.

"Sorry, do you mind? It's a getting a little crowded, I couldn't find an open table."

He glanced around. Indeed, it was now happy hour, and the bar was filling up. He needed to finish his drink and move on. After taking a bigger sip than the first time, he said, "No, that's fine. I'll be done soon, and you'll have a table for whoever you're meeting."

"Oh, I'm alone tonight. At least for now." She smiled before turning to wave down a server.

Leaning back in surprise, he almost spilled his martini. His intention had been to signal her that he was not interested in whatever she was offering or selling, but she seemed to have interpreted his comment as fishing for information on her availability. He smiled as well, not to encourage her, but amused at the misunderstanding. His work often created situations of surreal contrast. Here he was in a nice bar with an attractive woman at his table when just a short while ago he'd held a naked man tight to him, one hand over his assignment's mouth as hot blood gushed down Paul's own naked thigh.

"Vodka martini, dirty, heavy on the olives, light on the vermouth." She turned back to him and shrugged. "Yours looked good. Don't finish before mine gets here. I want to clink glasses."

"Of course." He decided to flow along with the situation. This was normal life, after all, people meeting in bars, making small talk. He wasn't concerned about his assignment; he'd hung the DO NOT DISTURB sign on the door. Barring unforeseen circumstances, the body wouldn't be discovered until at least the next day.

She fiddled with her necklace. "So what brings you to town?"

"Work."

"Not much of an answer. What kind of work?"

"Consulting."

She grinned. "Come on, that's like saying *workity-work*."

He smiled again, but actually with her, not at her. "Personal consulting. I fix people's problems."

She didn't look entirely satisfied, but any follow-up questions were pushed aside by the arrival of her drink. The server, a young man with excessively trimmed stubble, put down a coaster and the drink.

As she reached for her clutch, Paul said, "No, I've got this."

She looked up at him and lingered on his eyes. "You know what? How about we start a tab?"

He nodded his agreement at the server, who said, "Certainly, sir. Anything else for you? Something off our appetizer menu?"

"Yes, and yes." Paul pointed at his own martini to indicate he'd have another, then added, "We'll have the stuffed olive plate and the smoked salmon profiteroles."

"Excellent choices." With a nod, the server was off to place the order.

As promised, she raised her glass. Paul reciprocated, and they clinked them together.

"Cheers . . . ?" She hesitated, her eyebrows raised.

"Rick," Paul said. "And cheers to you . . . ?"

"Anne."

Paul took a drink. He looked forward to the appetizers. He'd noted them on the menu as soon as he'd entered the bar but dismissed ordering anything to eat. A man having a single drink and getting on his way was ordinary enough, but ordering appetizers by himself, sitting there alone like someone waiting for a date who never arrived, that could draw the attention of the waitstaff. As would a man sitting with a beautiful young woman and not talking to her.

"Nice to meet you, Anne."

"You too."

"I assume you're from out of town as well?"

"No, actually, I just really like this bar. And interesting people stay here."

He nodded. Anne smiled easily as she sipped her own martini. Paul realized he had little to say. He rarely socialized, and he couldn't talk about his job. He still fell back on the standards. "So what do you do?"

"I'm in med school. Not sure if I'm up to it, really."

"You don't seem like a student."

"I guess I clean up pretty well."

"That's not what I . . ." He stopped as she laughed.

"Sorry, I'm teasing. I know what you meant. The stress and the workload are a bit brutal. But every few weeks, no matter what, I sneak away to dress up and go out. It's nice to at least try to be normal for a change."

"I was just thinking the same thing."

"Well, you seem pretty normal to me."

Paul shrugged.

Anne leaned across the table. "I have a confession to make."

"Oh?"

"We've actually sort of met before."

Paul set his martini down, his eyes narrowing as he considered Anne's face. She didn't blink under his scrutiny. He was a solitary man by nature and that was only reinforced by his line of work. He couldn't imagine under what circumstance he would have both met this beautiful young woman and also not remembered it. His attention to detail was a point of pride for him. He kept his tone casual. "I don't think so. I have pretty good memory for faces."

"You couldn't see my face all that well. It was dark."

Years of lying openly to people as he looked into their eyes had given him a polished poker face, so no hint of suspicion would have been visible in his expression as he considered the implications of what she'd just said. Could she possibly be a witness to one of his assignments? That on its own seemed exceedingly unlikely, but when combined with the fact that she was sitting here flirting with him, it became a near impossibility. Before the moment stretched to awkwardness, he gave the typical response for the situation, what anyone who might have overheard their discussion would expect.

"I'm sure I would have remembered meeting you. Especially in the dark." He found the innuendo a bit crude, but he'd often used such banter to good effect when it served his needs.

Anne glanced away as if surprised by the flattery, perhaps even a hint of a blush appearing on her cheeks. She faced him again. "Well, thanks, but the circumstances weren't at all romantic." She paused, a silly grin spreading across her face. "I was your Uber driver!"

Paul found himself laughing. It was so rare an occurrence that it was almost as if it took him a moment to recognize what was happening. *Strange sounds are emanating from my mouth,* he teased himself. *This must be what normal people call "laughter."* The sense of relief after his initial suspicions was palpable. It was doubly amusing to him that there was a layer to his reaction that was completely unknown to Anne. She looked quite pleased with herself, like a person who's just pulled off a successful surprise party.

"I remember now. But I'm confused. To start with, what was all that about the chair?"

"Okay, let me give you the whole picture. I've been driving for a while now. It's a way to make some money that fits into my erratic schedule. And, like coming to this bar, it gets me out of that med school world.

"So I usually like the small talk with the passengers. Mostly because it's never about medicine. I don't say I'm a med student. But sometimes the chat about the weather, the family or friends being visited, or the drunken party they're trying to get home from . . . it's like everyone says the same thing, the same phrases. I could almost just play a recording. Then you got into my car a few nights ago, and there was just peace and quiet."

Paul nodded. His smile remained natural, but he was disappointed in himself. He'd made a mistake. Usually he did exchange the normal and expected pleasantries with the cabbie or other driver. But he had noticed his driver was a young woman. He'd wondered how often she was hit on by passengers. What would leave the least impression? Making some crass comment about her looks, or acting as though she were indistinguishable from other drivers? Instead, he'd opted to say the minimal and focus on the newspaper he'd brought with him. Reading was often a good way of avoiding interactions without being memorably rude. But she'd recognized him a couple weeks after giving him a ride.

The arrival of their appetizers interrupted his self-recrimination, which was just as well. He needed to keep this conversation light and routine.

After putting a couple stuffed olives on the small plate in front of him, he said, "Sorry, I wasn't rude, was I? I was just tired."

"Not at all. It was refreshing."

"But I can't be the only one who doesn't chatter away the whole ride."

"No. But there was just something different. You seemed so comfortable with the silence. You weren't fidgety. Sometimes with the quiet ones you kind of worry what they're thinking about. But you, with your paper, you could have been sitting in your kitchen having coffee. I started wondering about you. What's this guy's story, I thought. So when I recognized you sitting here, I just had to come over and find out."

"You still haven't explained the chair business."

"Oh, that." She smirked. "Just a way to make sure you weren't a creep before I decided to stay at the table. It's easier to get away if you haven't opened with, 'Mind if I join you?'"

Paul smiled back at her. By not engaging with this driver, he'd done the opposite of what he'd intended. He'd made an impression. But it seemed to have worked out all right for now. He'd never given much thought to having anything remotely like a normal relationship, but as he helped himself to a profiterole and watched Anne toss a stuffed olive into her mouth, he found himself wondering if maybe he didn't have to be alone the rest of his life. He smiled at her as he reached for his martini.

Paul opened his eyes, coughed, and blinked a few times. A medicated haze still clouded his vision. He wanted to rub his face, but his hands were tied to the headboard. His suit coat had bunched up under him uncomfortably, and his tie was too tight.

"I have a confession to make."

He turned his head toward the sound of Anne's voice. She sat in a nearby chair, now in jeans and a black t-shirt but still wearing the silver necklace. She ran her fingers along its length. Paul's throat was parched and sore. He managed to whisper, "What is this?" He tried to move again, but his legs were tied as well.

She leaned forward. "We actually met once before. I was your Uber driver."

Paul narrowed his dry, scratchy eyes. "I don't—"

"Well, we didn't actually meet. You didn't see me. It was dark under the table as I watched you murder my mother."

A jumble of insights. Anne's necklace. Her unblinking blue eyes. Drawing him back to that first time. The simple jewelry he'd left behind. Those other unblinking blue eyes staring. Not at her own blood running across the tile, but behind Paul. At her daughter huddled beneath the kitchen table, watching, terrified. And last night, he'd gotten drunk too fast. Staggered away with Anne into her car. The strong martinis and flavorful food covering the taste of whatever she'd drugged him with. Not thinking clearly, breaking his own rules.

"I'm in med school because of you. Because of watching my mother die. It was either become a doctor or a police officer."

Paul watched as she stood and started putting on scrubs she pulled from a small suitcase on the nightstand. There was nothing he could do. She had tied him efficiently; he could tell that even in his semi-drugged state. He'd had occasion to tie people up over the years, so he knew the common mistakes people made. She'd avoided them.

"I chose medicine because I didn't think I could handle the violence of being a cop. I didn't think I could kill someone if I had to. But when you got into my car the other night, I realized I'd been wrong about that."

What struck Paul at that moment was that one of the things that had made him the perfect assassin now made him the perfect victim. No one would be looking for him or calling the police to report him missing. His family and old friends had long ago given up on him as he retreated into the shadows of his calling. He'd perfected the art of no one noticing when he was gone.

Anne wriggled her hands into a pair of surgical gloves. "I knew what I had to do as soon as I saw you in the rear view. Without a doubt. I was as sure of my next steps as I was that it was you. I never forgot your face. You made a big impression on me."

Paul laughed weakly at her choice of words.

She pulled a surgical mask up over her mouth and nose. "Let's begin." ♜

RETURN OF THE INVISIBLE MAN

By Rob Nisbet

THIS FEELS UNCOMFORTABLY INTIMATE. I am unaccustomed to writing in my own voice. It is my normal habit to give thoughts and words to characters, into whom, like some god, I have breathed a semblance of life. But this is a tale of *real* men and women, including myself, and can be told in no other way. I freely admit to the changing of some principal names and an artful rejigging of circumstance, but I assure you, reader, that, in its essence, this account is as truthful as my memory will permit.

Let us start with the plain facts. I am pleased to record that the serialization of my story 'The Invisible Man' in Pearson's Weekly, was so favorably received that Pearsons were keen to publish it *ensemble* in the form of a novel. It was on the occasion of its release, in 1897, that I was persuaded to attend a reception, at the South Kensington Museum no less, to talk a little of the novel's themes and generally to publicize its existence.

Pearsons had hired a small lecture hall for the occasion. It was on the third floor, among the museum's science collections, appropriately adjoining a high-ceilinged gallery devoted to optics. The museum was very proud of its electric lighting, and lavished so much on me that, from my small podium, I could barely see the audience beyond its glare. The irony that the hall contained an invisible audience amused me, and I wondered if a similar

84

thought had occurred to the other dazzled occupant of the podium who was to prompt my talk with a series of questions.

Seated across a low table from me was, what I had gathered to be, one of the lesser Pearsons: a thin youth with an easy smile and the disturbing enthusiasm of his age. "Tell me, Mr. Wells," said he, "what was your inspiration for a tale of a man who could not be seen?"

I had expected this question and had already decided on a half-truth. To give a full account, I knew, would invite disbelief and scorn. "The story was suggested to me by two separate events." I smiled at the first, recalling childhood memories. "I have three siblings but, being the youngest, I felt somewhat isolated; I had no companions of my own age. So, when I was five or six, I invented one."

"You mean, you had an imaginary friend?" asked the junior Pearson, eager that the audience should understand.

I nodded. "His name was Timothy, I recall. Naturally, he accompanied me on many an adventure. I had, even then, a capacious imagination. We tracked wild animals in the garden. He partnered me in sensational form at cricket. We were the first six-year-olds to encounter aliens from the planet Mars. I must have appeared singularly strange to anyone observing me; talking with, and gesticulating to, someone they could not see."

Pearson leant forward eagerly. "And the second event?" he asked.

"My father was always keen to encourage my love of reading. When I was about seven years old, I broke my leg and became feverish. I was confined to bed and my father raided the local library bringing me tottering piles of books to keep me amused. There was a volume of verse that I will always remember: '*Old Peter vanished like a shot / but then - his suit of clothes did not.*'" I quoted. "It is a line from one of Gilbert's ballads, some time before he found fame in his collaboration with Sullivan. The idea that a man could become invisible resonated with my imagination, perhaps because of Tim, my unseen childhood friend. The idea for the book, I am certain, grew from there."

Pearson held up the handsome hardcover for the audience to see. On the red fabric, a line illustration showed an apparently empty dressing gown and slippers sitting in a chair, and beneath that, my name, embossed in gold.

"Scientifiction," said he. "It is a new term, but one I feel describes what is becoming a genre all its own." He turned to me, ensuring that the book was conspicuously on view. "Can you tell us a little of how you make plausible in fiction, what is, in reality, clearly impossible?"

I had never had trouble in imagining a sequence of cause and effect, especially in fiction. "I made Griffin, my main character, a student of optics," I explained. "The conceit being that he became able to alter the refractive index of his body to that of air." I waved a hand. "The rational mind knows it to be impossible but suspends its disbelief in favor of a compelling tale."

"A compelling tale, indeed." Pearson placed the book upright on the table while we discussed further the story's genesis and development from the weekly instalments. Then he squinted into the audience. "I wonder if we might invite questions now from the hall."

There were several questions comparing this latest book with my previous novels, principally *The Time Machine* and *The Island of Doctor Moreau*. One perceptive voice from the audience asked if there was some reason why I had written *The Invisible Man* from the third person perspective, rather than use the first person which had been my habit. This was something which I hadn't consciously considered before. I realized then that I may have been distancing myself from, if not the story, certainly the concept of an invisible man. I muttered something about thinking this the best way to tell the tale, but I knew that I had been avoiding putting myself, as the narrator, directly into the mind of my unseen character. That would have been too close to my personal experience. Too close to the truth.

The questions were generally of an amiable nature until a man stood from his seat in the front row. The lights obscured his features, but not his voice.

"Mr. Wells," said he, "is not the term 'scientific fiction' an oxymoron?" He paused. "*Science* implies a sensible grounding in fact, whereas *fiction* is the direct opposite."

"The term is not mine," I said, somewhat defensively, for this man's tone suggested some antagonism. "But it is a useful way to describe a fiction which explores, what we may loosely call, the sciences."

"There is currently a fad for *children's* literature," the man continued. This time there was no mistaking the derision in his voice. He listed several titles, including, I remember, *Through the Looking-glass*, *The Water Babies*, and *Journey to the Centre of the Earth*. "All have a pretention to literary merit, even the celebrated contrivances of Dr Conan Doyle, while being merely juvenile adventures. Would you, Mr. Wells, class your novels, as I would: boy's books for grown-ups?"

The mention of boys stirred in me a memory. There was a familiarity in this man's arrogance.

Sensing a hesitation in my response, Pearson at my side forced a strained laugh. "Best not to mock the invisible man," he said, waving at the space between him and myself. "He could be here with us now; we would not know."

The name *Southerland* came to me, and I raised a hand to shield my eyes, squinting to where the man stood. Sandy hair, worn longer than the fashion. Could it be? If so, I hadn't seen him for over twenty years. As if in reaction, my left leg twinged where it had been broken, something it had not done since I, Southerland and Kemp were schoolboys.

"The whole idea is bunkum," scoffed the man. "Your 'invisibility' is achieved by immersion in a medium that closely resembles air." He waved an arm around himself. "What could resemble air more than air itself? By your theory, Mr. Wells, we should all be rendered invisible – lest we walk around in a vacuum. Your warped idea of optics does not bear scrutiny." He smirked at his small witticism, and I knew then that this was indeed Southerland, now, like myself, an adult of his early thirties. "The eye, for example…" he continued. "The biology of the eye requires light to fall upon the retina which the brain then interprets as sight. Light would travel straight through an invisible man. Your central character, Bertie Wells, would have been blind."

That was confirmation. Only someone who had known me as a boy would have called me Bertie. I got to my feet and was aware of mutterings from the audience as they followed Southerland's reasoning.

An outrage gripped me, steering my words and filling my mind with unwanted memories. "Southerland," said I. "It appears that you are not content to have tormented me as a child. You have intentionally come here today to ridicule me as an adult."

"I am a critic of literature, sir," said he, his innocent-sounding politeness appealing to his audience, but marred again, I noticed, with that sly smirk. "I see it as my duty to point out the story's failings."

My leg spasmed again; I staggered slightly, and felt a rage begin to boil within me.

The young Pearson beside me also stood, his enthusiastic smile for once slipping. "Can't a novel, be simply *that* – a story?" he proposed. "It can illuminate human nature in the form of a fantasy without having to withstand a forensic analysis."

It was well said. I nodded, but I felt my hands bunch into shaking fists at my sides and tried to keep the anger from my voice. "My character, Griffin, serves to show an unseemly personality – and the depravity that can overtake a man of weak nature if he is given power over others."

Southerland clearly had more to say. He drew himself up, but then noticed, perhaps, the curled nails biting into my palms and the burning redness of my face. His sneer drooped in sudden apprehension.

The book which had been displayed on the low table, rose, seemingly unsupported, into the air.

The audience emitted a collective gasp and a startled murmur. Pearson at my side muttered an unbecoming oath, and Southerland, I noticed with some satisfaction, staggered back against the row of chairs with a look of wide horror in his eyes.

The book wavered in the air, and a voice rang out, clear and stark with warning. "You would be wise, sir," it said, "to keep your own counsel."

Southerland could but stare at the floating book. There was a general hubbub from the audience, some of whom now stood, some looked to the stage for signs of trickery, and some stared at my face, suffused with fury, for the disembodied voice they had heard was without doubt my own.

Southerland scrambled to the central aisle, addressing the space between me and Pearson. "What did you do to Kemp?" he demanded.

As if in response, the book dropped suddenly with a thump on the table. This horrified Southerland even more, for he had now no reference of where the voice might be.

"I did to Kemp," said the voice, edging from the podium towards

Southerland, "what I shall now do to you!"

Pushing his way past members of the audience, Southerland fled down the aisle.

"Run! Go!" roared the voice.

Southerland scrambled to the door at the rear of the hall, and out into the museum's gallery of optics beyond. The door slammed closed behind him, then, a few seconds later, opened again then shut, as if he were indeed being pursued by an invisible man.

Pearson looked to me as if to ask what had just happened. With an effort to relax, I unbunched my fists and appealed to the audience for calm. "Ladies and gentlemen," I called. "Thank you for your attendance here today. Some of you may know that, before I took up the pen, I was a draper. I could not resist this element of theatricality." I picked up the fallen book. "And it is truly amazing what can be achieved with a length of very fine thread."

Pearson's young face flooded with relief, and the audience swung from their nervous doubt to an applause of appreciation. It appeared that they now believed Southerland's jeering to be part of a stunt of book-launch publicity.

Pearson revealed a table to the rear of the podium, piled high with first editions. He began to organize a queue of those who might wish to purchase an autographed copy. I made ready my pen and added the book I held to the stack. There was, of course, no thread attached to it.

#   #   #

I had always hated what the school grandly called 'cross-country' running. It involved a group of seven-year-olds performing three circuits of the Burdock gravel pit every Wednesday morning, no matter what the weather.

"Faster, Wells!" came the habitual cry from the sports master. I was always left behind the crowd, sometimes so far that I only achieved two circuits before gasping wearily back to the changing rooms.

The bleak quarry landscape transformed in my imagination. It always seemed alien to me as I trudged alone over its slopes and boulders. "What do you think, Tim," I asked, "would the surface of Mars look something like this?"

My imaginary friend generally agreed with me. "Yes," he said. "If there are creatures on Mars, it's a wonder they don't leave somewhere this desolate to find a new home on Earth."

It was an interesting notion. Tim and I spent several Wednesday mornings exploring the idea of what we imagined to be a Martian invasion. With the excesses of our youth, we decided on much fire and destruction. London, certainly, would be destroyed. And there'd be human casualties too. Top of my list were two of my classmates: Kemp and Southerland. Even as I imagined their deaths by Martian hands, my two tormentors caught up with me.

"Talking to yourself, Bertie?" Southerland's voice was harsh from running.

"He's chatting with all his friends," jeered Kemp, pointing out that I was quite alone. "You're a lap behind, Wells. Get out of our way!" He pushed past, shoving me harshly.

I lost my footing and, in a cascade of gravel, fell from the path. The quarry sloped steeply at this point, and I tumbled down slamming my left leg into a boulder.

#   #   #

My leg was broken. The sports master had organized a splint to which I was strapped. I was then carried back to the school and thence to hospital. There were muttered comments among the masters as to my clumsiness. I said nothing in my defense. The glares from Kemp and Southerland told me it would not be in my best interest.

So, I ended up confined to my bed, surrounded by books which my father had brought from the library to keep me amused. My leg was uncomfortably raised on a pillow and encased in plaster of Paris.

Tim emerged from my imagination and shared my outrage at how unfairly I had been treated. Apart from the pain of my leg, I had also been feeling hot and increasingly unwell. Tim suspected that this might be the beginning of a fever. He was to be proved correct.

It was almost a week after my 'fall', that my mother appeared in my room with a plate of home-made biscuits. Two friends from school, she said, had called to see how I was progressing. She stepped aside as Kemp and Southerland sauntered in. She lay the plate on my bed then withdrew. There were four biscuits, I noticed, my mother liked to indulge me by including one for Tim.

"How are you, Bertie?" asked Southerland. His inquiry sounded concerned but was qualified by that ever-present sneer. He took a biscuit and wandered around the room fingering the books on my bedside cabinet.

Kemp too took a biscuit and sat on my bed. "Too bad about your leg, Wells," said he. "We just called round to make sure you haven't been spreading wild tales of how this happened." He tapped a finger on my plastered leg and leant his face in towards mine. His mouth was a grim line. "After all, we wouldn't want to have to break your other leg, would we?"

The threat was obvious. They were far more worldly than I. I was a scrawny frightened child, cowering before their oppression. I picked up a biscuit and shakily held it to my mouth but found myself too scared to eat it. A tide of heat surged through me, and the room wavered, seeming to spin in a whirl of dizziness.

Southerland had picked up one of my books. The verses of W. S. Gilbert. "Poems!" his voice grated with scorn, a critic even then. He flung the book across the room and joined Kemp seated on my bed.

"I'm sure you understand, Wells," said Kemp. "Keep quiet about the quarry."

My vision wavered again. I thought I saw Kemp reach for the last biscuit – Tim's biscuit. He snatched his hand back from the plate as if stung. It seemed to me that the biscuit rose impossibly into the air, out of reach, then floated down to settle again on the plate.

My memory is uncertain from that point. I remember vaguely that my mother returned to the room and, on seeing the burning in my face, bustled my visitors out of the house and sent for a doctor.

My fever broke that night, and I suffered a dream-like delirium for the next day. The doctor suspected an infection of my leg to be the cause and I was kept cool by the application of damp towels to my wrists and forehead, my mother staying with me night and day until the fever passed.

The day being a Wednesday no doubt affected my dreams. I had the impression that, while I raged with fever, Tim rose again from my imagination to take my place in the boys' cross-country run. Delirium makes no sense, but I saw the scene as if through Tim's eyes. Tim, my imaginary friend, who could not be seen even by me, stood, invisible, at the steep edge of the quarry path waiting for the runners to pass by.

Kemp and Southerland led the pack as usual. As they ran past, arms swinging, Tim joined them on the path. "Kemp!" he shouted.

Kemp drew-up sharply, looking about. "Wells?" He had recognized the voice.

"I heard him too," said Southerland. They scanned the path, but of course could see nothing.

Tim shoved at Kemp, as Kemp had shoved at me.

"Hey!" Kemp's eyes were wide. He circled, moving closer to his friend. "Did you see that? Someone pushed me!"

Southerland had seen Kemp's reaction, not the push. "It's like the floating biscuit," he realized. "Tim. Wells' invisible friend!"

"Tosh," said Kemp, but his eyes were frightened. He jolted again as Tim pushed him towards the edge of the path.

I should like to record here, that at home, delirious with fever, my mother states that I cried out from my bed: "No, Tim! Stop!"

But in the quarry, Tim seized his chance at revenge. Kemp was pushed and tripped from the path. He hurled down to the boulders below. He hit his head. His neck was twisted awkwardly. His eyes stared, open, but saw nothing.

#   #   #

A creative imagination is a powerful resource. And I would argue that an author's imagination is even more so. I *knew* instinctively that my fevered dreams were of actual events. As I lay ill in bed, I was spared the details by those around me but, by degrees, I learnt what had happened to Kemp. I was only a child; I knew that it was wrong of me, but I could not help a feeling of satisfaction that my tormentor was dead. I felt only mild remorse, though I knew that, in some fantastical way, I was responsible. I knew that, through Tim, I had got away with murder. For who could accuse *me* of pushing Kemp when I had lain ill in bed, my leg broken and nowhere near the quarry.

Southerland had told his tale, of course. But a distraught seven-year-old whimpering about an invisible foe would never be believed.

I think now that, while Southerland was still around as a potential threat to me, Tim persisted in my mind. But I had no further need of his protection. I'm sure that Southerland realized, to some extent, what had happened at the quarry, for he, though never civil, tended to leave me alone. Tim became, once more, my benign, unseen, imaginary friend – my inner voice. Through the years, when we were alone, we often whispered about that day, speculating, as we grew older, on the great power his incorporeal nature offered him.

These were the internal conjectures which led, eventually, to my writing of The Invisible Man, and thus to my fateful re-acquaintance with Southerland that day at the museum.

The death of his childhood friend must have affected him deeply – especially under such strange circumstances. I supposed Southerland saw in my imaginary friend, the inspiration for the novel. It is no wonder that he read my book with such avid interest. I fervently wish, however, that he had not decided to taunt me that day at the book's reception.

He had made it clear that he suspected my secret, that my imagination had substance enough to act independently.

Yes, an author's creativity *is* a powerful resource. I realized, with a sudden trepidation, that I, Herbert George Wells, signing books on a stage before a crowd of witnesses, could again kill with my imagination. This was not my conscious intention but, in my mind's eye, I sensed my protector, Tim, pursue Southerland out into the empty gallery of optics.

#   #   #

Southerland fled from the hall, slamming the door hastily behind him, and immediately found his way barred by one of the museum's glass cases. This was some years before the sciences were granted a museum building of their own, and the exhibits were crammed together making a maze of the cases and machinery on display.

He looked back and saw the door to the hall open, then close, apparently by itself. Scrambling around the glass case, his eyes darted uselessly back towards the door. "Where are you?" he demanded.

Tim gave a theatrical cough, only inches from Southerland's face.

Southerland jolted with terror, turning and weaving away between the exhibits. He moved behind a gigantic lens, so placed as to magnify the space before him.

"Even under such scrutiny," jeered Tim, "you will be unable to see me."

Southerland's wide eyes narrowed with confusion. "That voice… It's you, Wells!"

"I am his imagination," said Tim; "naturally, I have his voice. And his memories…"

Southerland could hear the voice approaching as if magnified by the lens he cowered behind. He moved cautiously to where a rainbow bank of electric bulbs glowed, demonstrating the effect of combining light of different colors. His face was lit in scarlet.

"You made Wells' young life a misery," the voice had jumped forward again.

"It was Kemp who broke his leg!" There was a trembling plea in Southerland's voice. "I'm sorry. I'm sorry!"

"Too late."

One of the smaller display cases was shoved aside, as blue and yellow lights cast the scene a sickly green.

"You created me, Southerland," accused Tim's voice, closer still. "You and Kemp. I am Wells' imagination imbued with the rage of a frightened seven-year-old. I have a semblance of existence, not real enough to be seen, but with intention enough to act on Wells' behalf."

"You can't exist!" Southerland twisted and fled again. He found himself canyoned towards a railing with a three-story drop beyond into the museum's atrium where Stephenson's locomotive 'Rocket' had been recently installed. "You are a figment," he yelled back into empty space. "A character in a fiction."

"The logic behind the fictional character is indeed flawed," said the approaching voice calmly, "as you pointed out so eloquently." Another glass case was shoved aside, and, though he saw nothing, Southerland felt the unmistakable jab of a finger in his ribs. He scrabbled along the edge of the gantry. "But then Wells could hardly tell the truth – that I am a product of his creativity, not of optics. You are correct, of course, that I am the inspiration for the novel – even its title. I am Tim. T. I. M. The Invisible Man."

Southerland felt his neck gripped by an unseen hand as he was slowly forced back over the edge of the rail. His pathetic cries for mercy were heard screeching throughout the museum.

#   #   #

H. G. Wells.

I looked up from signing another of my books. There had been a cry, and now there was some commotion from the gallery outside.

The tragedy would be announced shortly. Southerland was gone. And with him, I hoped, Tim's desire for revenge. I might, finally, lay to rest my persistent inner voice.

I felt already assuaged: The two childhood bullies that had first brought Tim into a form of corporeal existence, had, in effect, been eliminated by their own actions. It was, to me, a tidy and soothing justice.

I smiled towards the next customer in my queue and raised my pen. It was a genuine smile, for I hoped, truly, that this incident would be the last the world would see of the invisible man. ♜

FUTURE PERFECT

By Serena Jayne

THE STIFF FABRIC OF JUNE'S lab coat made her neck itch as she scrolled between photos on her work computer of Napa Valley, Forbidden Fantasyland, and Cabo San Lucas. While the wrong answer could spell the end of their relationship, the right one could cement her place in Charlie's life forever.

Kayla, June's assistant, jabbed a finger at the photo of a couple wearing virtual reality gear, and her holographic manicure flashed three-dimensional daisies. "Playing out kinky sexual scenarios via virtual reality doesn't scream put a ring on it."

"Okay," June said. "Hard pass on Forbidden Fantasyland."

Kayla practically skipped to the skeletal machine occupying the corner of the room. The machine, which resembled a giant albino spider, emitted a high-pitched hum, creating the illusion that the awful arachnid gibbered in some alien language. When in operation, the spiderlike machine seemed to feast on the client's brain matter.

"Want me to hook you up so Destiny can help with your decision?" Kayla's manicure seemed to send out a daisy distress signal.

June shuddered. "Nah."

Kayla shrugged and programmed an aromatherapy machine to emit a lavender scent.

With his sexy swagger and male model good looks, Charlie oozed confidence and charisma. Every time he came in for an appointment, June's feelings for him grew despite understanding the significance of the strip of untanned skin on his ring finger.

After they'd made love for the first time, he'd reeled her all the way in. It was one thing, however, to be the catch of the day, and another to be lovingly mounted in a prime position in his heart.

#   #   #

At the sight of Brooke Young, goosebumps crawled up June's arms. With blonde hair arranged in a messy bun and her designer workout wear, Brooke looked ready for downward dog inversions, not a catfight with her husband's mistress.

When June noticed Brooke's name in the appointment book, she'd swapped clients with another technician. She refused to pass up the opportunity to evaluate the woman against her own physical assets, trying to fathom what Charlie found lacking in his wife to cause him to stray, and what he found lacking in June that made him stay.

June plastered on a welcoming smile. "What brings you to Future Perfect, Mrs. Young?"

"Please call me Brooke." The woman settled into the treatment chair. "My husband has been using Future Perfect for years to make informed business decisions."

"We have a strict confidentiality policy," June said. "I can't discuss other clients."

"Oh good. Charles thinks I'm in an Astrospin class." Brooke crossed her Lycra-clad legs. "I need to make a personal decision."

June sucked in a breath, unable to tamp down the hope that rose in her heart. Hope that Brooke had come to look into possibilities for ending her marriage. The hope that shattered into a million shards to rain down despair at Brooke's next words.

"We want a baby."

June's ears buzzed with white noise and her brain went fuzzy. She took a deep breath to slow her thundering heartbeat. If Brooke got pregnant, Charlie would be bound to his wife and child forever.

"Are you okay?" Brooke's face scrunched with concern.

"Got a little lightheaded. I shouldn't have skipped breakfast." She didn't want Brooke's comfort. "What futures do you want to explore?"

"I've had several miscarriages." Brooke's lips quivered. "My doctor recommended using a surrogate, but that doesn't sit right with me. Neither does adoption. I get that tons of children around the world need good homes, but I'd prefer a child that's a product of our love."

The word "love" hit June like a laser blast. Swallowing the lump in her throat, she pressed the buzzer on her desk to summon Kayla.

"Seeing the outcomes of those three options will help me make the best decision." Brooke fidgeted with her rings and the meteorite-sized diamond nearly blinded June. "How's this all work?"

"The substance we administer via IV increases theta waves in the brain, creating the optimal state in between wakefulness and sleep for the procedure. The drug has an amnesiac effect, so you won't remember any of the outcomes. Don't worry though. I will record the images your brain produces for playback."

Kayla entered the room.

"Please prep Mrs. Young." June stepped away to get a dose of Seventh Heaven from her purse.

The highly addictive designer drug was something she saved for times when Charlie became distant. She didn't normally tote around illegal narcotics, but she'd packed a couple of pills in case Brooke's session went badly. And the possibility of a baby and losing Charlie's love was all kinds of bad.

With an euphoric wave of liquid pleasure riding through her veins, she returned to the treatment room. The IV line was in place, a virtual reality helmet hid Brooke's eyes, and the machine's spider spindly legs were positioned in brain-sucking aka *destiny exploration* mode.

Kayla tapped on the DESTINY7000 touchscreen. "Mrs. Young's vitals are good, and her brain patterns are within range."

"Take a long lunch." June handed her assistant a chip loaded with credits for Lure Lounge. "Treat yourself, and if you don't mind, please bring me back the daily sushi special."

"You sure? Lure takes forever since they have an all-human staff."

June nodded, donned her own headset, and once Kayla was gone, initiated the DESTINY7000 future exploration sequence.

"You're in a room with three doors." The swirling spectrum of colors in June's viewfinder shifted to an image of a room wallpapered in pink paisley. Against one wall, three shiny silver doors with matching doorknobs awaited.

Each client conjured up a different image. Everyone from astrologers to clinical psychologists weighed in on the significance of the room's design. June didn't care much about the room's appearance except for the time one resembled a medieval torture chamber complete with an iron maiden. June spent the next two days after that session on a Seventh Heaven bender. Some doors should never be opened.

"Place your hand on the knob of the first door." June used the soothing tone she had spent years cultivating. "Congratulations. You and your husband recently adopted a child. When you're ready, open the door to reveal this destiny."

Brooke complied, and the scene changed. She sat on a rug decorated with rainbow fish while a toddler stacked blocks.

The child constructed a shaky tower and clapped his hands in delight.

"Charles, come see what Brandon's created." Pride laced Brooke's words.

The man June loved stepped into the frame, and her breath caught. Charlie scooped up the child and bounced him on his hip. "Nice job, Buddy."

Brooke wrapped her arms around them both. "Who wants cake?"

"Me!" The little boy bounced in Charlie's arms. "Me! Me! Me!"

A sense of sadness dulled the edges of June's drug-induced euphoria. She asked her client to close the door on that future and explore having a surrogate bear the baby.

In the second scenario, the couple sat in a waiting room. Charlie wrapped his arm around a sobbing Brooke. "I'm sorry, honey, but it's within her rights to deny us access to the delivery room."

"But what if she sues for custody?" Brooke wiped her red nose with a crumbed tissue. "Going the surrogate route was a terrible idea."

"She signed away any rights to the child. I promise everything will be fine."

"I want my baby." Brooke sniffled.

"I know, honey." His com device made the special little chirp that signified June had sent him a message. "I'll step outside and give Harvey a quick call to inform him of our concerns."

Brooke paced for what seemed like an hour, her movements more and more agitated, until a nurse handed her an infant bundled in a blue blanket.

"I'll make sure you're ours. Always and forever," Brooke crooned, rocking the baby.

Charlie entered the room, stopping in the doorway to gaze at his wife and child in wonder. "Harvey's having a partner review the contract. Never hurts to have a second opinion."

"I'm not giving up this baby without a fight." Brooke's voice channeled a fierce mama bear's energy.

"Please close that door, Brooke," June said. "It's time for the last scenario, where you carry the baby."

Seeing Charlie leave his wife alone to communicate with her gave June a smidgen of hope. She was as ready as she ever would be to see Brooke give birth to Charlie's offspring.

Charlie stayed beside his wife, holding her hand and cheering her labor along. Once the baby was born and the couple quietly chatted about names, June closed her eyes to block out the image of the happy family.

The DESTINY7000 machine let out a shrill sound, signaling client distress.

June opened her eyes and silenced the alarm. Her heart thundered as she noted her client had gone into cardiac arrest. Brooke's death would solve all her problems.

There was something cold-blooded about watching someone die without trying to save them. June struggled to muster up the will to take action and do the right thing.

Adrenaline eventually overcame her Seventh Heaven-induced lethargy.

She fumbled for the defibrillator and worked to get Brooke stabilized, reclining the chair and adding an emergency rescue drug to the IV.

Sweaty and breathing heavily, June reviewed the recording. A client crashing typically meant that their choice resulted in their death. Sure enough, on the screen, doctors swarmed around Brooke, who was bleeding profusely.

"We're losing her," a member of the medical team cried, and the recording ended.

June eyed the woman, whose color was slowly returning. The woman whose life she'd saved. The woman whose choice could make or break June's future happiness.

June edited the file, deleting the footage showing the grim outcome of the baby's birth. Before Kayla returned, June disposed of all the evidence that showed Brooke had been in distress during her Future Perfect appointment and took the other dose of Seventh Heaven.

"Enjoy your lunch." Kayla handed over a bag of food. "I'll take good care of Mrs. Young."

In her workout gear and with the chair in the reclined position, Brooke looked to be in the savasana yoga position, also known as corpse pose.

\#   \#   \#

June flipped the picture frame face down on her desk, hiding the projected photos of her, Charlie, and his daughter, BeeBee. In each photo, June looked uneasy, biting her lip in one. Staring at the ground in another. Picking at her nail beds in a third. Charlie always gazed off camera as though he had somewhere more important to be.

BeeBee, however, sported a smug I-know-you-did-something-naughty smile. The little girl was a miniature doppelgänger of her mother. Besides Brooke's name, she possessed Brooke's slight stature, Brooke's shiny blonde hair, and worse yet Brooke's sky-blue eyes, which seemed to act as a portal for her dead mother's spirit.

BeeBee was as much of a product of June's actions as she was of Charlie and Brooke's DNA. The adopted child and the baby born of the surrogate were both boys. Had June not duped Brooke into choosing to have embryos implanted inside her own womb rather than that of the surrogate, BeeBee wouldn't exist. Instead, a different embryo would have thrived in the surrogate's uterus, or Brooke and Charlie would have adopted a child devoid of their genetic material.

June could mother one of those children. Children who didn't look at her like they held her scandalous secrets in one small fist.

When June had married Charlie a year after Brooke died in childbirth, she'd never considered that she'd end up spending more time with the baby than with her husband. Charlie had thrown himself into his work, leaving June alone with BeeBee whenever she wasn't working at Future Perfect. Hugging the child was like embracing Brooke's icy corpse.

With her life an actual nightmare, the spidery design of Future Perfect's DESTINY7000 machine no longer frightened June. If the machine came alive and consumed her brains, she wouldn't have to live knowing that she'd basically committed manslaughter to score a life that wasn't worth living.

The need for a hit of Seventh Heaven and the oblivion it brought made her grit her teeth and dig her fingernails into the flesh of her arms. Ever since Charlie had found precocious four-year-old BeeBee rattling June's metallic pill bottles like maracas, he'd demanded June attend rehab.

She wished Brooke had seen all three recordings in their entirety so she could have made an informed choice over her own fate. Sometimes she wished she'd never met Charlie and never had to discover her moral compass was so faulty. Other times, she wished she hadn't resuscitated Brooke.

Kayla righted the picture frame. "Want me to have maintenance hang this up?"

The displayed image of BeeBee posing with Charlie and the muskie he'd caught frost-burned June's soul, and she shivered. She was no better off than that poor doomed fish. "No, thanks."

June skimmed her next client's file. "Please bring in Hailey Parker."

"Sure thing." The door snicked shut behind Kayla.

June stepped away from her desk and the ever-rotating family photos. Dealing with BeeBee at home was unavoidable, and voluntarily bringing the child's image into spaces she didn't need to occupy was foolhardy. But Kayla had gifted her the frame, complete with photos she'd had Charlie upload. The thoughtful gesture nearly undid June, but she desperately needed a BeeBee-free space.

The woman Kayla led into the room wore form-fitting jeans and a flowered tank top. Three-dimensional tattoos of koi fish decorated her arms. Her hair glittered green with the latest sparkly celebrity-endorsed style.

Hailey's gaze lingered on the shoes BeeBee had scribbled on in purple crayon. The child seemed to leave her mark on all of June's things as though to serve as a reminder that her stepmother owed a debt that could never be paid.

"Our four-year-old fancies herself an artist." June made a mental note to leave a pristine pair of shoes at work. "How may we help you today, Ms. Parker?"

"My boyfriend and I are taking a trip to celebrate our two-year anniversary. I'd like to find out which destination will bring us closer. He's been all worked up about fluctuations in the scandium and helium-3 markets, his kid is super demanding, and his wife is a pathetic addict. Chuck deserves a break from all that bullshit."

Hot shame burned June's face. Other men traded commodities. Other men had children. Other men had marriage troubles. Other men were named Charles.

She sucked in a deep breath of lavender-scented air. Hope that Hailey's Chuck and her Charlie were two different men surged.

"Which destinations are you deciding between?" June's voice joined the tremble in her fingers.

"Forbidden Fantasyland, Las Vegas, and Cabo San Lucas. Forbidden Fantasyland looks fun, but I'm leaning toward Cabo. I've been dying to show off my new bamboo bikini. Not so sure about Vegas. Sin City's better for a bachelorette party. The pool and club scenes are phenomenal, but I want Chuck all to myself."

June couldn't deny that Hailey was indeed Charlie's mistress for a second longer. The travel options were too close to the ones he had given her all those years ago to be a coincidence. She remembered the trip she'd made with Charlie to Napa Valley. The vineyards they'd visited. The scores of wines they'd tasted. The love they'd made on the property of the quaint bed-and-breakfast. She remembered the sour feeling that had lingered in the back of her throat after her session with Brooke. She remembered how every moment she'd spent on that trip with Charlie seemed paid for in Brooke's blood.

At least Charlie had the decency to replace Napa with Las Vegas. Maybe taking Napa out of the mix meant something. Maybe it didn't, especially since Hailey said she'd been with her boyfriend for two years. Years June had spent raising his daughter. Years she'd spent being the devoted wife. Years she'd spent buried in guilt.

"Kayla will get you set up." June waved to her assistant, whose wide-eyed expression seemed to signify that she, too, had puzzled out that their new client was Charlie's mistress. "I'll be back in a few minutes."

In the restroom, June scrubbed at the crayon marks on her shoes with a damp piece of toilet paper. June was done mucking with fate. She'd put her feelings aside. Record Hailey's three destinies, play them back for her, and let her choose. Give her all the information she needed to make the right choice, as she should have done for Brooke.

After steeling herself to watching Hailey and Charlie's love fest in Cabo, Forbidden Fantasyland, and Vegas, June returned to the treatment room to help Hailey design her destiny.

But Hailey wasn't in the chair. The woman turned the photo frame in her hand, the fish tattoos swimming around her arms.

"I know who you are," Hailey said. "I know how you used to be in my shoes, then you stepped into his first wife's. Tragic how she died."

The image of Brooke's doctors trying in vain to save her life lit up June's brain.

"Thing is, I already ran the scenarios at a Future Perfect on the West Coast. I already know every outcome. None of them ends well for you."

June couldn't seem to catch her breath. Her legs wobbled and her heart pounded. She considered braining Hailey with the picture frame. As though she were hooked up to Destiny herself, she could envision ending up in prison, leaving Charlie free to marry Hailey. June could call her dealer and get more Seventh Heaven, but that would only be a temporary solution.

"You can have him." June imagined fixing her life. Kicking her addiction. Finding a new love. One who came without the baggage of a wife and child. "Take him and BeeBee."

"I don't want to raise someone else's brat." Hailey's lip curled. "You need to ask for custody. With your pre-nup, you won't qualify for alimony, but you can get child support."

June had been helping people make decisions long enough to know that Hailey wouldn't need her to take action if her desired destiny didn't hinge on what June did.

"Sure." A feeling of calm overcame June. Control was a heady drug. She eyed Hailey's designer shoes, imagining them decorated with their own crayon scribbles. "Treat Charlie how he deserves."

"I will." Hailey nearly knocked into Kayla on her way out.

"You okay?" Kayla put her hand on June's arm.

The warmth of her assistant's touch strengthened June's resolve. "Never settle for a man who is incapable of giving you his whole heart." She chucked the picture frame into the trash receptacle.

"Oh, honey," Kayla said. "You helped Charlie through the grieving process and built a family together. I'm sure that woman is just a fling."

June let out a bitter laugh. "Somehow I transitioned into the role of nanny with benefits."

"Charlie loves you." Kayla fished the picture frame from the trash.

June settled into her chair, her gaze moving back and forth from the image of BeeBee sticking her tongue out from the picture frame to Kayla. Kayla, who had spent months conversing with Charlie and carefully curating the photos that she'd loaded onto the picture frame.

She couldn't trust that Kayla was immune to Charlie's charm. Even if they weren't sleeping together, Kayla could report back to him anything June revealed.

"You're right. Charlie's a great catch. I'd be foolish to let him get away," June said. "Would you mind giving me a few minutes to collect myself before the next client arrives?"

Kayla nodded and squeezed June's shoulder.

Until Charlie served her with divorce papers, June would play the part of loving wife and mother, while keeping Kayla at a distance. If working together became problematic, June had other options. Recruiters constantly tried to woo her into starting a career with Brighter Tomorrow, Future Perfect's biggest competitor. Plus, her years of experience with the DESTINY7000 machine made her an excellent candidate for several technical positions outside of the future forecasting industry.

June dry swallowed the Seventh Heaven capsules she'd sewn into the lining of her purse and sent an alert to her dealer. She needed more, much more.

Over the years, June had collected information from sessions with influential clients. To keep their secrets safe, those judges and politicians would ensure she'd receive alimony along with a chunk of Charlie's assets.

Hailey could design her destiny through her actions, but so could June. After all, she was a big fish in the small pond of future-focused technology. The possibilities were endless.

A wave of drug-induced euphoria made June's blood sing. She let out a belly laugh, imagining the perfection of a BeeBee-free future. ♜

TO DIE LIKE A PHARAOH

By Katya de Becerra

WE COME AWAKE IN THE dark.

Hard ground, stale air. Everything hurts. Nails broken, knees scraped raw, feet banged up. We've put up one hell of a fight but still lost.

The acrid ghost of a chemical stench arrives like a slap. Our bodies remember being carried, dragged, packed into the boot of a car. Our bodies remember oblivion.

As we shed the aftereffects of chloroform, the imperfect darkness coalesces around us. A living thing, it breathes, it wants.

We push our hands against the unyielding floor, fingers seeking purchase.

"Who's here? I can hear you breathing," one of us asks, voice thin, breaking.

"Hey?" A reply comes, followed by another. "Hello?"

Three voices. Three hearts beating.

We take turns speaking our names into the dark.

Vika. Eileen. Maya.

The names ring high. There's power in the naming. Without it, we're all the same in the dark, features blurred, fates interchangeable. One anonymous victim on their way to the obscurity of bones.

But bones can sing too. They sing for the unnamed, for those without a voice. Those of us who couldn't find a way out.

We stand up.

We are women, we face each other in a loose circle, limbs tense, minds sharpening. Fight or flight. Live or die. As our eyes adjust and darkness dilutes, we come closer, reach for one another, to confirm we're real, that the dark hasn't erased us, that whoever brought us here hasn't erased us.

Our features have little in common. Maya is sharp and tall and young, wound tight. Her skin is brown, and her black hair is down to her waist in two braids, unraveled by the ordeal. She doesn't seem scared, a façade, a product of growing up with white neighbors who smile to your face but won't hesitate to call the cops if you misstep. She left the soft-hearted girl she used to be in the depths of her past, traded her up for the being of steel she is now. That steel comes in handy in the private security work Maya does for a living. If only she could pick and choose her clients—to protect only those worth protecting. But sadly, those in need of a bodyguard happen to be assholes more often than not.

Eileen, fifty-something, is short, muscular, and wiry, her physique a leftover from those immemorial days when she danced at seedy night clubs to help cover her med school bills. The curly mass of her silver-streaked red hair is too cheerful for this dungeon. Eileen's still wearing her hospital attire—practical, nothing fancy. Back in those days when her medical career was just taking off, her burlesque past vanishing in the rear-view mirror, she'd go out of her way to dress up, to match the looks of her wealthy clientele. Killer red-soled stilettos, fancy-cut office skirts that came from shops the impoverished student she once was wouldn't even dream of entering. But as her life turned into a monotonous dance choreographed to please her offensively rich patients, their wealth garish and unearned, Eileen stopped caring about appearances, swapping heels for flats and pencil skirts for wide-leg pants.

As Eileen finds herself in the dark now, her typically composed mind racing, instead of her entire life flashing before her eyes, she is taken to her time on stage, before she became a servant to the rich to pay off her student debt.

And then there is Vika. She closes the circle of the living. A porcelain-skin baby-doll, a sundress princess, a heart-shaped-face girl. At first, she is what you see. Pretty and fragile, oh so feminine. Easily dismissed. Which is what she wants you to think.

Here we are. We study each other before turning attention to the place that entraps us. This is not some expressionless basement a deranged serial killer would use to hide his victims. No. The walls fluoresce with vivid imagery, telling stories of conquests and victories and glory. The images bring to mind the glorious kings of old, the pharaohs with bronzed skin, their heroic heads adorned with lotus and snakes.

The paint glows in the dark. There recently was light in this dungeon. A door must've been opened, if only to bring in our limp bodies. How long will the fluorescence last? How much do we have? What about air? Does each hitched breath bring us closer to suffocation?

We are buried. Alive. We are buried alive. *Weareburiedalivewe areburiedaliveweare…*

Everything blurs, stretching, twisting out of proportion, the line between real and imagined, between thought and deed, becomes paper-thin.

But we *are* real, fresh and blood.

Confusion gives way to fear. United in crisis, our hearts rush ahead, hoping to jump out of our chests, to break free. Their beat is that of a metronome, counting down to our demise.

"Where are we?" Maya asks, keeping her voice low like she doesn't want the walls to overhear. She's good at hiding the quiver from her tone. "My head's so heavy. What happened? I remember…"

"I just got home from work. The doorbell rang. I opened the door and…" Eileen falls in sync with Maya's narrative, their accounts overlapping. "There was a man. He was smiling. It was not a good smile."

"That's right! There *was* a man. He reached for me," Maya picks up where Eileen left off. "I think he drugged me…" She trails off as she realizes something, recent memories flooding back.

"Do I know you?" Maya asks, suddenly suspicious of her companions. She renews her study of their features in the glowing dark.

An echo picks up Maya's question and bounces it around. Mocking her, or trying to help her remember.

"I don't think so," Eileen says. "I'd remember if you were a patient... I'm a doctor. I work at the Sekhmet clinic."

"You must be loaded," Maya says with a huff. "That's where the lucky few get to go, right?"

Eileen catches shade in Maya's tone and grows silent.

Vika listens, observes. Underneath the Barbie smokescreen, there's a calculating brain. It's putting things together. Vika learned about survival the hard way. Long ago, in a different life, a trip abroad turned into a nightmare. Once Vika was in his clutches, a gorgeous boy who doted on her every whim dropped the pretense and revealed his monstrosity. Vika hated herself for a time, hated how naïve she'd been, a sad statistic. She'd never forget the bitter oblivion of drugs or the stale smell of sweat that wouldn't go away no matter how hard she scrubbed her exploited body. She escaped, put that hellish summer behind her. But now it's coming back. That rotten taste of hopelessness, of disempowerment.

Last summer, when Vika met *him,* she saw an opportunity. If she looked and behaved a certain way, maybe some of the power he wielded would be hers too. But instead, she's ended up here. Did he see right through her pink lipstick and blond curls? Did she do or say something to show her hand? And what about these two women, dumped in this tomb with her? Her fellow victims. No. She hates that word, refuses to apply that label to herself. Not again. She'll tear her way out of here, break through stone, dig until her fingers turn to bone. Whatever it takes. She won't be trapped again. And these two better be helpful. She won't hesitate to leave them behind in this crypt the powerful man who once was her lover had built for himself.

Here we are again.

We study our shapes, the way our fear smells, the clammy skins we're in. We're reluctant to tell our stories, but as the reality presses on—*we are trapped here together, in this tomb*—we have no choice but to open up. And so, we do, forest critters braving the open despite the fear of the hunter.

"I think I know where we are," Maya says, with an uneasy sigh.

It's *him.* The asshole she was assigned to guard, the one with delusions of grandeur. Maya glimpsed the blueprints for this place while snooping in his office. And there was a ledger too, a list of things he was planning to take with him into the next world. Gold bricks, Armani suits, emerald cufflinks. His wealth, all of it. He'd rather be buried with it than leave any to his ex-wives, mistresses, offspring. As for the blueprints—the man was building himself a giant tomb, to be like the mighty pharaohs with their impressive mortuaries built off the backs of the exploited and the enslaved.

But what really set Maya's nerves on fire was that there were *names* on that list of possessions. The rich asshole wanted to take his people into the next world with him too.

The moment she understood what the list meant, Maya knew she was in serious trouble. Her name wasn't on it—she wasn't important enough, an interchangeable pawn—but her snooping might've just added it to the list all the same. Aware of the surveillance cameras' watchful eyes, Maya thought about running, disappearing. But her elderly, arthritic mother needed her and, besides, maybe Maya was just being paranoid. Surely, the man didn't have someone go through daily surveillance footage of his empty apartment?

Two days later she found herself here, in the tomb. The rich asshole wasn't taking any chances when it came to his plans for the afterlife. Now, Maya was to be his bodyguard for all eternity.

Maya starts to move, exploring this underground space, running her hands against the walls, checking the limits of their prison, learning its shape. There must be a way out. As she searches for it, she tells the others what she knows. About her last client, his tomb. Eileen gasps at hearing the man's name. One of her patients. Vika flinches, as if the name is a curse.

"He's dying," Eileen says when Maya grows silent.

"Aren't we all?" Maya drops, her fingers exploring every dip and crack.

A door, there must be a door. *God, let there be a door.*

But all she finds is stone, cold and unfeeling. Her hope dwindles.

"I mean he's dying *soon*," Eileen clarifies. "I'm his oncologist. We've tried every experimental treatment there is... Wealth can certainly buy you time, but it can't keep you alive. What I don't understand is why he'd put us all in here."

Her gaze lingers on Maya, then shifts to Vika, who is still silent. But as Eileen voices her question, the terrible answer dawns on her.

She knows this patient of hers well, knows his ideas. He sees the world as a Gobelin, a tapestry stretched around the shape of his choosing. He calls himself a student of history, singing praises to the powerful men of old, his appetite for power rivalling theirs. He's enamored with the pharaohs. Thutmose III, the Napoleon of Egypt, his army unstoppable. Ramesses II, the terror of Egypt's enemies. Khufu, his famous mortuary guarded by the mighty Sphinx.

As Eileen recalls their private conversations, she remembers the odd glint in her patient's eyes, the fervor. He isn't just enamored by the pharaohs. He thinks he is one. He has his own private army, he's amassed unspeakable riches, he has servants and anything one could wish for and more. But he's dying. Way ahead of 'schedule'.

"He wants us close by, waiting on him in the afterlife," Maya says, confirming Eileen's own conclusions. "In his rotting head this means I'll continue guarding his ass even when I'm dead. And you"—she glances at Eileen—"will continue looking after his health, as ridiculous as it sounds, and you—" she looks at Vika. "Are you his girlfriend or something?"

"Or something," Vika says, darkly. "More like his side piece. A side piece who knows too much."

"Your name must've been on that list," Maya says. "There were so many names... Why only us three are down here?"

"Maybe he's working his way through that list," Vika says. "I knew the architect who designed this place. She went missing three months ago. Women in his life have been disappearing for years, ever since his terminal diagnosis. He's a collector by nature."

Maya stops her pacing and leans against the nearest wall. She wants to slide down, to slump on the floor and bury her head in her hands. She wants to scream and rage and cry, but it's no use. Crying isn't going to change their predicament.

"Who was she? The architect?" Eileen asks, coming to study the wall art. She recognizes her patient's face. One picture shows him seated on an elaborate golden throne, faceless figures prostrate on the floor at his feet. In another, he wrestles a lion to the ground. She wouldn't put it past him to actually kill some poor lion on a deranged oligarch safari.

"I've only run into her a couple of times," Vika says, her face tense with memories. "I overheard them talking about chambers and bluffs and…"

"*Bluffs*?" Maya interrupts.

She knew that word from somewhere.

Those fateful blueprints on the rich asshole's desk… She closes her eyes and sharpens her focus. On her rare days off, Maya binges on the History Channel, anything that would take her far, far away from the routine. Underwater worlds, the planet's driest deserts… Ancient civilizations, their ways of life and death. The Sumerians loved beer so much that they had a goddess dedicated to the drink. The Minoans traded saffron and worshiped matriarchal deities. Egyptians included bluffs in their pyramid designs, to confuse would-be robbers.

Maya is on the move again, but this time instead of tracing the outline of their prison she knocks against it, searching for that shallow sound. "Bluffs are fake walls!" She says. "His henchmen who brought us in here had to get out somehow—it's more likely that they covered up an entry with a fake wall than moved a granite slab around."

Eileen and Vika join Maya in her quest to locate the bluff, their combined hope gaining momentum, turning into a powerful hum perforated only by taps and knocks.

"Here!" Vika calls out to them. She's kneeling in the far corner, her hands pressed against the stretch of the wall at her feet. Her heartbeat is electric.

We come together and push. The wall, fake or not, refuses to be moved. The despair threatens to consume us, it settles on our shoulders, whispering defeat into our ears. Our inhales turn ragged, our exhales are a dirge. Or a prayer.

We scream our hope.

We may be no one, already ghosts, but we are many, the living and the dead united. When our bones sing, they accuse, and they reveal. In the next chamber, there lies the architect—she designed this place and then took her knowledge to the grave. Next to her is the prized chef who cooked this dying pharaoh's meals. Here are some former lovers—no longer desired, but kept, nonetheless. Here we are, those who served him in life, those whose skills or looks impressed him. Bones upon bones. There's no limit to his greed, his desire and want. This tomb is a storage, where the collector stores his favorite things. Because that is what we are to him. Things. A child's toys to be gathered up and placed in a box at the end of the day.

But a silent chorus has been building in this tomb from the moment the first stone was laid over bones. The dead wake up, hearing the prayer of the living. The architect's broken neck moves with a creak. The chef's bullet wound mends just enough to empower her spirit. We, the ghosts, come to help the living. We fill their limbs with strength, their minds with determination. Now, it's not just three women attempting to move a wall, but many.

Vika cries out in relief when the wall gives. Eileen and Maya join her, their breathing victorious. The tomb is thick granite, but this short stretch of the wall is fake stone painted to look like the rest. Breaking nails, tearing skin, three pairs of living hands, helped by the ghosts, break the bluff apart. The opening is a black gasp, the way out. One by one, we drop down to our bellies and crawl.

We find ourselves in a bigger chamber that smells of decay and desolation.

We, the living, proceed across it, while the ghosts trail behind like a mantle. Chamber after chamber, interconnected beehive cells, each containing bodies, with still more space left to fill. We are the accumulation of bones. This modern-day pharaoh has been burying us here for a while, some already dead by the time we got here. But not all.

And here's the central room, reserved for the pharaoh himself. Everything is ready. The canopic jars. The sarcophagus. His body will be mummified, to rest in this unholy temple until the end of days.

We crawl and break through the walls and grind our teeth into fine powder. It's been hours or days. Maybe years have passed. Maybe when we at last dig our way from this grave, the world as we know it will be no more, turned into an inhospitable wasteland by greed, ruled by a desperate few.

We lose track of time, leaving behind the endless stream of chambers and bluffs and corridors. But then we emerge from yet another windowless room and into an… underground parking garage. Empty of people, filled with sleek cars.

Maya can't suppress the sudden giggle. "We're in the Braun Tower," she says, recognizing the building's austere walls and gunmetal fixings. "He built his pyramid underneath his company's HQ."

In the industrial lighting, we study each other anew, committing our features to memory. We're alive, having left the ghosts behind in the dark. But we brought with us their desires, their thirsts for justice.

We move toward the exit, not caring about the cameras tracking our progress, not thinking about how the surface world will receive us, our clothes torn and bodies bleeding from the effort of survival.

The light outside is blinding.

"He has to die," says Vika, her features stern with rage.

"He's already dying," Eileen says, the darkness in her voice matching that in Vika's heart.

"He needs to die *sooner*." Vika thinks about the bodies they glimpsed on their way out, in various stages of decay.

"If he loves pharaohs so much, maybe he…" Vika says.

"Maybe he what?" Maya takes in Vika's determined expression.

"Maybe he should die like one," Vika replies.

"What do you mean, exactly?" Eileen asks as they begin to walk away from the Braun Tower, taking turn after turn, uncaring where they are going as long as it's putting the distance between them and their would-be tomb. "You want to kill him? How are we ever going to get close enough?"

"I know the access codes for his apartment. And I know his security schedule. I bet I can get us in," Maya says, her heartbeat steady, determined.

"I can get chloroform," says Eileen. "Among other things."

Vika nods and smiles. She may not have the access codes to his penthouse, and she can't procure tranquilizers or poisons, but she has rage and that's got to be worth something.

We, the living, fall into step, ignoring the looks from passers-by as our plan takes shape. We, the ghosts, trail behind. Together, we'll turn the tables. Together, we'll give this pharaoh his death.

#   #   #

He comes awake in the dark.

As chloroform wears off, he understands two things: he's alive and he's buried. The confines of his prison are tight, so tight. He bangs his hands against the unyielding wood.

We, the silent ghosts, float toward the sound, surrounding his extravagant coffin. His sarcophagus, sealed.

We press on the lid, adding weight, and trapping this pharaoh inside his own gaudy creation.

The walls swallow all sound inside the tomb. ♜

THE SUICIDE TREE

By Carmen Gray

AS SHE RAISED HER GAZE slowly, she spied a person's head moving in tandem in the reflection. But it wasn't her. Or was it? She lifted her hand, extending the index finger to her right. The image followed her movement almost exactly, except that the finger in the reflection was straight, not crooked. Was this mirror magical? Or was she still dreaming?

\#   \#   \#

Irmalina's biggest worries were accumulating enough cleaning jobs to make her rent. Again. She had put flyers out all over the fancy neighborhoods advertising her services as the housekeeping agency she worked for was slowly eliminating her hours each month. More and more younger people were seeking employment, and they were willing to take less and less for the same job. This city was full of people without jobs while just a handful of very wealthy folks needed their services. God forbid she end up living on the street like so many she walked by on her way to the bus stop. She didn't risk her life all those years ago to come to this great country to end up without shelter. Back then, everyone had told her the streets of America were practically lined with gold.

She had been able to make something of herself on her own for a while here. Cleaning houses, getting her own place, and being free of her abusive husband back in Mexico. They'd never been able to have children, but that hadn't stopped him from having a family with another woman. She figured that would have made it easier for her to leave him, but he wasn't willing to let her go. A good friend convinced her to leave the country entirely and start her life over again. All had been good for a long time. But now she was in danger of losing her place.

With no family in this country to help her, she could only truly rely on the one friend she made here to help her out, Nell. In her late fifties herself, Nell understood the problems she was starting to deal with– her health wasn't what it used to be. Years of manual labor had aged them both much more quickly than people whose jobs didn't require so much stress on the body. Irmalina had developed arthritis in her right hand, and she noticed she was running out of energy faster. Her age was catching up to her and she knew she was a liability for the agency. Mr. Fitzgerald, the manager, warned her that she'd better hustle harder lest he cut her hours completely. He was probably the unkindest person she knew, next to her ex-husband. Sadly Nell had recently died unexpectedly, leaving Irmalina to feel very much alone in her situation. But God must have answered her prayers in the form of Cecelia Rutherford. If she could just make it until the end of her lease, she could move into Ms. Rutherford's attic as promised. Only three months left to go, but it turned out she would not have to wait after all.

Irmalina was assigned to clean Ms. Rutherford's home by the agency. The woman liked her so much after that first cleaning that she asked her to come by daily to tend to her three fat, aging cats. Although Irmalina was not accustomed to pet sitting, she couldn't turn down the offer of getting paid directly. No portions of her pay would be taken by Mr. Fitzgerald, who grew heavier by the day as he sat in his office bossing the workers around and throwing insults at Irmalina, who wasn't as pretty or young as the others.

Cecelia Rutherford lived in a beautifully restored Victorian home on the west side of the city. She was a quiet woman in her mid-forties who was a bit of a hermit. She quickly took a liking to Irmalina because Irmalina did not ask too many questions nor bat an eye at her quirky requests. "Ni modo, hazlo," she could hear Nell's voice in her head. *Just do what she asks and who cares.* The money was an unexpected windfall, and after taking care of the cats, she would now be able to use pet sitting as another skill to earn extra income to offer to clients. It was also less wear-and-tear on her body and would be a good path to move toward if she could get more clients lined up on her own. It was becoming increasingly clear that she needed to find some other form of work outside of the agency.

Some of the strange quirks of Cecelia Rutherford presented themselves immediately on the first day of cleaning. Irmalina could not help but notice the many unusual terrariums throughout the house that contained plants that she'd never seen before. She paused to peer into one, observing the tiny world of spindly green vines inside a beautiful glass enclosure, looking like a miniature greenhouse.

"Wardian Cases," came a soft voice from the other side of the hallway, "which are from a bygone era, like my home. Never touch them, please, as some of the plants growing inside them are well over ten years old and I rooted them from seed. Just clean around them gingerly." Irmalina complied and Ms. Rutherford retreated.

Irmalina finished tidying up the entire downstairs without too much fuss. She sighed as she looked up the wooden spiral staircase. She slowly climbed to the top where a landing opened up to a large window, overlooking a rose garden. Her heart rate had sped up from the ascent and she took a moment to rest on a green velvet chair. She sighed as she massaged her fingers on her right hand. "Nell, tu sabes cómo es," she spoke aloud to her deceased friend. Nell would understand how it was. The two of them had plans to buy a small one room condo, start their own business, and grow old together. But it was not to be. She sighed again. Her own mother had died of a heart attack when Irmalina was a teenager. Maybe she had also inherited a bad heart. Was death imminent for her? A large orange cat meowed, peeking out from underneath her chair. He leaned into her leg, vigorously rubbing his head against it. She petted him, feeling like Nell was somehow here with her at this moment.

"I see Leo approves of you. He never comes out to visit anyone. Not that many people ever come by," Irmalina was startled by being caught sitting on the job and leapt up to her feet.

"Rest anytime you need to, it doesn't bother me," Ms. Rutherford reassured her, her quiet voice sounding slightly demanding.

Irmalina, not wanting to appear lazy, glanced over at the glass knob on a door to a room. She headed in that direction with her dust rag and bucket full of cleaning supplies, but Ms. Rutherford stopped her.

"Don't go in there. Not even my beloved cats go in there. The room contains over one hundred vintage books on exotic plants... and other things. They are worth a fortune. Please ensure the door is always secure in case I forget." She locked eyes with Irmalina's. Hers were an icy blue, with pale golden flecks inside them.

Irmalina nodded her head in agreement, casting her own dark eyes downward. "Yes. It may take me a bit longer to clean, but I'll do everything you ask me to do, Miss," Irmalina promised.

"You can call me Cecelia." She stared at her long and hard and paused before adding, "What only matters to me is that my rules are followed. I'm a very private person and I don't often invite people into my home." Then she disappeared again to another room.

Irmalina finished the job after another two hours and Cecelia was pleased. To Irmalina's shock, the woman said, "I really like you. You seem the type to keep to yourself. Would you like a cup of tea?"

Irmalina had never interacted with any of the other clients before. The agency definitely frowned upon that, but before she could decline the invitation, Cecelia took her by the hand and led her into the dining room, instructing her to sit.

As if she could read her mind, she said, "We won't tell the agency about this."

Something about Cecelia's voice felt comforting to Irmalina. She did not have any companionship anymore and it was clear she needed it. Ever since Nell had passed away, she'd just kept her head down, doing her job. None of the other owners of the fancy homes she cleaned even noticed her. It was as if she were invisible.

"Do you like hibiscus tea?" Cecelia held up a glass jar of dried petals.

The shriveled burgundy flowers brought back childhood memories.

Irmalina nodded her head, recalling the tea her grandmother made for her as a child in Mexico. Though she had a very different life than her own, Cecelia felt familiar to Irmalina.

Over the tart-flavored tea, the two women chatted about life. Cecelia learned of Irmalina's plight and offered her the job of tending to the cats daily.

"I am very busy with my research, Irmalina. I often forget to feed the cats," Cecelia began.

"What do you study?"

"Gothic female monsters from the late 1800's," Cecelia answered, arching one eyebrow.

Irmalina sucked in her breath and made a sign of the cross. Maybe Cecelia was a witch herself. She could hear Nell in her ear, "Bruja Blanca." She recalled Nell telling her about a white witch who had saved her life as a child.

"Oh, not that I believe in them. It's for my dissertation," Cecelia smiled, the corners of her eyes crinkling.

"What is…what is a disser..?" Irmalina tried to repeat the foreign word.

"Dissertation. It's a long paper I have to write. So I may earn my PhD."

Irmalina cocked her head. She did not know what a PhD was.

"My doctorate in Victorian feminism. From the University."

Irmalina nodded her head, not completely following along.

"Anyhow, I sometimes spend days locked in that study with the books. I take my meals with me and really get into my work. Leo, Violet, and Miss Kitty are left to their own devices. It would be wonderful to have someone like you come daily to tend to them. There's something about you that I like, and I don't like a lot of people."

"Maybe it's because I'm lonely. Like you?" Irmalina said, before realizing that could have been an insult. Sometimes she was too honest. Nell always said that and often told her she needed to be more careful around Mr. Fitzgerald as more than once Irmalina had offended him with her honesty, which had resulted in some passive-aggressive punishment like delaying her paycheck.

Cecelia stared at Irmalina again, then broke out in laughter. "Yes. That could be it. I'll pay you well."

And that's when Cecelia hired Irmalina right on the spot. Irmalina sensed that Cecelia was generous and trusting when she pressed a key to the house into her hand.

"You know, Irmalina, if everything works out, there is an attic apartment upstairs. This house has more than enough space for one person. I inherited it from my aunt, who had no heirs. I lived in the apartment during my twenties and when she passed away eleven years ago, I took over the entire estate. The apartment has remained empty all this time."

"Oh, but I'm not sure I could afford the rent," Irmalina began, glancing around at the mahogany wainscoting below the dark blue floral wallpaper surrounding them. It still needed a good dusting.

"No, I wouldn't charge you. I don't need any money. It might be good for me to have some company. I'm nearly finished with my studies."

"I only have three months left on my lease," Irmalina noted.

"Well, then, it is settled. Next week when you come to clean, I'll have you work on the attic. You can get it prepared for yourself, little by little until your lease is completed. There's not much up there. Just some old furniture and boxes. If you like the furniture, you can keep it up there. Otherwise, I'll get rid of it," Cecelia replied.

"You must be the answer to my prayers," Irmalina said, her eyes moist.

"And you to mine. I've been looking for a good cat-sitter. Come every morning and every night to feed the cats and give them fresh water. Leo wanders upstairs, as you saw. Violet is rather independent and can be found lingering in the rose garden out back and Miss. Kitty…" before Cecelia could complete her sentence, a very senile white cat crept slowly into the room and yawned, then licked its paws. "Well, she must have known we were talking about her. That's Miss. Kitty. She's old, but she's my favorite."

Irmalina smiled. She felt like Miss. Kitty.

The week went by, and she got to know the cats and found the cat-sitting job very easy and satisfying. The cats, like their owner, kept to themselves. Except for Leo. He liked to rub against her legs and follow her around as she filled the bright red glass bowls with kibble and refreshed the water bowls. She whistled happily as she did this. Life was looking up for her. By the end of the week, she realized that she had made as much money in one week as she did for a month's worth of house cleaning with the agency. However,

Mr. Fitzgerald must have sensed something was off, because when she went into the office to collect her paycheck, he held the envelope to his chest and looked at her suspiciously with his beady eyes.

"Irma, have a seat," he said, cocking his round head. He never called her by her full name. She hated that about him.

"Yes?" She replied, complying, sitting on the cold, metal chair, spying a strange-looking plant on the corner of his desk.

"Here, have one of these," Mr. Fitzgerald interrupted her thoughts, thrusting a rectangular piece of black candy towards her. He kept a jar full of licorice on his desk. He'd never offered her anything before. Very peculiar. She eyed her check and took the candy.

"Eat it," he commanded.

She bit into the candy. It tasted like fennel to her. And something else. Her lips slightly tingled.

"I've heard some complaints about you. You're taking too long to get your job done with Mrs. Tarrytown and Mr. Clark."

Irmalina thought about the two other clients whose houses she cleaned weekly. She used to have six a week until three months ago. Mr. Clark was a flamboyant art collector. His house was very easy to clean as he was meticulous. It never took her long to do that job. Mrs. Tarrytown was a young wife who played tennis and seemed to have affairs while her husband was out of town. Irmalina had found evidence of other men's belongings in the bedside table, but she never said a word. Mrs. Tarrytown was too busy focused on her looks to notice how long it took Irmalina to clean her house. These claims seemed suspect. She stayed quiet, as always, and looked down at her lap while Mr. Fitzgerald continued. She continued to chew the licorice, but she didn't like the taste of it. Something wasn't right– it was bitter. She wondered how she could get it out of her mouth discreetly.

"Also, Megan told me she saw you at Ms. Rutherford's place on Wednesday. You only clean her house on Monday. Why exactly were you there?"

"Oh, that," Irmalina was annoyed that young Megan, who seemed to be getting the clients that Mr. Fitzgerald was taking away from her, was spying on her. She pretended to cough and spit the licorice into her hand.

"Yes. Why on earth would you be at that house? Ms. Rutherford keeps to herself. Her blinds are always drawn. What are you doing over there?" Mr. Fitzgerald shifted in his chair. He popped a long slice of rope licorice from a different jar into his mouth now, loudly chewing it.

"Oh, I left something in her house and went back to get it," Irmalina responded, proud that she came up with a good excuse on the spot. She just needed him to hand her the paycheck. If she could just fast forward three months, she'd be out from under his thumb. At least he didn't find her attractive anymore. She didn't have to fend off his disgusting advances like she did when she first began cleaning with the agency years ago. Now he bothered the younger, desperate girls. Like Megan.

"What?" He demanded.

"What?" Irmalina repeated.

"What did you leave at her house?" Mr. Fitzgerald sucked his teeth, moving his tongue around his mouth, like a worm moving in dirt. He reached over to squeeze her thigh.

Irmalina's cheeks flamed red. She was too old for this nonsense. But she needed the paycheck. Her heart rate was going up. Thump, thump, thump. Suddenly she felt hot and dizzy. A whooshing sound filled her ears before everything went black.

#   #   #

"Irmalina, would you like some tea?" was the next thing she heard.

She blinked her eyes. Was that Nell's voice she heard? It couldn't possibly be her.

"You okay? Your face is still a little pale," came the voice again.

Irmalina felt a cool cloth on her forehead. She looked up into those clear blue eyes. Cecelia was holding her hand.

"Where am I? What happened?" Irmalina stammered.

"You had a dizzy spell at the cleaning agency. I had stopped by to drop off paperwork for Mr. Fitzgerald and you were slumped over in the chair across from his desk," Cecelia said, "So I offered to lend assistance and have you brought back to my place."

Irmalina looked around. Sure enough, she was in the front living room of Cecelia's beautiful home. She saw a glimmer of gold from the spiral staircase and heard Leo's familiar meow. She was processing everything.

"What, what did Mr. Fitzgerald say? Does he still have my paycheck?" Irmalina suddenly panicked. She needed that money for rent. She attempted to sit up but felt too weak and lay back down.

"Oh, he was very surprised to see me. I got your paycheck for you. Truth be told, I think you should just work full-time for me now. I don't see the point in you toiling away to make ends meet at that place when I can pay you much better. Pardon me, but I did glimpse at your paycheck. That man is a thief, among other things. You shouldn't have to deal with him anymore. He gave me a very nasty feeling. Creepy and letchy," Cecelia rolled her eyes at the thought of Mr. Fitzgerald. "Had I known he was like that, I would not have hired someone from his agency to clean my house in the first place. But I'm glad I did. Because I met you."

Irmalina smiled weakly. She considered this proposition.

"I would love nothing more than to quit that agency, but what can I do for you? As you can see, I am probably not up to doing more than cleaning once in a while and feeding your cats."

"I'm fine with that. I have my personal doctor coming to check in on you. Do you have dizzy spells often? I'll let Mr. Fitzgerald know you are done myself, if you like. I've dealt with men like that," Cecilia responded. "Why don't you rest here on the couch for a bit. I have some apple scones I bought just this morning. I'll bring you one."

Irmalina had not been waited on like this since she was a little girl with her grandmother. She sighed and closed her eyes. If she truly could just quit the agency, maybe her health would improve. Nell had told her that stress was probably causing her heart to race. If only she was still here to give her advice. But that awful accident had taken her away in an instant. Irmalina could still hear the nurse's words at the hospital, "I'm sorry, but she is gone. It was a hit and run. She died before she even got here. We call that DOA. Dead on arrival." Irmalina had wanted to see her, but the nurse said only family members were allowed. Of course, Nell had no family members here. Like Irmalina. But the nurse was just following protocol. A tear slipped down her cheek.

"Here you are, Irmalina. Please rest. Dr. Carmilla is on her way. She's wonderful and will make sure all is well with you." Cecelia set a platter with a scone and some marmalade next to her.

"Thank you, Miss. I am very grateful," Irmalina said, "I don't know why you are so kind to me."

"Please call me Cecelia. I am kind to you because you deserve it."

"Thank you, Cecelia," Irmalina whispered.

She rubbed her eyes. Her fingers were still sticky from the discarded licorice that she'd spit into her hand. She was curious about the attic apartment. Did it have its own kitchen where she could cook her food and stay out of Cecelia's way? Or would Cecelia want her to come downstairs and join her for meals? She had a lot of questions to ask Cecelia. The doorbell rang and Leo tiptoed back up the spiral staircase.

Cecelia opened the front door and a petite woman with short dark hair stepped inside. She moved into the living room and pulled up an ottoman to sit close to Irmalina.

"Hi, I'm Dr. Carmilla, Irmalina. Who is your doctor?"

Irmalina didn't have a doctor. Doctors were expensive and she had no healthcare. She didn't get sick often and had never broken a bone. When she had the flu a few years ago, Nell took her to an emergency clinic and the doctor there just told her to rest and take Tylenol. Irmalina stared back at Dr. Carmilla blankly.

"She probably doesn't have one," Cecelia offered.

"I don't have a doctor," Irmalina confirmed.

"Okay. Have you had dizzy spells like this before? I'm going to check your vitals and take a blood draw to ensure there's no underlying situations."

"I've never had dizzy spells. It was strange. But I also know I've been under a lot of stress. Especially since my friend died," Irmalina said.

Dr. Carmilla was taking Irmalina's blood pressure and raised an eyebrow. "Your friend died? That's difficult. I'm very sorry to hear this. Your blood pressure is a bit high."

Dr. Carmilla had Irmalina make a fist as she poked her arm to fill up two vials of blood.

"Yes, actually it was unexpected. She was walking home, and a car hit her," Irmalina added.

"That's awful. Was the driver under the influence?" Dr. Carmilla inquired.

"Influence?" asked Irmalina.

"Was he drunk?" Cecelia intervened.

"Who knows? It was a hit and run. The driver just left her on the street to die. The nurse at the hospital said she was DOA." Irmalina said morosely.

Dr. Carmilla glanced over at Cecelia before fishing around in her bag for a bottle of pills. The two women exchanged knowing looks.

"Listen, Irmalina. I think you've been through some serious distress. You probably have PTSD from your friend passing away and all of the stress from your job. You need to rest. I don't want you so much as lifting a finger for the next three days. I want to get the results back from your blood tests to ensure you are well otherwise. I'm giving you three-day's worth of anti-anxiety medication to help you. It will also temporarily help your blood pressure not go too high."

Cecelia thanked Dr. Carmilla and led her to the door, shaking her hand and whispering something inaudible in her ear, then she returned to Irmalina's side.

"I'm inviting you to rest here. The attic apartment obviously isn't ready, but there's a bedroom upstairs by the study that I don't use with a twin bed, and you are welcome to sleep there. I can order us some dinner. How about some soup?" Cecelia smiled at her, the golden flecks in her blue eyes dancing.

"I don't know how I deserve this, but I am so grateful. I'm happy to eat anything you bring me. Except licorice," Irmalina said.

"Licorice? I don't have any, so no worries. What a funny thing to say, Irmalina," Cecelia said.

"Well, that's the last thing I had before I fainted," Irmalina mumbled, feeling the stickiness on her fingers.

"Oh?"

"Mr. Fitzgerald offered it to me. In fact, he insisted I have it," Irmalina was starting to feel strange thinking about this.

Cecelia could sense Irmalina's anxiety and brought her a glass of water and opened the bottle of pills that Dr. Carmilla had left for her.

"Take this and no more talk of that horrible man. I'm going to tell him you are done working for his agency. I'll take you up to the spare room."

Cecelia helped Irmalina go up the stairs and tucked her into bed under a homemade cream-colored quilt with lavender circles on it.

"Pretty," Irmalina noted, looking at the design.

"Oh, this is a very precious heirloom. It's a quilt pattern that can be found as early as the late 19th Century. It's called the Double Wedding Ring. My grandmother gave it to my aunt, hoping she'd use it one day. But she remained single until she died. My aunt thought it might give me good luck in the romance department, but I've never been into romance. Besides, I'm too involved in my studies to be in a relationship."

"Tell me about your studies," Irmalina said, feeling relaxed as she nestled into the bed.

Cecelia smiled, the edges of her eyes crinkling. "You remind me of my aunt in a way. She was also a very hard-working woman. She didn't clean houses, but she owned a successful bookstore and sold it for a small fortune when the city grew. That's when she bought this house and invested the rest of her money. She didn't have any children, but she treated me like her daughter and left me this place and a nice inheritance. Oh, and a hell of a collection of rare books that I keep in the study."

"Yes. Tell me something interesting. About one of your monsters," Irmalina said, feeling like a child being put to sleep.

"I study about female monsters from the Victorian era, that's the period between 1820-1914. There's a story from around then called *The Great God Pan*. In it, the main character is a man named Clarke. At the beginning of the story, he has a doctor friend whose goal is to open the mind of a patient to experience the spiritual world. Of course, it is a woman he experiments on, and her name is Mary. This mind-opening experience is what the ancients referred to as seeing the god, Pan. Dr. Raymond performs the minor brain surgery, and she awakens from the operation awed and terrified but goes downhill fast. This mind experiment haunts Clarke throughout the story. Years later he hears rumors about a beautiful, mysterious woman named Helen Vaughan. Helen has caused all kinds of strange things to happen in her town and much of it has to do with deviant sexual activities involving other women and men. Clarke is a writer and is writing a book about proving the existence of the devil and includes these stories in his book. Clarke takes part in an investigation of this woman, Helen, eventually, as it is suspected that she either killed or drove her husband to his death."

Irmalina was drifting in and out of sleep as she listened to Cecelia's story. She mumbled to her, "So who is the monster? Is it the doctor who tried to experiment on the woman?"

Cecelia laughed, replying, "Oh, no. The monster is the woman, Helen, who disappears from America. However, Clarke learns about a series of perfectly happy men in London who commit suicide. In these cases, it turns out that the last person known to have been with them is a Mrs. Beaumont. Clarke, along with this other guy band together to confront Mrs. Beaumont, who is in fact Helen Vaughan. They take a noose with them and demand that she kill herself, or they will expose her. Her death is very abnormal as she transforms between human and animal, male and female, until eventually turning into a strange substance and dying. Basically, Helen is a supernatural creature– from beyond this realm."

Irmalina, her eyes barely able to stay open any longer, added, "Well, I don't think she is a monster. I think the doctor who messed with the first woman's mind is a monster. Just because this Helen woman makes men crazy does not make her a monster. And besides, who knows what those men were like."

Cecelia laughed again. "I have to agree with you on that, Irmalina. I'm going to add that to my dissertation. The point is that female monsters in Gothic literature challenged perceptions and expectations of women. This book was very frowned upon at the time because Victorians did not dare talk or read about female sexual behavior. Helen the monster challenges this concept, as do the supernatural transformative powers that she has in the end. Anyhow, it's time for you to sleep now. I'll see you in the morning, unless you wake up hungry later. I'll have soup downstairs in the kitchen. Just help yourself to it."

Irmalina fell into a deep sleep. In it, she floated out of her body and into the landing at the top of the stairs. She could see the grey-and-white cat, Violet, darting in and out of the rose bushes from the window. Turning back toward her room, she passed by the locked door of the study. Her curiosity got the best of her as she floated through the door and into the study. The floor was covered in a dark ruby-colored carpet with paisley designs on it, surrounded by floor-to-ceiling shelves full of books on either side of the room. At the end of the room, a big window with an antique desk sat in front of it, a heavy velvet rolling chair inviting her to sit. She took a seat and opened the notebook on the desk. A slender green leaf from a plant lay inside it with some undecipherable scribbling in the notebook. Before she could focus on it more, she heard footsteps approaching and glided back toward the door, where there was a full-length oval mirror that she hadn't noticed when she entered. Pausing in front of it, she peered in to see if she could see her reflection. As she raised her gaze slowly, she spied a person's head moving in tandem in the reflection. But it wasn't her. Or was it? She lifted her hand, extending the index finger to her right. The image followed her movement exactly, except that the finger in the reflection was straight, not crooked and the finger was beckoning her to step into the mirror. She froze, lifting her gaze again to meet a pair of familiar, amber-colored eyes.

"Nell?!" Irmalina wanted to shout, but she found she had no voice. The image nodded its head in affirmation. Again, she noticed the fingers gesturing to bring her into the mirror. Irmalina followed the apparition into what seemed to be an open space beyond the mirror. In it, Nell held up her bloody clothes and pointed to a sign in the distance. It was the cleaning agency. Irmalina gasped in horror. Was Nell saying the agency had something to do with her death? Irmalina suddenly felt nauseous and didn't want to stay in this place anymore. She turned away, noticing Nell's hands were now on her shoulders, gently guiding her back out. Wanting to say goodbye, she paused, but was afraid to turn and look again. Her heart was racing.

#   #   #

"Are you okay?" Irmalina heard as she blinked her eyes open. She was in a pool of sweat and her heart was still beating fast as she looked up into the pale blue eyes of Cecelia.

"I had a very strange dream," Irmalina began, trying to sit up.

"There, there. I heard you cry out and came in to check on you," Cecelia said soothingly.

"What did I say?" Irmalina asked.

"You called out the name, Nell. Wasn't she the friend you told me about?"

"Yes. Hmmmm," Irmalina mused, recalling her vivid dream.

"Was she in your dream, then?" Cecelia prodded.

"She was. This is going to sound strange, but is there any way you could let me into the study?" Irmalina suddenly wanted to see if it looked like it did in her dream.

"Yes, it's fine if I go in there with you. I just don't want you to touch anything in there. But, why?" Cecelia asked, frowning.

"In my dream, there were things that seemed so real inside that room."

"You went into that room in your dream? Hmmmm. Interesting. Well, gather yourself and let's go take a look."

Cecelia led Irmalina to the door of the study and took out an old-fashioned skeleton key, sliding it into the keyhole and turning it clockwise until there was a loud click. The door creaked open, revealing the same ruby-colored rug and the walls lined with books from her dream. Irmalina gasped, walking toward the desk by the window.

"It's like it was in your dream?" Cecelia somehow knew.

"It is. And this is the same looking leaf I saw," Irmalina reached out to touch the leaf on the notebook when Cecelia's hand grabbed hers in mid-air.

"Do not touch it-highly toxic," Cecelia let go of her grasp on Irmalina's hand and she recoiled from the notebook.

"What is it? Why is it here?" Irmalina was very overwhelmed. How did she know what this room looked like in her dream? And was that mirror in the room as well? She turned to check. Sure enough, it was right by the door.

"Irmalina," Cecelia began, asking her again, "Is this room the same one you saw in your dream?"

"It is, let me see this mirror," Irmalina went to the mirror. She saw her reflection in it. There was a flash of light from the right-hand corner. Probably it was just her imagination, she told herself.

"Let's go downstairs and have some soup. We can talk more about the plant and your dream," Cecelia led her gingerly down the stairs.

After they were settled at the dining room table, each with their bowls of chicken soup, Cecelia began to talk.

"Irmalina, I believe you are more powerful than you realize, and you've proven it to me with your dream."

Irmalina rubbed the temples on her head. Such strange things were happening to her lately. She could hear Nell's voice in her head, "Escúchala." Yes, she would hear Cecelia out.

"As you know, I'm a bit different. And as soon as I met you, I could tell you were also…different," Cecelia started.

Irmalina nearly spit out her soup with a laugh. She was the most boring, normal person she knew. There was nothing unusual about her. Patting the corners of her mouth with a cloth napkin, she looked back at Cecelia, who looked quite serious.

"Sometimes we cannot see the power that lies inside of us. But I saw it in you. I can see people's auras."

"Bruja Blanca, cómo yo te di," Irmalina heard Nell's voice, reminding her again that Cecelia was in fact a White Witch.

"What is an aura?" Irmalina asked.

"It's the colors that surround your physical body. Your spiritual colors. For example, some people have yellow auras– people who are cheerful and magnetic. Others may be blue– -they are good at expressing their deep thoughts. And a few rare ones are white. These are people who have extremely good intuition and healing abilities. These people have pure hearts and can do no harm to others. You have a white aura. It does not surprise me that you have the ability to see beyond the things in this world. That is why you could see into my locked study. And why you are able to go beyond the veil between this life and the afterlife. To see and hear your friend, Nell."

"Oh, my goodness. Do you really think I saw her?" Irmalina started to recall that she had had visitations from her mother, too, when she was a teenager, after her mother had passed away.

"Yes. And what message did she tell you?" Cecelia peered intensely into Irmalina's eyes. Those golden flecks were practically glittering.

"I think she was telling me that the agency had something to do with her death," Irmalina whispered.

"Me, too," Cecelia replied. "In fact, I think Mr. Fitzgerald killed your friend."

Irmalina made the sign of the cross, sucking in her breath. She knew that's what Nell was telling her in her dream.

"And…I believe he was going to kill you, too," Cecelia said.

"But, why? What did we ever do to him?" Irmalina didn't doubt he was capable of this act. She shivered, thinking about it. But she didn't put it past him. It was clear he did not like them because they were getting too old for him to harass.

"Some people have black auras. They are full of darkness and their souls are lost. They have no compassion. That is what I saw in him. And I believe he poisoned that licorice he gave you. That's why I had Dr. Carmilla test your blood."

A chill went down Irmalina's spine. What kind of poison would he have put in that candy? She wondered.

As if Cecelia could hear her, she responded, "That leaf you saw in my study, it comes from a plant known as The Suicide Tree. It grows naturally in faraway places like Australia. It is called this because it can kill people. I believe Mr. Fitzgerald tampered with that licorice he gave you. I saw that he had that plant on the corner of his desk. Only someone such as I, who studies such rarities, would recognize it. With how you responded in his office, he could have killed you had you not spit out the licorice. I put it all together when Dr. Carmilla and I spoke after she treated you."

"That horrible man! How could he do something like that? And Nell?" Irmalina was aghast at the thoughts swimming in her head. How she hated Mr. Fitzgerald now more than ever.

"It's okay, I took care of him," Cecelia continued, her blue eyes suddenly a steel grey.

Irmalina looked up at Cecelia. The golden flecks of light from her eyes seemed to beam out and permeate all around her body.

"Come again, Cecelia? And is that sunlight surrounding you? It's so bright," Irmalina asked, squinting her eyes. Maybe she didn't hear Cecelia correctly.

"That's my aura you see, Irmalina. It's golden, very rare. The rarest.

You're so pure you would never hurt a soul. But I am from beyond this place. I have no problems righting the wrongs that happen here. And you and your friend have been truly wronged. So I took care of Mr. Fitzgerald. Like Helen Vaughan took care of the men exploiting her in the story I told you about."

"Are you a monster, then?" Irmalina asked Cecelia.

"Did you think Helen was a monster?" Cecelia asked.

"I did not," Irmalina answered.

"Exactly. So, there's nothing to worry about anymore. I took a sample of the leaf and delivered it to Mr. Fitzgerald in the form of a cupcake while you were sleeping. He ate it right up, with a little persuasion while telling me how much he liked you and Nell. He tried his best to convince me that he was innocent." Cecelia pictured Mr. Fitzgerald, whose piggy eyes looked pitiful as he panted and vomited on the tile of his office, crumbs from the smashed cupcake spread over his lips. Death would come within the next couple of hours for him. She smiled at him before leaving him writhing on the floor, sweat pooling below his large body.

"Won't you get caught?" Irmalina asked.

"No, Dr. Carmilla will take care of that." Cecelia smiled. "Dr. Carmilla is my best friend. She will be the one to do the autopsy. Mr. Fitzgerald died of natural causes. Or accidental ingestion of a toxic plant. No matter. I was not involved. And neither were you."

Miss. Kitty slinked into the kitchen to join them. She purred loudly as she plopped herself at Irmalina's feet, her white coat shining unlike it had ever before. ♛

SMALL RETRIBUTIONS

By Michael Joseph Tharnish Roby

IT WAS TWO WEEKS TO the summer solstice when I touched down for food miles west of Dublin. The city folk with their gas lamps and rugby matches didn't pay much mind or offer much tribute to fae anymore, as my brothers warned me. When I returned to my ancestral glen in Knocknarea I'd be swallowing pride to my friends and family and admitting I wanted to return to our pastoral homeland. I thought on all of this as I descended to the shabby old farmhouse. The sun beat hot on my black feathers, and I was ready for a break. A saucer of milk fresh enough to have not curdled yet, sippets, and honey sat on the farmhouse's windowsill. At least some of the rural folk still had respect for tradition.

SNAP!

A moment after I landed on the saucer, a pressure plate beneath it triggered and a cage snapped up around me. I jumped in surprise, my mouth half full of soggy bread, the iron of my prison sapped my strength, broke my veil of invisibility, and I fell to my knees. My glamour burned away, my head went hazy, sickness racked my body. Sweat beaded on my head as I looked about in fear. "What? Why?" After that, the scare shifted to annoyance as I spat out the food, too weakened to keep it down. "Damn it, such a waste."

I sat caught in a faerie trap, and the farmer probably just wanted to cut a deal with me. Mum and Da warned me about such things, but that was my first experience with one. Apparently, the big people were displeased that petty food offerings led to petty blessings, and some figured the threat of imprisonment could earn them more. I laid as close to the center of the dish as possible to keep distant from the iron bars and waited. A few old stories told of humans who sought to eat fae, but I figured no one setting a food trap would be so desperate, it would be like eating gold instead of trading it. Fantasies of how I could corrupt the wishes of my captor crossed my mind to kill the time. If the farmer asked for a great harvest, I figured I could speed the growth of his weeds, that'd teach him a lesson.

An hour passed before a bespectacled man with a dark beard and rough, sun-tanned skin entered the house and checked the trap. Mum and Da always told me, "Stand up straight and look confident if you must make a deal with humans, Lonán. Wings aside, you look pretty human yourself, work their empathy. Tuck them away and look the big folk in their eyes."

I put on my toughest face, crossed my arms, and glared up at him. "All right, you caught me. I suppose you've already decided what you want to trade me to open this damned cage then?"

With his great size and stoney face, the farmer looked like Manannán mac Lir, the god turned into a mountain. He studied me and, when he finally spoke, it was in a ragged brogue. "Are you a changeling?"

"Eh?" I frowned and referred to my black wings. "No, I'm a púca."

"Don't you lie to me." He snarled like a dog.

I took a step back from the center in fear and afront. "Lies are not in my nature, sir. I can no more lie than you can fly."

Mac Lir continued to stare, no change in his expression. "Do you know any changelings around here?"

"I've been living in Dublin," I said. "I don't know what kind of folk you have prancing about."

The farmer grunted as he picked up the cage. Milk spilled from the saucer, I lost my balance and a hand slipped against the iron. I yanked the hand and bit back a shout of pain. "Wait, what are you doing?" My words came fast, edged by pain and confusion. "Let's make a bargain."

"Oh, we'll make a bargain all right." Mac Lir carried the cage into the house. A sitting room sat opposite us under a layer of dust and hair like it was long since anything within had been much cared for. The giant crossed the kitchen, opened a door half-off its hinges, and thrust the cage inside. From what I knew of human homes, the windowless room seemed to be a larder.

A scream belted out from within. I looked up, from a hook latched to the ceiling hung another iron cage like my prison. The inside wasn't clear to me in the dark, but from the shrill cries, it sounded like he'd already caught another fae before me.

"Now think back and think hard." Mac Lir shoved my cage against another, far larger one on the floor.

A new sickness rose in my belly as the shape within came into focus: a body, big for a fae, but tiny and starved for a human, sat in the center of the cage. Dark, clumped locks covered most of her face, with a layer of grime beneath. Within the cage was barely enough room for the child to do her broken little rock back and forth.

"A changeling took my Eliza," the farmer spoke over the screams above. "Stole away the last little bit of my wife I had and left this—this—" he struggled for a moment before he continued, "Abomination in her place. Now think good and proper if you've never seen her before."

I studied the pathetic creature in the cage, more to be cooperative than anything else. She was maybe six or seven by human count, but something in her look made her seem decades older. The child looked beyond me with wide eyes, neither thought nor soul seemed clear in them. Of course I didn't know anything about her. "I don't. But it seems to me you've done as the remedies say," I had to speak up to overcome the shrieks of my fellow fae. "When you torment the changeling's child, it is supposed to take pity and return."

Mac Lir jerked my prison up to his face, which showed red with rage. "I know all that already." He shook the cage and again I slammed against the searing bars, a shout of my own joined the ones above. "But clearly it's brought me nothing. What wretched parents this thing has."

I tried to bring my hands together in pleading supplication, but the stings on my palms where the iron touched me made the pain too great. "Please," I said. "I don't know why this has happened, and I'm sorry it's happened, but there's nothing I can do—"

"But there is." The farmer took the other cage down and hung my prison in its place. With one big, grubby hand he opened the door, and reached in. Mac Lir pulled out another whimpering púca with long, scabbed over rabbit ears atop his head. The farmer pushed open the larder door and thrust my kin onto his kitchen table. "It's all very simple. A changeling took my daughter—my beautiful, handsome little girl— and left that putrid brat in her place. All I want is my little one back." He pulled something out of a nearby drawer. I realized with a sinking dread in my belly it was a nail. "But until I get her back, it'll be the blood of you lot for hers!"

Mac Lir smashed the nail into my brethren's ear, the púca screeched in agony, the pierced flesh sizzled like he'd set it aflame. The farmer grabbed a meat tenderizer off the counter and beat the nail deeper, then beat a second nail through the púca's other ear. I lost what was left in my stomach in an awful retch. I'd meant what I'd said, we couldn't tell lies, the best we could do was obfuscate. If the poor púca stabbed into the table knew anything of the madman's child, it would be impossible for him not to say so. Surely the giant already knew all that.

The farmer picked up a milking pail with a heave and held it inches over the babbling púca's face. "Can't be caging all you abominations at once, one is already enough. Do you have anything left you want to tell me?"

With a voice scratchy from screams, the púca said, "I don't know what happened to your girl—I'd have told you by now if I did! P-p-please, you don't want to do this—"

"Whoever said that fae can't tell lies? Because you said something very wrong just now." Mac Lir tilted the bucket and a steady stream of white fell onto the púca's feet.

My kin screamed and jerked about as the salt ate through him like a slug. The farmer directed his pour slowly upward and drew out the púca's harsh cries. As his leg disintegrated, in the midst of a thrash, one of his rabbit ears sliced loose from the nail. The púca rolled over and tried to dig his other ear free. The farmer tipped the pail over and unleashed an avalanche of salt. I curled into myself, shut my eyes tight, and held my hands over my ears.

"And lest you find some way out of that cage—"

There came a *creak*, Mac Lir opened the door of my cage. I threw myself toward the exit and beat my wings, but the giant caught me before I could escape. Out from one of his drawers he drew a butcher knife.

"No, oh gods, please no!" I kicked and writhed in his grip, but the movement meant nothing to him. Mac Lir slammed me onto the table and raised the knife high.

He slashed. My back exploded with agony. One wing split off, blood and screams burst from me. I pled, "No more—please no more—." It came out as babbling. The fight slipped from my body as Mac Lir slashed through my other wing. Unconsciousness rushed toward me, and I pled for it. Mac Lir said something more as he shoved my limp body back into the cage, and I fell into darkness as he slammed the door shut.

...

"Looo…nán."

"Loo… nán."

"Lonán!"

A new wave of phantom pain rushed through where my wings once sat as I awoke. With a scramble backwards I searched around for my caller. It was bad enough the giant had me locked away. If he somehow knew my name as well, he'd have such power over me—

"Lonán."

The voice sounded like a woman's husky tone run ragged. I turned to the front of the cage. Just outside floated a mass of phantasmic green energy. Every few moments it bent and shifted like it struggled to maintain its form.

In disgust and fascination, I stared for a few seconds. "What are you?"

"A lingering regret that waits to be free of his cursed place."

With a squint I made out the contorting silhouette of a woman in the center of the mass. I tried to look straight at her when I asked, "Can you help me?"

"There is usually little we can do in the madman's domain," the wisp said. "But so near to the solstice, when magic and mortal are intertwined, some rules of this world have been suspended." The mass stretched out toward the door of my cell. "Even still, one great favor requires another in exchange."

I crawled as close as I dared to the door. "Anything, declare it."

"Other fae are doomed to fall into his clutches, so long as she remains his bartering chip." The creature extended like a pointing hand and motioned toward the cage below. "I can open the door of your prison, but you must do the same for her."

"Wha—what?" My heart fell into my stomach. "Can't you just open her cage as well?"

"You are a captive, cheated out of his freedom, I can help restore it to you. But even in this state, the madman has some sway over her. Not by my hand can she be saved."

"I don't even have my wings," I said. "I would if I could, but I just don't think I can."

The writhing creature in the center took on a solemn stance for just a moment. "Very well then." And then began to fade away.

"No, no, wait!" I clasped my hands and knelt like I was in prayer. If the wisp ensnared me in a deal, I wouldn't be able to escape the house until the deed was done. I'd almost certainly die in the attempt. But I had no doubt at all I'd die when the giant came for me. "I'll do it, please, I'll do anything!"

The wisp did not rematerialize, and for a moment all hope slipped through my fingers. But then came a little metal *clink*. The door of my cage popped open. "The madman keeps a key in the drawer beside his bed," the disembodied voice said. "Bring it back and you can free the girl. But beware, his hatred runs through this whole house."

I struggled with whether or not to say thank you to the creature who'd saddled me with an impossible burden, and decided she'd already gone where she couldn't hear me. Head leaned over the lip of the cage I looked down at the floor below. No fall ever looked so tall back when I had my wings. With a running start I leapt out of the cage, the ground below rushed to meet me. Teeth grit, I bit back a shout as my legs hit the floor, and thankfully the ache passed soon after. Damage from salt or steel could take months to heal, but I come from hearty stock when it comes to most other pain.Up and down at the larger cage I looked until I identified a lock at the bottom. The whole damned thing was metal, exactly how I was supposed to open was still unknown to me. "Changeling," I called to the pathetic creature inside, but she did not look toward me. "Changeling!"

She still did not react.

After a moment's consideration, I called, "Eliza?"

The changeling turned her look to me for just a moment and her eyes narrowed. But then she looked away again.

Pity ran through me. For however short a time, Mac Lir must have mistaken her for his own, his daughter's name may well have been the only one she'd ever known. "I'll do what I can to get you away from that monster. But if he finds I have gone and captures me again, I'm sure it will be the end of me. He doesn't want to kill you; he still needs you to make his trade. Keep me safe so I can do the same for you."

For an instant that felt much longer, Eliza glanced back at me. I wasn't sure what I felt in that look, maybe just that there were words she wanted to say but couldn't. After what looked like consideration, she opened her mouth wide. I took a horrified step back as the implication came into focus: a tiny, scabbed over nub was all that remained of her tongue. She was giving me assurance the only way she could: she couldn't turn on me to her captor, even if she wanted to.

I swallowed hard, turned away, and slipped out of the larder. An almost full moon shown in the window and illuminated the kitchen. No footsteps or creaking floorboards from above reached me, Mac Lir probably laid fast asleep. Still, I kept to the shadows and moved quick through the dark room. The thought the beginning of my journey was the easiest step ran a stab of dread through me. Most human stairs were nearly as tall as me, I'd have to slowly climb each individually, and after that I'd still need to sneak up on—

My body froze up as I rounded the corner into the entryway. Another body only a little bigger than mine stood beside a door carved into the staircase, back turned to me.

"Oh gods, what are you doing here?" I ran toward the fae, my kin remained stock still. Bits of the body came into focus, strongest among them the tall pair of rabbit ears atop the head. "You need to get out of here, the farmer is a monster—"

The body opposite me turned slowly and, as he did, I brought myself to a stuttered stop. His eyes opened wide, but within them was nothing but bottomless black. The skin across his face clung tight to his skull as if his flesh was dried for leather.

"It's you." It came out as a stutter, and I took a step back. "The one in the cage before me, but you're—I saw you—"

"Eliza." The púca drew the name out long on rotted lips. "Find them—get them—kill them!"

He threw himself at me, decayed hands wrapped tight against my throat, and we fell to the ground.

I gagged. "Wait, stop! I'm not your enemy, I—"

"Your blood for hers." His intonation matched Mac Lir's perfectly. "Your blood for hers!"

Kicking and beating against the ground I struggled against my dead-eyed cousin. A constant refrain of the call for vengeance slipped from him over and over as he pressed to steal the air from my lungs. As he gripped my throat, I slipped my arms between his and pressed outwards, expecting a slip of his grasp. Though he held tight, the grasp did begin to weaken, so I kept pressing. With one great push I shoved at the inside of his elbows. Meat shredded from bone, bone turned to dust, and the púca screeched as his arms split from his body. I scrambled to my feet and made a run for the cupboard beneath the stairs.

Mum and Da's old warnings rushed through my head. "A fae that dies young leaves a bit of themselves in the place they breathe their last," Da said. "Their magic clings, it becomes poisoned and enthralled by the place of their dying."

If that púca still lived, we wouldn't be enemies, but all that was left of him stood poisoned by the hatred of the farmer. The dread and fear ran together as I closed in on the cupboard: did Mac Lir know he'd done this? And just how many other fae had he already killed?

The púca uttered a last, raspy scream of, "Your blood for hers!"

And chorus of echoes burst from the cupboard with the reply of, "Your blood for hers!"

A deluge of undead fae burst from the cupboard like wasps knocked from their hive. Nearly all were as I was—human apart from animalistic distinctions—but all glared at me with the same rotted faces and dead, empty eyes. In the same raggedy tone they all chanted, "Blood for blood, blood for blood."

With a racing heart I diverted my dash and pumped legs hard to the left. The small sitting room stood down the hallway. It felt like only luck that got me past the first of my kin, the rest of Mac Lir's undead army had the numbers ready to hold me down and rip me apart. I jerked my head left and right in search of some kind of escape. A mousehole, another closet—

A small wicker basket sat beside a roughed-up sofa. I pushed the top off. A new sense of sickness washed over me, but a new hope awoke inside me. Inside the wicker sat scraps of cloth, thread, and a half-dozen thin sewing needles. I had to act fast, I grabbed one of the scraps to protect my hand and drew out a needle as long as my arm.

A pair of claws dug into my back. A scream slipped from my lips as talons reopened the wounds from my slashed wings. A dead-eyed, black feathered fae woman clutched me tight and took to the air. Blood seeped through my scars, and I had to bite back both shrieks of pain and pleas of, "You can't do this—I'm one of you!"

"Kill," my kin said with a snarl. "Kill, let him kill, always he who kills."

I fought back the need to struggle as she flew over the mass of snarling fae below us. If she intended to hand me over to Mac Lir, I could bypass the legion ready to tear me apart. Tears leaked from my eyes as her claws bit deeper into me, but I kept still as I could as she flew up the stairs.

As we reached the second floor, my captor slipped into her own chant of, "He who kills, he who kills," and clawed ever deeper into my shoulders. When we cleared the last stair, I took my chance.

Hands tight around the cloth for protection, I thrust the cruel iron up through her chin. For just an instant she let loose a sharp *screech* and then fell silent. The stab went clean through her head, and her whole body went limp. My victory lasted only a moment as, without her wings for support, the floor again rushed to meet me, and we crashed hard. The needle pricked my side, my innards felt like they'd erupted in flame. Even slowed by my exhaustion, I forced myself up and pushed my kin off me as her body turned to dust. I stood up straight, needle raised like a sword, and waited. One death was not enough to hold her down, I couldn't be sure two would either. After half a minute's wait, I relaxed, just a little.

As loud as the chants were downstairs, I barely heard a word of them from the second floor. It was a relief to think they didn't seem to have the power needed to wake Mac Lir up with their words alone. My relief was then overwhelmed by both assurance and dread by a great roar from behind. I turned, two doors waited for me, one at the end of the hall, one to my right. With the constant, glutaral roars from the door at the end, I slipped into the other for anything that could help my cause.

A truly desolate little girl's room waited on the other side. In one corner sat a bed with a headboard lined with cobwebs next to the window, dresses and socks laid thrown about on the floor. A small bookcase that bore nursery rhymes, a copy of the Bible, and the image of the Catholic Madonna stood near the entryway. And just in front of that stood a half-finished, shambled bit of wood. By the little characters made of sticks and paper before it, my best guess was it was a dollhouse. Mac Lir clearly wasn't much of a craftsman, and as a farmer in the country probably couldn't afford the kinds of toys I'd seen in Dublin.

The thought the cruel giant was once a caring family man stirred up sickness in me, and I put the reflections out of my mind. I stepped into the dollhouse, planted one foot firmly against the floor and pushed against the back wall. It took some struggle, but eventually, the walls began to separate and revealed its inner workings: a line of nails that held the two pieces together. Unsheathed from the wood, the rusty nails wore on me, but I pushed past my weakness and dragged the floor of the dollhouse down the hall and positioned it in front of the second, roaring room. If I slipped out with the key, I might need any way to slow down Mac Lir I could get. In and out like breath came the roars from within. I recovered my bit of cloth and the needle and walked down the hall, a reunion with my captor awaited.

Within the dark room moonlight was again my only illumination. The giant laid in his great bed, a small table with a drawer flush against the headboard. Every few seconds he took in a deep breath and let out another long, congested roar. I wrinkled my nose, disgust fought with fear as I slowly approached the bedside table and tested how climbable it would be. The damned thing may as well have been an oceanside cliff too steep and slick to climb, there was nothing to grip onto. An answer already felt clear, and I already dreaded it.

Steps slow and gentle, I sidled up to the bed and gauged the climb. With my needle raised I stabbed into the side of the mattress deep enough to maintain a solid hold and pulled myself upward. With my free hand I bunched up bits of the bedspread until I got a solid handful and used that as my next handhold. The effort proved tiring and time consuming, but I kept pushing myself. My arms and legs started to ache with new pains as I pulled myself up over the lip of the bed, got to my feet for a moment, and then collapsed.

Mac Lir laid with his back to me and continued his foul-smelling roars. If he'd faced me, it seemed the exhales alone could knock me off my feet. I made careful movements past the sleeping giant and slipped up to the bedside drawer. With a jump I landed on the table, walked to the edge of the surface, dropped onto my hands and knees, and wedged the needle into the top crease of the cabinet. It took some trial and error and much of my remaining strength, but after a few seconds' fiddling, I pulled the drawer open. A braid of red hair formed a circle around a small, metal key. My phantasmic benefactor hadn't given me any other instruction, so I had to assume—

"Got you, you little blighter!"

Mac Lir slammed a cupped hand down into the drawer, I clutched my knees and ducked to keep from being squashed. The giant's hands covered me in darkness save for little slits of moonlight that slipped between his fingers, again my heart raced.

"Slipped out from the cage, did you?" His tone sounded one part amused to three parts furious. "In a hurry to be put out of your misery then?" Mac Lir tightened his grip as if to crush me. "I'd be glad to—"

I thrust the needle into Mac Lir's palm. For an instant, he didn't react, and I feared I'd done nothing but waste my one opening. Then a thin stream of blood burst from the wound, the giant screamed, and wrenched his hand away. I abandoned the needle, threw my bit of cloth over the metal key, gripped it tight, and leapt out of the drawer.

"You goddamn, miserable cockroach!" Mac Lir's voice went shrill with the shout. "I'll tear your head from your shoulders!"

I hugged the key to myself and rushed for the staircase. Mac Lir stomped fast on my heels until I heard another scream from his direction, seemed the floor of the dollhouse served its purpose, and the nails tore into his feet.

Down the flight of stairs I saw the legion of undead fae slowly ascending the steps one step at a time. At halfway down the stairs I had enough space to leap off the side. Another burst of pain rushed through my feet and a *crack* rushed up my bones. I swallowed my shout and turned to look back at the mob hunting me. They looked between themselves, maybe in confusion from my turnaround. My bones quickly mended themselves back together and I rushed back through the kitchen and into the larder.

"Eliza, Eliza!" I rushed in and shoved the key into the lock by her feet. "Wake up, time to run."

The girl looked at me, wide eyed.

Both hands pushed and twisting against the key, I tried to unlock the cage. But the cloth over the key impeded my progress, and no matter how I struggled my grip kept slipping.

The girl reached out a bony hand, I backed away. With two slight fingers she slipped off my cloth cover.

"Wait a minute, what are you doing?" I said. "Don't just touch it, it's made of metal—"

Eliza turned the key until the cage let out a little, *click.* No sizzle sounded from her bare skin, no wails of agony escaped her lips. My jaw went slack, and a hundred confusing thoughts rushed into my head. All of them had one simple answer I hadn't considered.

A wave of power rushed through me. The lingering pain from my injuries remained but faded into old stiffness. The favor to my benefactor was to free the girl, and now that the cage door was open, the task was complete.

"I'll kill you, you little bastard!"

The larder door swung open. I turned and faced Mac Lir, the giant seething with fury, both of his hands full of salt. I tried to back away, heart racing again, but that just brought me closer to the cage. My eyes darted about, I felt certain I couldn't outrun him, I had to—

The little girl grabbed me off the floor, hugged me to her chest and ran. I heard, then felt, the burst of the salt handfuls as they cascaded down her body and burned me like blazing flakes of snow. Head up, I opened my mouth to scream at her for a senseless sacrifice. But like with the metal, the salt did nothing to deter her.

Oh gods, there could be no doubt: she was never a fae at all.

Eliza, surely pushed by that wild will to survive humans on the brink feel, ran. Mac Lir went to grab her as he screamed a new line of curses, but with the bloody holes in his foot he couldn't keep up with his lithe daughter. Right next to the kitchen window I'd been captured on stood a door out to the fields, Eliza threw open the door and ran. At last, back in the outside world, my next deep breath revitalized me as I shook free of the rank of intrusion that hung over the fiend's house.

"You stop right the hell where you stand, girl!" Mac Lir hobbled out of the house and leaned hard against the doorway, blood seeping from his foot as he pushed past the threshold.

Eliza came to an abrupt stop and turned back toward him.

Mac Lir raised one hand and lowered a finger in command. "Get your arse back over here, or I'll do to your eyes what I did to your tongue."

"Don't listen to him," I said. "Keep running, he doesn't have any power over you."

But even if it wasn't the same, of course he did. He was her father.

As Eliza looked back and forth between me and the hobbling giant, the rush of the phantom fae pushed one past another outside. As soon as they did, however, each one of them froze, the fury on their faces shifted to dazed confusion. I thought on it for a moment before I realized that, outside of the house, Mac Lir held no influence over them.

I leaned far as I could out of Eliza's grip and shouted, "He's the one who killed you, his blood for yours, his blood for yours!"

The undead fae looked between one another and, in an instant, the realization struck them, and they chanted, "His blood for ours, his blood for ours!"

A legion of undead faeries threw themselves at Mac Lir's legs and dug claws and teeth into his bloody foot. The giant lost his balance and fell into the dirt. He struggled and kicked, some of the fae flew off, but others took their place in seconds.

Through all this, Eliza remained frozen save for her looks back and forth between me and the struggling heap of her father. Tears ran down her cheeks and sniffles took her breaths. I owed her my life after she'd taken the handful of salt for me, and that could fuel some truly powerful magic.

I asked, "You don't want to return to him, do you?"

Eliza shook her head, hard and fast.

"But you do wish he wasn't like this, don't you?"

She nodded and resumed her stare.

I thought back on how I swore to myself I'd corrupt one of Mac Lir's blessings when I got free. There came no pride in the idea that came to me, but it seemed my best solution. "Do you wish he had a bigger heart?"

Eliza turned her stare at me and, after a few seconds consideration, slowly nodded. I nodded back.

With a bite to her finger, Eliza flinched and released me. I ran at Mac Lir fast as I could and didn't look back. If she sensed any deception, Eliza could spoil the wish she'd just given me. For at least that moment, thank the gods she had no tongue to shout, "No," with.

Mac Lir kicked another mass of fae off himself as I closed the distance. Their wild magic buzzed in the air and as I reached out, both with a favor to fulfill and vengeance of my own to take, their power became mine. All I had to do was draw close enough—

Mac Lir rolled onto his stomach, reached out, and clasped one hand around me. I shouted in his clutch as he squeezed.

"Should have run when you had the chance." He spoke through gritted teeth. "I'm going to squash you like a bug."

The phantom fae behind Mac Lir faded away as their power flowed into me. As the clutch forced air from my lungs, I slipped a hand into his grip and felt where my needle first punctured him, the wound still bloody. I began my own weak chant of, "Blood for blood," as my power flowed into him.

"I'll shut you up for good—"

"Blood for blood, blood for blood!" As I chanted, the calls of the dead fae joined me.

Mac Lir released one hand of his grip as his breaths grew short. "Wha— what in the—the—" The giant felt at the left side of his shirt. After a moment of gasps, he yanked it down. Something pressed at him from within and pushed his ribcage outward. "Oh God, what in the hell is this?" He released his grip as he clutched at the growth in his chest.

A tiny laugh slipped out of me. "I asked your daughter what she wanted me to do," I said. "That's what she really is, you know. I don't know where you got it in your head otherwise, but it's true. She told me she just wished you could have had a bigger heart."

"You monster, you devil, you—you—you—" Mac Lir gasped for breath in a last desperate cry. Then the growth erupted. The giant got a last, struggled look at himself before red burst from his eyes, nose, and mouth, he fell into the grass, and breathed his last.

A little girl's scream ripped through the air behind me. Eliza threw herself down on the body of her gored father, tears hot in her eyes. After a moment with her hands bloodied by him, she jerked her head in my direction. I held my breath, threw up my veil, and vanished from human sight. The girl rose and looked around, frantic, but her eyes remained elsewhere as I ran off.

…

The day of the solstice arrived just as I made it to Knocknarea, carried on deals I made with ravens for flights. Mum, Da, and my brothers and sisters all looked over my scars in horror and demanded, "Lonán—poor child— what kind of monster did you make enemies with?" After the journey, my phantom pains finally started to fade away.

When all was done and I finally laid down to rest, I saw that farm one last time. Whether it was in a dream or a vision, I do not know.

A fae with shimmering skin of light blue, the size of a short human woman, descended down from the skies and settled just outside a window on the second floor. After seconds there alone, the mass of phantasmic green that first approached me materialized before her.

"This is the place," the green spirit said. "She is just ahead."

"This isn't typical, you know," the fae said. "Usually, we must have a child at the ready to trade."

"But it is the day of the solstice," the green spirit said. "Some rules have been suspended."

The fae nodded. "Indeed, they can be."

"Be good to my Eliza," my benefactor said. "She has suffered enough already."

"I know she was your girl," the fae, a changeling, it suddenly seemed so clear, said. "But was she your husband's?"

The little figure at the center of the green mass dissipated a bit, as if looking away in the only form it could. "… I do not know. She may not have been. But that doesn't mean she should have been punished for it."

The changeling nodded. "I understand, dearie. Be at peace and leave the rest to me."

As the green phantom faded away, the changeling passed through the walls into Mac Lir's empty bedroom. She crossed through and into the hallway, singing the old Garten Mother's Lullaby.

"*Sleep oh babe, for the red bee hums the silent twilight's fall.*" The changeling opened the door to the bedroom on her left, where a tiny body laid beneath blankets on a bed in the corner. "*Aoibheall from the grey rock comes, to wrap the world in thrall.*" She stepped up and laid a hand on the child, the girl's hair still wet from a recent washing, and showing red.

Little Eliza rolled over and looked up at the changeling.

The fae smiled gently at her and sang, "*A leanbhan oh, my child, my joy, my love, my heart's desire.*" She held the last note, as was tradition, and took in a new breath.

Eliza leapt up from the bed, the glint of a kitchen knife revealed from under her covers, and threw herself at the changeling. In a fury she stabbed the fae over and over, my kin screeched as the bane ripped her apart. Her dark blue blood stained her light flesh, and the girl kept up her attack. Struggles turned to twitches which turned to the frozen yield of the dead.

Wide eyed, blood splattered across her face, and still with no tongue to form words, the girl moved her lips over and over. "Yours for his. Blood for blood. Blood for blood." ♜

THE TERRORS OF THE GRAVE

By Charles R. Rutledge

No event is so terribly well adapted to inspire the supremeness of bodily and of mental distress, as is burial before death... — Edgar Allan Poe

France, 1810

JULIEN BOSSUET TOILED HIS WAY up a muddy slope toward the grave of his beloved. A slow rain surrounded him, soaking through his clothing and stealing away what little warmth they provided. Dense fog lay all around, and he had to make his way carefully through the old churchyard to avoid tripping over the scattered headstones and grave markers.

It didn't help that Bossuet had to keep the shield of his lantern mostly closed. The churchyard was a considerable distance from the village, but someone might still see the wavering progress of his light through the fog. Once he was on the other side of the hill, where Victorine's grave lay, he would be hidden from the eyes and ears of the village, so he could proceed with his grim labors and be on his way before anyone knew he was about.

The rain began to fall with more vigor as he crested the slope and started down the other side. Now he was able to open his lantern, which not only made his progress swifter, but allowed him to find the sad and hallowed place where Victorine Lafourcade slept the sleep of ages.

Bossuet had not been prepared for the rush of anguish that washed over him at the sight of the simple headstone. But he drew a shuddering breath, threw off his cloak and set to work. His shovel sank deep with the first thrust. The grave was scarcely three days old and the ground still soft. The smell of damp earth rose around him.

As Bossuet worked, he couldn't help but think of Victorine as she had been a few years earlier when he had loved her as only a young man can love. He had been struggling to establish himself as a journalist in Paris and his prospects had not been promising. Victorine, the daughter of minor nobles, had been expected to marry better than him.

Bossuet truly believed she had loved him, but in the end, she had done as her parents bade and accepted the proposal of an eminent banker and diplomatist, Monsieur Renelle. Renelle had been ten years her senior and was an influential and powerful man.

Bossuet had heard the marriage had not been a happy one and that Renelle had been neglectful and possibly worse to his wife. When Victorine had died unexpectedly, rather than having her interned in his family cemetery on his estate, Renelle had shipped her off to the town of her birth to be buried in a common grave.

Bossuet was bereft when the news reached him, and he resolved to secure a lock of Victorine's hair to remember her by, even if he had to resort to graverobbing. And so, here he was, long past midnight, in this remote churchyard in this nameless town.

Bossuet had been so deep in thought that he was surprised when he heard a hollow thump as his shovel struck Victorine's casket. He gritted his teeth and continued working until he had cleared the casket lid and made a hollow to one side where he could stand. He was fortunate that the sandy ground on the area was porous, so the water from the rain soaked through, rather than collecting around the casket.

The casket was simple but well-made. At least Monsieur Renelle had provided that much for his unfortunate wife. Or perhaps it had been her parents. It didn't matter. Bossuet girded himself and began unfastening the casket top. The moment had come. He took another deep breath and flung back the lid.

The light from the lantern cast flickering shadows over the face and form of Victorine Lafourcade. Bossuet wasn't sure what he had expected, but it wasn't this. Had he not known she was dead, he would have thought her merely sleeping. Her cheeks still held color and her auburn hair was as lustrous as it had been in life. Bossuet stifled a groan of despair. Ah, what he had lost. What they had both lost.

But enough. He could not linger here. He would do what he had come to do and then put the grave back as he had found it. He fumbled in his coat pocket for the shears he had brought. Finding them, he leaned forward and began cutting a long lock of hair from the beloved head.

And as he did so, Victorine opened her eyes.

#   #   #

France, 1830

"Whatever Victorine's strange malady was, Kharrn Mon Ami, it had given her the semblance of death," Julien Bossuet said. "You can well imagine my reaction when she opened her eyes and looked at me."

"I can," said the man Bossuet knew only as Kharrn.

The two men sat at a small table at a café on a side street on the northern edge of Paris. Bossuet and his wife had met Kharrn during their voyage from America. Like them he had been traveling in "cabin passage" on the packet ship and had access to the central saloon which was denied to less fortunate passengers in steerage. They had struck up a conversation and had found the man an amiable and interesting companion.

Kharrn was a giant, easily seven feet tall. His hair was dark, and his eyes were a cold shade of blue. He said little about himself, but Bossuet had determined he was a mercenary soldier and that he was very well-traveled.

"Once I realized what had occurred," Bossuet continued. "I somehow managed to carry Victorine to my horse and take her back to my lodgings in town. I have an uncle who is a physician, and I had some knowledge of restoratives, which I quickly acquired from a local apothecary.

"It took time, but I was able to slowly nurse Victorine back to health. I had to be careful, for her husband had a long reach, and I didn't want him trying to reclaim her before her faculties had been fully restored."

Kharrn said, "I assume he never found out what happened."

Bossuet shook his head. "No, by the time Victorine had recovered she had made up her mind never to return to that cruel man. Together we fled to America. I made no demands upon Victorine, but in time our love grew, and we became man and wife while living in New York where I had secured work as a journalist at last."

"So Victorine was insensate throughout her ordeal?" Kharrn said.

"Yes, thank God. She never knew the terrors of the grave. She didn't recover from her trance until the rain fell upon her when I so fortuitously opened her casket. I later found out her parents had arranged for her transportation and burial. It was they who did not want her buried in Renelle's family cemetery. Thus she had been well cared for as she was taken from Paris to the remote province. I mentioned before how porous the ground was there, and I believe that allowed her to receive what little oxygen she required in her death-like state."

Kharrn said, "You have been very fortunate. Remarkably so."

"I agree, Mon Ami. And now we have returned to France after 20 years. I think we have both changed enough not to be recognized by anyone we once knew. Still, as you have seen we have been careful to stay away from the more popular areas of Paris, and our lodgings are outside the city."

Kharrn said, "Probably best if you don't tell your story to any other strangers, as well."

Bossuet smiled. "I pride myself I am a good judge of character, Kharrn. But as you see, I waited some time before revealing all to you. Ah, but here Victorine comes now, returned from the shops. I beg you to say nothing of her history. She does not like to be reminded of her ordeal."

"Of course," said Kharrn.

Victorine smiled as she saw the two men. She was carrying several boxes and parcels of varying sizes. She wore a simple, but elegant dress, though Bossuet suspected she would soon be attired in the latest fashions, given the number of packages she carried, and those already in their rented house.

"What are you two speaking of so earnestly?" Victorine said.

"What do men always speak of?" Bossuet said. "The wickedness of the world and the ways of women."

"Not too much about other women, I hope", said Victorine.

"Not at all, my dear," said Bossuet. "Perhaps we should carry your spoils home so that we may prepare for the theater this evening."

Victorine nodded. "Will you accompany us, Kharrn? I should dearly like to show you the farmhouse where we are staying, and I can promise you an excellent dinner."

"How can I refuse?" Kharrn responded.

Bossuet said, "Let us return to our coach, then."

They had left their coach and horses at a commercial stable close by. The trio left the café and made their way through the narrow and twisty streets of the shop district. It was a fine day, and though he now considered America his home, Bossuet was happy to see Paris again.

They ascended a hill and turned toward the stable yard and almost collided with three men coming from the opposite direction. Bossuet begged their pardon, but even as they passed the group, he had a sudden premonition of something ill.

"Bossuet?" a voice said. "Is it you?"

Bossuet turned and found he was looking at Monsieur Renelle. In all the city, in all the country, to meet this man here. Renelle had not aged well, his once handsome features blurred by time and indolence. He glared at Bossuet and Victorine with bulging eyes.

"It is you," Renelle said. "Good God, and Victorine as well. How can this be? You are dead."

"You are mistaken, sir," Bossuet said. "I do not know you."

Renelle said, "Do you think me a fool? Even after all this time, do you think I would not recognize my own wife?"

"I am not your wife!" Victorine said. "This man is my husband."

Ranelle said, "We shall see about that. So, that was your plan so many years past. To make a ruse of your own death and escape with your penniless lover. What a fool I was to ever think you possessed the qualities of a noblewoman. Why, you are nothing but…"

Renelle didn't finish his comment because Bossuet slapped him across the face hard enough to make the man stagger backward. A moment later, Renelle's two companions rushed forward and seized Bossuet roughly. Bossuet recalled now that Renelle, always a man with enemies, traveled with bodyguards. That apparently had not changed.

"I will give you cause to regret that," Renelle said.

"No," Kharrn said. "You won't."

With that, the giant man grabbed one of Renelle's ruffians by the back of his collar and jerked him away from Bossuet with such force that the man was thrown to the ground. The other bodyguard released Bossuet and lunged toward Kharrn.

Kharrn struck the man in the face with one massive fist, destroying his nose and crushing his teeth. The man fell without a sound and lay motionless on the cobbles. Bossuet saw the first man had regained his feet. The ruffian fumbled inside his jacket and produced a long, slim dagger as he ran at Kharrn. Bossuet shouted a warning.

Kharrn turned, but the man was already upon him. The man drove the dagger down toward Kharrn's chest, but Kharrn turned so that he took the blade in his left shoulder. He immediately reached out with his right hand, grabbed the ruffian around the throat and lifted him off the ground. Kharrn hurled the man at the closest wall, where he struck the brick and plaster surface with a sickening crunch. Bossuet was taken aback by Kharrn's sheer savagery.

Kharrn grabbed the handle of the knife still embedded in his shoulder and pulled the blade free. He tossed it aside almost casually. Then he turned back to Renelle.

"Stay away from me," Renelle said, holding out his hands. "I have powerful friends in this city."

"None of them are here now," said Kharrn.

"Leave him, Mon Ami," Bossuet said. "He can do nothing to harm us now."

Renelle said, "You think not? I shall contact the authorities. This woman is still legally my wife."

Bossuet said, "No tribunal would uphold your claim, Renelle. The long lapse of years has extinguished any legal claim you may have. More importantly, Victorine and I are now American citizens. Would you argue your case to the American ambassadors?"

Kharrn said, "Enough of this, Bossuet. Let us leave now."

"I am not done with you," Renelle said. "None of you."

Kharrn stepped up to Renelle and loomed over him. "If I see you again, I will kill you, Renelle. As simple as that."

With that, the trio walked away from the fuming Renelle. Bossuet didn't look back, but he knew the man was still staring holes in his back.

"We had planned to stay in France for two more days," Bossuet said. "But I think it would be wise for us to leave for London tomorrow. Despite what I said, Renelle does indeed have powerful friends and he could cause us some trouble."

Kharrn said, "I think that wise. I think it would also be a good idea if I slept at your accommodations tonight. Renelle strikes me as someone unlikely to let today's encounter pass without retaliating."

"Nothing would please me more," said Bossuet. "I would feel much safer with you there. Wouldn't you agree, my dear?"

Victorine said, "Most certainly. I have never seen the like of how you dealt with those men. Oh! But I had forgotten your wound, Kharrn. Should we seek a physician?"

"It's nothing," said Kharrn.

"That ruffian drove a knife into your arm," said Bossuet.

Kharrn said, "I've had worse. There is only one thing I require, so let us stop at my hotel before we journey to your house."

#　　　#　　　#

Bossuet was awakened by a pounding on the door of the front room. After dinner, Kharrn had refused the offer of a bedroom and said he would sleep there, and Bossuet had decided to join him. Bossuet had taken a couch and Kharrn had simply thrown his greatcoat on the floor and reclined upon it.

Kharrn kept the mysterious object he had retrieved from the hotel close at hand. It was a flat, leather case. As Bossuet sat up, he saw what that case had contained. Kharrn was already on his feet, and he held a huge, twin-

157

bladed axe in his hands.

There came another loud crash and then the lock broke. The door slammed open and a group of a dozen or so men spilled into the room. They were armed with bludgeons and knives. The first man to cross the room lost his head to the huge axe, and Kharrn caved in a second man's chest with the backswing of the weapon.

With a loud bellow, Kharrn leaped into the midst of the other ruffians, killing two instantly, and for a moment, Bossuet thought the giant would kill them all. Just then there was a flash of light and a loud report, and Kharrn fell to the ground. Beyond the fallen man, Bossuet saw a tall, dark-haired man in a blue coat holding a calvary flintlock pistol. Bossuet could see a terrible wound on the side of Kharrn's head and blood began to pool on the floor.

"So much for your champion," Monsieur Renelle said, stepping through the door.

"I've lost four men, Renelle," the tall man said. "And had I not come armed, I think that bastard would have killed all of us. I'll need extra money for the men's families."

Renelle said, "Yes, yes, of course. I am certain that money would reach their families. But first do what you already were paid for, Andre. Bind this fool and find his whore of a wife."

Bossuet lunged toward Renelle, but three of the remaining brigands latched onto him and wrestled him to the ground. They pulled his hands roughly behind him and bound them with heavy cords. He heard Victorine scream and he struggled more fiercely, but there was nothing he could do.

Bossuet's captors pulled him to his feet in time to see two of the ruffians leading Victorine into the room. "Listen to me, Renelle. Do whatever you wish with me, but please don't harm Victorine."

Renelle said, "You? You are merely an appendix to my vengeance. It is my *late* wife who has deceived and betrayed me. Rest assured you shall share her fate, but she is the one I intend to punish. Now, Andre, take these two to the carriage. And do not harm them. I want them in perfect health for what is to come."

Andre, who was crouched near Kharrn, said "Believe it or not, this one is still alive. Shall I finish him?"

Renelle seemed to consider that for a moment. "No. Bring him along. I will adjust my plans to include him, since he threatened to kill me on sight."

The brigands complied and forced Bossuet and Victorine outside and into a waiting carriage. It was an old vehicle, obviously not Renelle's private conveyance. It took three men to carry Kharrn out and dump him unceremoniously onto the carriage floor.

Andre came last, carrying Kharrn's axe. "I've never seen such a fine weapon. I can scarce lift it, but I think I will add it to my collection."

One of the ruffians sat in the coach to keep an eye on the prisoners. The others climbed on their mounts and the grim procession rode away from the farmhouse. The next hour or so seemed like a nightmare to Bossuet as the carriage rattled along. The moon was high, and its baleful glow illuminated the countryside in stark shadows.

Bossuet tried to help Victorine by looking stoic, but he was almost consumed with fear by thoughts of what fate might await her. He would gladly face any death, no matter how horrible, if she could escape.

Finally, Bossuet saw the outlines of an ancient pile loom in the distance. He recognized the place at once. It was the family home of the Renelles. As the carriage rolled through huge iron gates, he knew he had little chance of leaving the estate alive.

The carriage passed beyond the main house, past stables, and other outbuildings. Finally, it halted before a low, stone wall. Bossuet and Victorine were pulled from the carriage to stand before a smiling Renelle.

"Welcome, dear wife, to my family cemetery. Your parents did not wish for you to rest here after your first death. But now you shall sleep here in an unmarked grave. You see how I honor you."

Bossuet said, "Listen to me, Renelle. Please, just listen. I…"

"I have listened to enough of your prattling," Renelle said. He made a *follow me* gesture to his men. "Bring them along. And drag that lummox from the coach as well."

Renelle and Andre led the strange procession along a winding path through the graveyard, past ancient mausoleums, and massive gravestones. A cracked and broken statue of a winged angel bore mute witness to their passing. The cold moon shone down.

They made a turn at another huge family crypt and walked to a far corner of the cemetery. Now Bossuet could see more of Renelle's men. They stood in a circle of lantern light beside two freshly dug graves.

"Good God, no," Bossuet said.

"God is not here, my friend," said Renelle. "I know not how Victorine managed the appearance of death, but this time neither she nor you shall escape the cold embrace of the grave."

Bossuet glanced over at Victorine. Her eyes were wide with horror, but her mouth was a tight line. She would give Renelle no satisfaction from tears if she could help it. He hoped he could go to his death as bravely. Now Bossuet saw that two large packing crates sat near the yawning black holes in the ground.

"Yes, I'm afraid there was no time to acquire proper caskets," Renelle said, following Bossuet's gaze. "Originally, I had planned to bury you separately, but that was before your beast of a friend survived being shot by Monsieur Andre. Now you and Victorine must share the narrow house. Fitting, really."

Bossuet said, "Surely you cannot mean to bury us alive?"

"Can I not? Victorine escaped the grave once before, though I know not how. But I do not think she will be so fortunate this time. We are far out in the country on my estate. No one knows you are here. No one will come to help you. But I grow weary. Andre, have your men bury the giant first. I want Victorine and her dear husband to see what awaits them."

Andre barked some instructions to his men. They moved one of the wooden crates close to one of the graves and lifted the lid off it. As Bossuet and Victorine looked on in helpless horror, the men dragged Kharrn to the packing case and deposited him none too gently inside. Then they replaced the lid and nailed it in place.

Using several ropes, the men lowered the crate into the ground. Bossuet saw the graves were deeper than normal, perhaps eight feet. Renelle was taking no chances. Once the crate was at the bottom of the pit, the ropes were withdrawn, and the men began shoveling damp soil into the hole. Not until the grave was filled and the earth patted down firmly down did Renelle turn back to Bossuet.

"Untie their hands," Renelle said. "I want them to be able to scratch at the lid of the coffin until they can no longer breathe."

Andre's men did as they were bid. Bossuet tried to grapple with them, but they were too many. And what good would it do if he could escape their clutches? They would still have Victorine. The ruffians pushed the box close to the grave as they had done with Kharrn.

"Now," Renelle said. "Get into the crate. There is plenty of room if you lie on your sides. You'll be able to look into one another's eyes until the lid is nailed on."

"For the love of God, Renelle," Bossuet said.

"I told you. God and his mercy are not here. Only I, and I have no mercy to bestow."

Andre's men urged Bossuet and Victorine into the crate. Once they were in place, Bossuet whispered to his wife. "Be brave, my dear one."

Bossuet did not feel brave. He was filled with panic at the prospect of being buried alive. He wanted to beg and plead and cry, but he knew none of that would do any good. Renelle would never release them.

The crate lid was put in place and Bossuet flinched at every strike of the hammer as the nails were driven home. Some of the slats didn't quite meet so a little light filtered into the box. Bossuet could see Victorine's eyes shining with tears as the crate lurched and began its journey into the cold earth.

Bossuet could feel the case bumping the sides of the grave as it was lowered. He felt the final thud as they reached the bottom of the pit. He stifled a scream as the first clump of earth struck the lid and dirt sifted down through the spaces between slats. Shovelful after shovelful of soil rained down upon the box until finally all light was blotted out and there was nothing but the sound of the grave being filled. At last even that sound was gone, and they were alone in the dark.

Bossuet willed himself not to claw at the lid. He knew no exertions of his could free them. Now he could hear Victorine crying softly. She had held it in as long as she could. Around them the crate groaned under the weight of the earth atop it. In spite of himself, Bossuet gave a moan of anguish and despair and began vainly to beat upon the inside of the box's lid.

\#   \#   \#

Kharrn opened his eyes and saw nothing. His head ached abominably, but when he reached to touch his wound, his hand bumped against a wooden surface close over his face. He felt around and found he was in a wooden box. The air was stale and filled with the smell of freshly turned earth. The conclusion was obvious. Someone had buried him.

He had a moment of panic but pushed it down. He had been in some terrible spots in his twelve thousand years of life. Sometimes remaining calm was all that had kept him alive. Despite the tight confines, he managed to get his fingers to his head. His hair was matted with blood. Now he remembered. The tall man in the blue coat had shot him. The ball must have grazed the side of his head, not quite deeply enough to kill him, but sufficient to render him senseless.

The wound was almost healed now, so from long experience, Kharrn reasoned he'd been unconscious for about three hours. The air trapped in the coffin was bad but not exhausted. Still, it wouldn't last long now that he was awake. Kharrn smiled a rueful smile. Renelle and his men had stumbled on a way to actually kill him.

Thousands of years in the past Kharrn had struck a bargain with a goddess named Samra. She would help him gain vengeance on the man who had killed his wife if Kharrn would become her paladin. Her weapon of revenge. She had made him immortal and virtually invulnerable, though if enough damage was done to his brain or heart he could be killed like any man.

And he did need to breathe.

Kharrn put both palms against the lid of the box and pushed. There was a small bit of 'give' because the ground above had just been dug up and the soil was loose. Still, the weight was going to be a problem. He had no idea how deeply he had been buried, but there were likely hundreds of pounds of dirt between him and fresh air.

Loose earth spattered down on him as he pushed upward. He was apparently in some sort of crate and the slats didn't quite meet. That was good. An actual casket would have been harder to get out of.

Kharrn decided that the lid had to go. Trying to push the wooden panel to the surface would be all but impossible, even as strong as he was. He would have to break out of the box and dig his way upward. But once he was through the lid he would be surrounded by dirt, unable to breathe. He would have to move quickly.

Kharrn steeled himself and took a deep breath. Then he drove one huge fist up through the top of the crate. Dirt immediately began to pour in on him, but he kept punching until he had shattered the lid, then managed to get to a seated position. The dirt surrounded him, making it hard to move, but he kept twisting and pushing until he was on his knees and then his feet.

Kharrn's efforts were exhausting the air in his lungs. He struggled to a standing position. Had the grave been merely six feet his head would have been partially out of the ground but apparently the hole was deeper than that. He pushed his arms up through the clutching earth and felt his hands break free of the ground.

Moving as fast as he could, Kharrn pushed upward again and again, sending the loose earth flying. His head was swimming from lack of air and his lungs were trying to force him to take a breath. Finally, he dislodged enough soil that he felt the night breeze on his face. He gulped in a grateful lungful of precious air. He was still for a few moments, regaining his strength. It had been a close thing.

When his head was clear, Kharrn struggled toward the nearest side of the grave. Once he could get his hands on firmer ground, he was able to pull himself out of the hole. Another man might have rested on the edge of the pit, but Kharrn got to his feet. There still might be enemies close by.

Kharrn looked all around him. The moon was low on the horizon but there was enough light that he could see passably, if not well. His blood froze as he saw there was a second freshly filled grave about six feet from the one he'd just escaped. Bossuet and Victorine!

Kharrn quickly moved to the other grave. He glanced behind him and was overjoyed to see two shovels leaning against a tree. He hurried to the tools, and snatching one up, rushed back to the grave and began to dig.

The nature of Kharrn's immortality was that he had been frozen in time. He didn't change. If his hair was cut short, it would grow back to its original length overnight. His numerous scars had all been acquired before his bargain with the goddess of vengeance. Thus, despite his ordeal, he was back to full strength now, and he dug into the grave like a man possessed.

When he reached the crate, he tossed the shovel aside and grasped the edges of the lid. Ignoring the flesh ripped from his fingers, he tore the lid off the box and hurled it away. There wasn't much light now, but he could see Bossuet and Victorine lay facing each other. As gently as he could he lifted each in turn and deposited them on the edge of the grave. Then he climbed out.

In the waning moonlight he saw Bossuet yet breathed. Victorine seemed without breath, but placing his fingers at her throat, Kharrn could detect a slight pulse. Both of his friends yet lived. Bossuet awoke first and sat up, rubbing his head.

"Kharrn? You…how did you…"

"Try and rest for a moment. And see to your wife. She needs those medical ministrations you spoke of."

Bossuet gasped Victorine's name and dragged himself to where she lay. He slapped her face gently and massaged her wrists and throat. At last, her eyes fluttered and she saw Bossuet.

"Oh, my dear," Victorine said. "I cannot believe we are still alive. How could we have escaped?"

Bossuet said, "Be calm, dear one. It was Kharrn. Somehow, he escaped his own grave and rescued us." He looked back at Kharrn. "But how, Mon Ami?"

Kharrn said, "I'll explain later. Right now we need to get you two away from here. We passed a stable on the way to this accursed boneyard. Let's find horses and you can get far away. You should go directly and get your things and get out of France. Do whatever it takes."

"But will you not come with us?" Victorine said.

Kharrn shook his head. "I have business with Monsieur Renelle and his friends."

"But what will you do?" Bossuet said.

"I will keep my promise to Renelle and kill him on sight. The man who shot me must die as well, and anyone who gets in my way. They tried to kill us, and I won't let that pass. Now go. I will find you in London in a day or so."

"I wish you would come with us," Bossuet said. "You're injured and have endured much."

"I'm well enough."

With that, Kharrn led the pair to the stables and helped them hitch two horses to a carriage. He said nothing else, and only when they were well on their way did he turn back toward Renelle's estate.

Dawn wasn't far away, but he could still see light streaming from the windows on the ground floor on one side of the great house. He moved across the grounds, staying in the shadows. As he passed one of the outbuildings two of Renelle's men came around a corner and almost walked into him. Kharrn struck the first one a crushing blow to the jaw and grabbed the other around the throat, pinning him to the wall of the small building, keeping him from crying out.

The man's toes didn't touch the ground. He clawed at Kharrn's hand, trying to get free, but Kharrn held him against the wall until he stopped struggling. He let the dead man fall, then knelt beside the other man, and grabbing his hair with one hand and his chin with the other, he twisted until the man's neck snapped.

Kharrn loped across the remaining distance to the house. He slipped over a small railing onto a wide porch and peered into one of the windows. He was looking at a book-lined study. A cheerful fire still burned in the hearth and Renelle lounged in one chair and the tall man with the blue coat in another. Kharrn grinned as he saw his axe leaning against the tall man's chair.

Kharrn looked around the porch. He saw a small stone bench and lifting it over his head he hurled it through the window. He followed close behind the bench. The tall man was on his feet even as Kharrn dropped into the room. He clawed at the axe, but it was too heavy for him to wield easily and Kharrn snatched it away from him.

With one smooth movement, Kharrn whirled the axe as another man might use a hatchet and brought it straight down on the man's head, splitting his skull. As the man died, Kharrn saw Renelle hurrying for the chamber door. Kharrn vaulted over a sofa and caught Renelle before he could reach the doorway. He flung the man to the ground and loomed over him.

"Please, please," Renelle said. "Do not kill me. I will give you whatever you want. I'm a rich man. I have gold here. Jewels. Just please don't kill me."

Kharrn grinned. "The only thing I want is your life. I told you I would kill you if I saw you again. If I had time, I would drag you to that graveyard and bury you as you buried me. But I can't wait around for you to die, and someone might help you when I'm gone."

"What are you going to do?" Renelle said.

Kharrn seized the trembling man by his lapels and pulled him to his feet. He twined his fingers into Renelle's hair and pulled his head back. Then he struck Renelle in the throat with his fist and let him fall. Renelle twisted and spasmed on the floor, clutching at his throat.

Kharrn said, "I've crushed your windpipe. No one can help you. Now you can spend your last moments on earth trying to take a breath you'll never get, just as you intended for me and my friends. That is my vengeance on you, Renelle."

Renelle twisted and writhed and dug his fingers into the fine rug on the study floor. When he was dead, Kharrn returned to the window and without a glance back, climbed out the way he had come into the last remnants of the night. ♜

SEVERED CAPE

By Melanie Schubert

Trigger warning: readers should be aware this story involves themes of sexual assault.

YOU MIGHT BE WONDERING HOW I got here—smart, well-dressed businesswoman turned vigilante with a cape of mess and gore.

Words bind me. I taste blood.

But that's a story for another time. First, I need to deal with *this* guy. I can't see him yet, but I feel him—boy do I ever. This level of asshole pings my abilities the way a fresh pile of bullshit summons a dung beetle. I don't need my X-ray ability to tell me which house it is. The unassuming cottage at the end of the street bleeds darkness to my eyes, which see the auras of things since that night. I've been doing this for a while now, but auras like this never stop rattling my body with chills. Because I know this level of darkness only blooms when it's someone close. A father. A brother.

"I'm sorry Ma'am."

I fall to my knees.

Not her. Not her.

My girl.

No.

No.

No...

I close my eyes and suck in a short, hot breath and surge forward. Rage takes claim of muscle and sinew, propelling me. I have no weapons—I need none with this remodeled body of mine. And I wear no mask. I want my haunted mug branded on my victims' brains forever in warning. My super speed kicks in instinctively and I'm on the doorstep in a blink. I stare at the ivory-white door with the cross-shaped doorknocker. So mild, so unsuspecting.

I give the cross doorknocker three hard raps—it would be rude to just barge in.

I wait.

Their mouths keep moving. I can't hear words anymore, but their eyes murder my soul, and all I know is my darling, my perfect girl, is gone. She's gone, and he hurt her. I boil and break. My bones are dust and then lava.

"I'm waaaiting," I sing out to the door, as I rap the cross against it harder this time.

Knock

Knock

Knock

Knock

Knock

Knock

Knock

The door cracks open. "Can I help you?"

My heart shatters. She's young. Too young. She can't be much older than twelve.

The same age as my Sarah.

Something screams and unwinds in my head.

Her eyes are afraid. But I might not believe it myself if I didn't see how her beautiful gold aura is choked with reds and greys. I want to barge in and do it now, but I swallow down my rage. Put it on pause and ask. I always ask.

"I'm here to help you. But it's going to be messy, and things will change. Is that what you want?"

Her big eyes take me in. A haunted silence hangs in the air for a moment. I'd find it hard to leave now if she said no. Impossible to not stalk him forever, but I always ask.

"Help me," she whispers.

They always do.

"Do you have somewhere safe you can go?"

She nods.

"Go. Run."

She squeezes my hand, eyes wide as she takes in the twisted cape that flows out behind me, she pauses, and for a second, I wonder if it's too much, if my methods are too harsh, then I see her aura lighten and I remember it's never enough.

She sprints away down the street, and I wait until she's out of sight, then surge down the corridor.

"Lara? Lara! Who is it?"

The voice sounds frustrated, and it pricks my fury all the more.

He's still busy tucking his shirt in and doing up his fly. He hasn't noticed me here in the shadows.

"Finished?" I ask.

He jumps a little. "Who's there?" He frowns as I peel myself out from the shadows. "Who are you? What are you doing in my home?"

I give him my sweetest smile and the frown fades. "I'm sorry, are you one of my wife's friends?"

"No. I'm here for *you*."

I can see his brain scrambling for answers but the thing inside me is tired of waiting. It's been uncurling moment by moment.

"Where's your daughter, sir? What were you doing a moment ago?"

His face grows red and angry.

"I don't know who you are, but I'll ask you kindly to leave my premises this instant—"

"I'm not going anywhere." The words leave my mouth like steam; I barely recognize my own voice. It grows deeper and darker every time.

"Get out!" He grabs my arm and the fact that he dares lay hands on me so quickly is enough for me to begin. I will take my time with this one. He will feel every muscle rip and every bone break.

I start with the fingers, the ones currently latched on my arm.

snAp

The man screams, "What the hell are you doing?" He swings at my head with his other hand, and I let it land. Watch with pleasure at the pain that ricochets through his arm as it bounces off my iron hard head.

I grab it before he can nurse it and rip and break.

His screams interject the snaps and pops and soon I have ten pretty trinkets to add to my flowing cape, but I'm still missing one thing…

My eyes trail down to his belt buckle. He catches them and freezes a second, then tries to scramble away.

I don't bother lecturing him, and he doesn't ask why I'm doing this, because he already knows. I can see it carved in sweat and fear, in every movement and glance.

I take my time coming after him. I want him to feel the same horror his daughter has felt all these years.

I hear him start to pray for deliverance. He thinks I'm some demon, I guess.

I am.

I unbuckle his pants delicately, like a lover, and see a fresh wave of confusion wash over him. Then I rip. I tear.

I deliver him to the hospital when I'm done—I'm not a barbarian. And I don't want him to die. Death is too kind for ones like these. He must live and suffer.

Back at home I knit my gory treasures into my cape carefully with the rest of them. It might seem strange, tasteless to keep these bloody little vestiges of the hunt, but my cape keeps me calm. Without it, rage would consume me completely. The fire in my blood would never be quenched. Each act soothes the same thing it exacerbates, because each time I find a new daughter or son I must protect from this filth that roams the earth unchecked—well, not the way I want it checked. Why aren't they all checking it harder?

There are too many.

Their deeds swept beneath dirty carpets. Their victims guilted into silence, afraid to speak lest they be ridiculed or not believed.

They don't see what it does to them. How their auras turn black and grey and red. They don't hear how their souls scream.

But I do.

I will check it.

I will make the guilty pay a price that's enough.

When I'm done stitching, I throw myself onto the bed, but sleep doesn't come. It abandoned me months ago. Instead I seethe and remember.

Wading through glue with no air. I can't breathe and I burn. I burn. I run. I run and run and scream. I'm in the forest. I don't know when I got here or where this forest is, but I scream until I taste blood. Until my body splits with hot red light. I writhe in the dirt and moss of the forest floor in pain. Something is wrong. I've been in agony for weeks, but this is different. My blood whistles in my ears and my bones shudder and quake. Something is happening to me. I scream and I scream and I change.

And that's how I wound up like this. Super fast, super strong. Able to hear feelings and see auras. I'm your perfect superhero. It's not the cape you're used to, but it's the only one keeping me together. I need sleep. I know it. Just as well as I know I'll never sleep until I find *him.* The one that started this all.

I check over the sprawling map that claims every space on my living room walls. The gashes of red paint that mark areas I've already been, and the blank spaces of the world that wink cruelly, reminding me he might be anywhere.

I will know him when I feel his rotten presence. This I know in my bones. But my abilities have limits. I sense things within ten kilometers and no more.

I will search all of it.

I've lain in bed for barely a minute before I'm bent over choking. I cough and vomit bile at the feelings assaulting my senses.

Time to go. Someone needs me again.

I follow a shrieking trail of malice and fear into the city. The alley is dark, and I am its wraith.

There are no actual screams. The alley is quiet. Save for some scuffling that could be anything—a cat, a rat. But I feel the silent screams of a victim in my soul, and the thing growing inside me demands payment in blood.

I taste iron in my throat and see nothing but red.

It's over in moments.

My heart pounds. I barely remember any of it.

It doesn't escape my attention how my fingers bleed shadows now too. I'm changing again. Turning into something more than human and less. It aches. Rips away pieces of my soul.

Let it.

I will become this thing of darkness, if I must, to protect the light.

My head snaps violently to one side and my senses catch wind of something that cuts up my insides into gore.

Him.

I feel him.

I surge after the feeling on the wind. The sick, twisted feeling guiding in whiffs here and there, but I can't quite pin it. Can't make sense of where to go.

I scream.

I coil.

I burn.

The vapors are gone, and I can't catch the scent of it again.

I will find someplace else to exact my rage tonight.

It won't be hard.

It never is.

The pounding music of the club throbs, a steady beat in time to my rage.

I lost him.

But he's here somewhere. Still living in the same fucking city.

How dare he.

How dare he.

"You look like you could use a drink?" The kind-eyed barperson assesses me with a quirked brow.

I hesitate a moment, then nod. I've been busy today. A drink might be nice. Might make me feel a little more human again. The club seems surprisingly un-haunted by creepy perverts tonight. Maybe I can take tonight off. Maybe goodness will prevail, and I can stay human a little longer.

"I said fuck off. I'm not interested."

"Ohhh! Attitude this one!"

My ears prick.

I close my eyes and follow the voices and emotions like ribbons of color with my heightened senses into an upper room marked PRIVATE.

I can't see them from here the way a regular person would, but I see their auras and emotions. These boys are early in their journey. They've not hurt anyone. *Yet.* But their auras are tinged with shades of things that easily lead that way. Entitlement. Lust. Narcissism. And a buttload of toxic patriarchal shit they've had slammed down their throat by men far worse than them.

It's enough to make me slam back my drink and stalk up the narrow staircase.

A group of boys laugh, and one spanks the Kardashian-esque ass of the very hot girl they've dragged into their private booth.

One guy bites his lip, lets his eyes rake over her form. "Sheesh girl. If you're not interested you've no business being dressed like that."

The other boys' laughter congratulates him on the comment, and he continues, encouraged. "Come onnn—smile for me, baby. Stop playing hard to get. I know you can't *not* be wanting all of this." He flexes a massive bicep in the girl's face. It's almost as big as her head.

I can sense that individually, they are not "bad" guys specifically— well, most of them aren't. Bicep guy, I sense, is much further gone than the others. He has darkness in his own past. Blacks and greys that take the breath out of me a little. I almost feel sorry for him, but he's egging the others on. And together, like this in a pack, it catches on something ugly in them all.

The girl regards him with distaste. "Yeah…I'm good actually."

The room is filled with reds and blacks and greys from her emotions splashing everywhere and I realize this is not her first time experiencing this. She's had encounters like this before, but she's holding her head high and trying not to let them get the better of her.

Bicep guy laughs and grabs her by the wrist. "Did you boys hear that? She said, 'yeah'. That counts as consent, right?"

He pulls her in and kisses her deeply and lets his unwelcome hands roam.

"You kiss like a horse. I'm out of here," the girl says in disgust, pushing herself out of his grip and putting some space between them.

"I think you should stay."

"Whatever. I'm leaving."

She's so poised on the outside. Her perfectly made-up face shows no evidence of being rattled, but I see inside her has become a maelstrom of fear.

The storm inside her intensifies when the same boy who took liberties to kiss and grope her walks over casually to block the only exit. "What kind of fun would that be?"

He hasn't seen me, melting out of the shadows behind him, and neither have his friends, too drunk, and horny from being drunk. And making little allowances many of them would be ashamed to justify in the stark, sober light of day.

I lean in close until my lips are right by his ear. "She said she's leaving." I stick my tongue down his ear canal, and he jumps away.

"What the fuck are you doing, freak?"

I make a face and rear back in mock surprise. "Wait…so you *don't* like having tongues shoved down your orifices uninvited? That's a surprise given your actions a moment ago."

I tap my blackening fingertips along the soft leather walls of the private room. They've grown so charcoal dark I half expect they'll leave a trail.

"Go home, lady." One boy laughs. "You're not invited to this party."

I ignore him and lock eyes with the girl. "Get out of here, honey."

She stares at me a moment, eyes widening as she takes in my cape. The others haven't noticed yet.

She nods, her eyes growing watery for a moment. Then she power walks out the door. I don't miss how her hands shake, how her steps quaver.

"Heyyy….are you happy now? I was about to score with the hottest bitch of my life."

I take in a long, calming breath as I close the door to the private booth and lock it.

"Ohhhh shit! Looks like Stacey's Mum wants some of this." The main boy laughs, and the others join in, a bit less sure than before. Some of them squirm in their seats, but the power of peer pressure has bound them to silence.

"I hope you boys don't mind, but I've been listening in to your conversation, and, I have to say. I'm very disappointed in you all."

Some of them are still grinning at me, not understanding the danger.

The leader of this sorry pack wears oversized shades even though it's practically dark in here. He lowers them to assess me carefully. "You're pretty fine yourself for an older bird. I mean, just look at those tits! Like, damn!"

A few laughs from the other boys pepper the room.

His hand stretches out towards me but I'm there before it reaches.

SnAP

Screams absorb into the soundproof walls all around me as I rip off one thumb, then the other.

I pause for a second, the mother in me feeling sorry for some of them for a moment. They haven't actually done anything yet. But the thing growling in my bones says it's only a matter of time. That they must learn their lesson.

snAP

SnaP

sNAP

SNap

I snap and tear and soon I have a lovely assortment of thumbs of all kinds of shapes and sizes.

Blood has sprayed everywhere, but they'll be fine. I wonder if it's enough. A part of me wants to shred them all, to let my unquenched hunger from earlier be fed. But I'm still human enough to know that these ones yet might change.

But just in case…

"Consider this a warning," I growl, taking my time to make close, intimate eye contact with each of them. The main boy, so arrogant and self-assured just moments ago, whimpers and wets his pants. "I'll be watching," I whisper, "always watching. And if I'm not happy with what I see…" I lean in close, letting my pretty cape hang where they can see all my trophies.

Their eyes rake over its bumpy leather-like composition, taking it in properly for the first time. Two boys start vomiting immediately. One screams and throws himself at the door trying to get out, the other passes out.

A smile stretches across my face. "Good. So we have an understanding."

I place the new additions in my pockets and use my super speed to exit the room so fast I will vanish to their simple eyes.

It's all a part of my plan. Let them think I'm some vengeful spirit. Let them wonder if I watch every step.

I'm weary to my bones, but further from sleep than ever.

He was here. Right in this town. And I let him slip away.

I speed through the city all night, searching and feeling the fibers of the air, seeking that rotten core I long to destroy.

Night turns to day, and my phone rings at eight.

"We got him," says the voice on the other end. "But…"

My heart stills in knowing, but my brain is taking longer to register the words.

Apparently, even hardened criminals think men like this must pay a heftier price.

Several days later I stand in the cemetery. A cop with a kind heart gave me details when I told him I needed to see this.

Even in death, there is a befoulment on the air around this freshly dug gravesite.

It is done. I'm quenched but empty and changing. Always changing.

I could stop it now, perhaps. My goal met. The villain in my personal narrative dealt a fitting end by Karma. But there are other daughters and sons who need me. I will claim my revenge on the others. I will strike fear into their hearts until they never dare strike again. I will be justice; I will be terror. I will haunt the dark corridors and spaces behind closed doors.

I leave my severed cape behind in the cemetery along with the final fragments of my humanity as I breathe and stretch out into my full form and fly back out into the world.

I feel the auras of pain and darkness waiting on the wind.

I'm coming for you.

I'm coming for you… ♜

THE CLOWNING

By Heath W. Shelby

Friday, October 4, 2024
White County Fairgrounds
Searcy, Arkansas

WHITE COUNTY JUDGE LOUIS WILSON looked forward to his Fridays, but he always dreaded the first Friday in October. This particular Friday meant that Louis would have to get up extra early, make his way to the White County Fairgrounds, and wait for the arrival of the Chilcott family and their traveling circus.

Louis had never been a fan of any circus. The smells and the creepy clowns were nightmare-fuel for Louis, but the county judge knew good revenue when he saw it.

The Chilcott Family Circus had been stopping in Searcy, Arkansas the first Friday in October for a weekend run for the past 15 years. Over the years, children and adults of all ages had flocked into the county fairgrounds to soak up the smells, snack on the food, and marvel at the trapeze artists, animals, and creepy clowns, bringing lots of money to the circus and the county coffers.

Louis parked his beat-up Ford pickup up next to the fairground's main gate, got out, and unlocked the rusted swinging gate. Just as he pushed the gate open, Louis could hear the unmistakable sounds of the approaching circus caravan.

Louis checked the time. Straight up 6 am. Louis could set his watch by the arrival of the Chilcotts every year. Their promptness was one of the attributes Louis liked most about working with the circus family, along with their willingness to always pay the fairgrounds' rental fee in advance.

A car honked. Louis raised his right hand to wave as a beige Station Wagon pulled up next to him.

"Good morning, Miss Chilcott."

A raven-haired lady with dark sunglasses shook her right index finger at Louis.

"Louis, what have I told you? We have this same conversation every year. As long as we've known each other, you call me 'Moira.'"

Louis grinned and blushed a little. "Yes, ma'am. Good morning, Moira. It's good to see you and your family again."

The matriarch of the Chilcott Family Circus smiled at Louis, extended her right hand out of her car's window, and produced a bulky envelope.

"It's even better seeing my money, though, right?"

Louis took the offered envelope and smiled.

"Well, ma'am, I will admit both you and your money make me smile."

Moira shook her head and smiled at Louis.

"Louis Wilson, you're a funny man. A *good* man. It's always a pleasure doing business with you. We'll have a good weekend and we'll be gone by Sunday at noon. Why don't you bring the missus out for one of our shows this weekend? I haven't seen Miss Danielle in ages."

Louis chuckled as he walked back toward his pickup truck.

"That's okay, ma'am. I'm not much for the circus...or for the creepy clowns."

Moira called out to Louis as she slowly led the caravan through the open gate, "Oh, Louis! Our clowns may be creepy, but they don't bite!"

\#   \#   \#

"Mother, I don't think this is going to work."

Moira Chilcott looked up from her vanity to see her daughter standing in the doorway of her travel trailer.

"Selina, this is the best we can do until the baby gets here." Moira walked over to take her troubled daughter's hand and led her over to the small bed in the back of the trailer. "Darling, you are over six months pregnant. I can't have you up on the trapeze with Luca. We've discussed this…Until the baby comes, it's best for you to just be a happy little earthbound clown!"

"Mother, I am *not* happy, and I am certainly not a clown. I hate this outfit…these giant shoes…and I can't *stand* this greasepaint. I don't know the first thing about being a clown!"

Moira grabbed a tissue from her vanity and began to dab the tears that began to appear in the corners of her only child's eyes.

"Nonsense, my dear. You know everything you need to know to be a clown in the Chilcott Family Circus. You just make the little boys and little girls smile. And don't be creepy!"

Selina looked at her mother and produced a small grin that allowed her mom to know that she had somewhat eased her daughter's worries and fears.

"Now, you stop crying. You're smearing your makeup and we've got less than thirty minutes until our first performance of the day."

#   #   #

Moira Chilcott poured herself a glass of red wine to prepare herself for the last performance of the day.

The matinee performance went off without a hitch and was like most matinee shows: lots of children fresh out of school, hopped up on the cotton candy they managed to convince their parents to buy for them.

The evening performance could have gone better, but the low attendance was expected. People getting off work at 5 pm didn't have time to rush from the office to the big top. Those working Joes and Jills would turn out for the final performance of the day, along with the rowdy teenagers and rednecks the area was notorious for.

Thinking about the possibility of a raucous night at the circus made

Moira down her drink in one gulp and then pour herself a second glass of wine.

There was a knock at the door. "Come in."

The door to Moira's trailer slowly swung open and her son-in-law Luca Boswell stepped inside.

"Mother Chilcott, we have ten minutes until we open the front gate for the last show of the day."

"Thank you, my dear. I will be right there."

As she gathered up her tarot cards, Moira noticed that Luca was still standing in the trailer's doorway.

"Luca? Is there something else?"

"Well…"

Moira noticed that Luca couldn't bring himself to look her in the eyes.

"Luca? What is it?"

"Do you think it's safe for Selina to be out there tonight…for a third show…the last show of the day is always a little…rambunctious…"

Moira walked over to her son-in-law and took his hand.

"Luca, Selina will be fine. She's just going to hand out some balloons to the children walking up and down the midway."

"I just have a bad feeling about tonight…"

Moira laughed and slapped Luca on his left shoulder.

"Darling, I am the fortune teller around here. Not you."

#   #   #

Caitlynn Taylor checked her iPhone for what felt like the hundredth time in the last twenty minutes. Caitlynn was crazy about her boyfriend, but Dylan Matthews was always chronically late.

"Cocoa? Do you believe this? Twenty-five minutes late."

Caitlynn's Boston Terrier cocked her head and gave her master a look of confusion and concern.

Caitlynn smiled, patted her dog on the head, and walked to the front window of her home in Searcy to watch and wait for her date's arrival.

Date night with Dylan was always a big deal for Caitlynn, but tonight she was especially excited. Dylan was taking Caitlynn to the circus, and she loved the circus. Caitlynn's dad used to take her to the circus when she was a kid. That's when Caitlynn fell in love with the sights and sounds of the circus, especially the animals and the clowns.

She heard the honking of a car outside. "He's here! Cocoa, you be a good girl. I will be back after a while."

Caitlynn grabbed her purse, locked her front door, ran down the sidewalk, and climbed into her boyfriend's Dodge pickup.

"It's about time…"

"Honey, I am so sorry. Dad left his phone at the house, so I had to drop it off at the Sheriff's Department."

"You would think County Sheriff Matthews would send one of his deputies on his errand runs…or at least hire his son as a deputy…"

Dylan put his pickup in DRIVE and gave Caitlynn a side glance that left no doubt in her mind that that would never be a possibility.

"Not in this lifetime. It's bad enough that my dad is the sheriff, and my best friend is the mayor's son. That's more than I ever wanted to be involved in local politics. I'm happy being a mechanic."

Caitlynn smiled, looked out the passenger window and began to nervously tap her right foot.

"What's wrong?"

"Huh?"

"You're gonna wear a hole in the floorboard if you tap your foot any harder."

Caitlynn blushed a little with embarrassment as she made herself stop tapping her foot.

"Sorry about that…"

"We have plenty of time to get to the circus. The gates don't even open for another fifteen minutes."

"Yeah?"

"Yep. You're really excited about this, huh?"

"Dad used to take me to the circus all the time…it's been years since I have been, though."

"How long has it been?"

"Probably ten years or more…the last time we went, Dad and I rode an elephant!"

Dylan laughed and said, "Well, I don't think you could get me on an elephant…maybe they have some pony rides or something…"

"You'll be off the hook for elephant or pony rides if you just get us there on time."

"We'll be there in plenty of time. Oh, one more thing…"

Caitlynn squinted and hesitantly asked, "What would that be?"

"Uh…Ethan and the rest of the gang are going to meet us there…"

"Really? The gang? You mean the Yee-Yee Boys?"

Caitlynn really loved her boyfriend, but she wasn't too crazy about his group of redneck friends known as the Yee-Yee Boys, even if they dated her best friends.

"Your friends will be there, too. How often do you get to say you went to the circus with the Yee-Yee Boys?"

"What? Does the circus not have enough clowns on the payroll?"

#   #   #

"Yee-Yee, my brother!"

Ethan Sypolt ran to greet Dylan as he parked his pickup in the White County Fairgrounds parking lot.

"Yee-Yee, E! Where's your girlfriend?"

Ethan pointed toward the carnival midway that led to the big top.

"Maggie is over there with the rest of the gang. They're throwing darts at balloons trying to win a big ole stuffed unicorn. Hey, Caitlynn!"

"Ethan. Dylan, I'm going over to talk to Maggie, Gracie, and Courtney. Are you coming?"

"I'll be there in a few minutes."

"Hurry up so we don't miss the show."

As Caitlynn ran to join her friends, Ethan slapped Dylan on his shoulder. "Runnin' late, my brother?"

"I had to run an errand for Dad. I got us here in plenty of time."

"Hey, speaking of dads, I raided my dad's liquor cabinet. You want to smuggle some 'happy juice' into the big top?"

Dylan stood back and looked at his best friend.

"Let me guess, you've already smuggled some 'happy juice' into your stomach?"

Ethan smiled at Dylan and confessed, "Maybe…a wise man once said it's five o'clock somewhere! The bar is open over here in the trunk of my car…"

"No. I'm good. Caitlynn would kill me and if my dad found out…"

"Hey, my dad is the mayor, and I am not afraid of him."

"Well, my dad can not only ground me, but he can also lock me up for public intoxication. All your dad can do is threaten me with those giant scissors he uses at ribbon cuttings."

#   #   #

"Caitlynn, do you want some popcorn? Candy apple? How about some cotton candy?"

"No, Gracie. Maybe just a Dr Pepper."

Gracie Lawson and her boyfriend, Brison Turner, walked past their friends in their front-row seats to make a run to the concession stand before the show began.

"Y'all hurry up. The show's about to start."

"Caitlynn, chill out. We'll be back in no time. Plus, if we miss a second of it, I'm sure Courtney will record it and stick it on social media."

Courtney Vess and her boyfriend, Sid Jones, took a selfie before she responded, "You know it, girl! I got you covered!"

Maggie Still leaned over and whispered in Caitlynn's left ear, "Why buy a ticket if you're gonna be on your phone all night…and not even watch the show?"

Caitlynn shrugged as the lights inside the big top went out.

"LADIES AND GENTLEMEN! BOYS AND GIRLS OF ALL AGES! PLEASE, DIRECT YOUR ATTENTION TO THE CENTER OF THE BIG TOP!"

A lone spotlight illuminated a man decked out in a red tuxedo, holding a microphone in the middle of the big top.

"WELCOME TO THE CHILCOTT FAMILY CIRCUS!"

Caitlynn grabbed her boyfriend's hand and squeezed hard.

"It's showtime!"

\#   \#   \#

At intermission Dylan asked, "Well, what do you think so far?"

Caitlynn kissed Dylan's left hand, beamed her biggest smile, and exclaimed, "I LOVE it!"

"You need me to get you a Dr Pepper or something?"

"No. I am good. I'm ready for the rest of the show!"

As if on cue, the lights inside the big top dimmed and a lone spotlight directed the crowd's attention to a lithe figure on a small platform near the top of the circus tent.

"LADIES AND GENTLEMEN! PLEASE, DIRECT YOUR ATTENTION ABOVE THE BIG TOP TO THE MARVELOUS MARCEL, AS HE WALKS THE HIGH WIRE WITHOUT A SAFETY NET!"

"Ooooohhhhh!"

As a collective gasp echoed through the big top, Caitlynn squeezed Dylan's left hand tighter.

"LADIES AND GENTLEMEN, AT THIS TIME WE REQUEST ABSOLUTE SILENCE AS THE MARVELOUS MARCEL BEGINS HIS WALK."

A hush fell across the crowd as the circus performer took his first step onto the barely visible wire strung high above the ground.

"Don't fall!!"

The crowd erupted in laughter. Caitlynn cringed because she recognized the source of the rude silence breaker. It was her boyfriend's obnoxious best friend, Ethan.

"Don't look down, clown!!"

The crowd laughed, albeit a little uncomfortably when everyone noticed that the Marvelous Marcel was trying to regain his balance high above the big top.

"Whoa! He's gonna fall!"

The Marvelous Marcel slipped and managed to grasp the high wire.

As the crowd gasped in shock, a couple of circus workers wheeled out a safety net, while another worker began climbing the ladder leading to the in-peril Marcel.

"I'm sorry, but you folks are going to have to leave."

Caitlynn's attention was brought back down to Earth by the sound of a burly gentleman wearing a black polo shirt with the words CHILCOTT FAMILY CIRCUS STAFF embroidered over the right chest pocket. The staff member was talking to Ethan and looking at Caitlynn and all of her friends.

"Excuse me, sir? Who has to leave?"

"Ma'am, you all have to leave…unless one of you wants to fess up and tell me who was over here causing all the commotion."

Caitlynn looked to her left and settled her eyes on Ethan.

"Ethan?"

"Caitlynn?"

Caitlynn squinted angrily at Ethan.

"Ethan, do you have something you'd like to say?"

"Yeah…I wish one of you rednecks would come clean and tell this nice gentleman what you did so we can get on with the show!"

"Okay, that's it. All of you. Out. Now!"

#   #   #

"Dylan, take me home."

"Caitlynn, please, calm down. Let's just all go get something to eat… or we can go hang out at Sonic and get a Dr Pepper."

Caitlynn wheeled around and pointed at a laughing Ethan.

"I am not going anywhere with him!"

"Ah, come on, Caitlynn! I was just messin' around in there. It was funny!"

"It wasn't funny! That poor guy could've fell! He could've died!"

"But he didn't…it was just a joke."

Caitlynn turned back to Dylan.

"Take me home. Now. I mean it."

"Caitlynn…"

"You knew how much I wanted to see the circus tonight. But you had to go and invite your idiot friend. You can either take me home or I'll walk."

Caitlynn walked toward the parking lot, leaving her boyfriend feeling torn and hurt.

"Dylan, drop her off and come back and hang with us. Yee-yee!"

Dylan gave his friend a disgusted look and took off across the parking lot to catch up with his girlfriend.

#   #   #

"Ethan, can we go now?"

Maggie Still had been sitting impatiently on the trunk of her boyfriend's Dodge Charger in the White County Fairgrounds parking lot with her best friend, Courtney Vess, and Courtney's boyfriend, Sid Jones.

"Girl, y'all just chill out."

"Why are we just sitting here in the parking lot? Let's go somewhere and do something…anything besides sitting here outside of the circus you got us kicked out of. We're not getting back in. The show is already over, and everyone has left but us!"

"I am just waiting…there's someone I want to talk to…"

"Who?"

"Maybe that clown!"

A clown wearing a pink costume with red buttons and a long blond wig atop her head walked from the shadows behind the big top.

"Hey! Hey! Miss! Over here!"

The clown looked across the parking lot as Ethan jogged toward her.

"Hey! I want to talk to you really quick!"

Ethan sprinted across the parking lot as the clown picked up the pace in an attempt to avoid the oncoming confrontation.

"Ethan! Get back over here!"

Maggie took off in pursuit of her boyfriend and was soon joined by Courtney and Sid.

Ethan stopped in front of the startled clown.

"Hey! Do you work here?"

The clown looked at Ethan with startled wide eyes and a painted mouth that hung wide open in shock.

"Well, silly me. Of course, you do. Hi. My name is Ethan."

Ethan stuck his hand out and the clown reluctantly took his hand and timidly shook it.

"And you are?"

"Uh…Selina…"

"Selina! Nice to meet you! Over there is my girlfriend, Maggie. And that's Courtney and Sid."

Selina gently waved at the gathered friends and suddenly grew even more anxious when she noticed Courtney raise her iPhone.

"Are you filming me?"

"Oh, that's just what Court does. She lives on social media."

Selina tried to walk past Ethan.

"I've gotta go…"

"Whoa! Whoa! Whoa! Not so fast there, Selina! I had something I wanted to talk to you about."

"Ethan, maybe we should -"

"Maggie, chill out! We got kicked out of the circus tonight and I'm trying to find out how we're supposed to get our money back."

"Sir…you will need to go to the box office for something like that…"

"Hey! What are you doing there?! Get away from my wife!"

Luca Boswell ran from the shadows behind the big top to Selina's side.

"Whoa! Whoa! Whoa, hoss!"

Ethan took two steps back and held his hands up in the hopes of calming down the angry man.

"What are you doing to my wife?"

"Your wife? You mean you're married to this…chubby clown?"

Luca took a step toward Ethan and snarled, "She's pregnant, you ignorant redneck."

Ethan tried to stifle his laughter, but failed miserably once his friends began chuckling behind him.

Luca angrily shoved Ethan and yelled, "Get out of here! NOW!"

Without hesitation, Ethan regained his balance and returned the shove, forcing Luca backwards into his unsuspecting wife. Selina stumbled and fell hard against the ground.

"Selina! Are you okay?!"

A terrified look swept across Selina's face as she grabbed her stomach and whispered to her husband, "Luca…something is wrong…it hurts…"

Luca glanced down and noticed the pants of his wife's outfit had suddenly turned a bright crimson.

"Someone call 911…"

Luca turned around and saw Ethan and his friends standing together in stunned silence.

"You! With the phone in your hand! Instead of filming all this, CALL 911!"

#   #   #

Deputy Chandler Smith hadn't been working for the White County Sheriff's Office long, so he was still working the weekend shifts. Chandler had been on a routine patrol around Center Hill when he received a call to report to the White County Medical Center over some kind of incident that originated at the White County Fairgrounds.

As he entered the emergency room waiting area, Chandler was stunned to see a group of men and women dressed in colorful attire, as well as a couple of clowns.

"Officer!"

A small lady carrying a black cane and dressed all in red approached Chandler.

"Ma'am?"

"My daughter was assaulted at the circus! She's in surgery right now! The doctors are trying to save the baby!"

"Mother Chilcott, I'll take care of this. Go sit down and try to relax."

Moira Chilcott nodded at her son-in-law as Luca directed her to an empty chair.

"Boswell family?"

The waiting room fell silent as Doctor Dillinger Carr entered the area.

"I'm her husband…Luca. Is…Selina okay?"

"Mr. Boswell, your wife is fine, but I'm afraid I have some bad news…"

Moira slowly rose from her chair.

"Mr. Boswell, we couldn't save the baby. I am so sorry."

As if struck, Moira fell to her knees.

Luca looked at Dr. Carr in stunned silence. "I don't understand…"

"Mr. Boswell, your wife lost too much blood. There was nothing that could be done."

"Wrong…something could have been done…"

Moira stood up with tears streaming down her face. Moira's makeup was streaked, and her eyes looked crazed.

"Mother Chilcott…"

Moira pushed Luca aside and walked up to Dr. Carr.

"Something will be done…"

Deputy Smith felt like the situation was getting heated, so he walked toward Moira and Dr. Carr. Moira wheeled around and pointed at Deputy Smith. "Stop."

Deputy Smith couldn't help himself and came to an immediate stop. What unfolded in front of him kept Deputy Smith glued to the ground in complete shock.

Moira took her pointed index finger and turned the long red fingernail at the end of it toward the palm of her left hand. With a quick swipe of her fingernail, Moira opened a gash in the middle of her hand. Moira closed her fist and blood seeped between her fingers. Moira then shook her fist at Deputy Smith, throwing blood on the floor and on the unsuspecting deputy.

"Until those responsible are brought to light, vengeance will reign day and night!"

Luca grabbed his mother-in-law and led her back to her empty chair.

"Deputy, she didn't mean to -"

"UNTIL THOSE RESPONSIBLE ARE BROUGHT TO LIGHT, VENGEANCE WILL REIGN DAY AND NIGHT!!"

Deputy Smith slowly wiped blood from his face.

"Sir, it's okay…I understand…if I could take your statement on what happened, I will leave y'all to…grieve…"

\#   \#   \#

"Sheriff, that's what her husband said. It was the mayor's kid. Did you want me to go pick up Ethan and bring him in?"

Sheriff Jerry Matthews couldn't believe he was in the office on a Friday night.

"No. I will take care of this one. You get back out on patrol."

"Are you sure, Sheriff?"

"Yeah. With the mayor's kid involved, I need to handle this one personally…"

\#   \#   \#

Friday night was Mayor Blake Sypolt's favorite time of the week. No city business to deal with coupled with time on the couch with his wife Tori watching *Blue Bloods*.

"Honey, could you bring me some popcorn on your way back from the kitchen?"

"Sure. Do you want something—"

\#   \#   \#

Tori heard the doorbell ring. "Blake? Who would be ringing the doorbell this time of night?"

"I don't know, honey…Hang on and I'll find out."

Blake walked to the front door, looked through the peephole and was stunned to see Sheriff Matthews standing on his front porch. Blake opened the door and instantly knew from the look on Sheriff Matthews' face that he hadn't dropped by to watch television with him.

"Sheriff? What's up?"

"Mayor, can you step outside so we can talk?"

Blake stepped out onto the front porch and closed the door behind him.

"Jerry, what's going on?"

"It's Ethan."

"*What happened?* Is he okay?"

"Yeah. It's nothing like that. Ethan is fine…but he's…done something…"

The initial panic he had felt faded, replaced by something else. Maybe something worse. Blake sighed and placed his right hand over his forehead. "What did my son do now?"

"Well, Ethan and his friends - including Dylan - went to the circus. Ethan apparently got the kids kicked out for being disorderly… he might have been drinking—"

"Are you serious?!"

"There's more. Ethan hung around after the circus and had a… confrontation with some of the circus workers. According to the circus folks, Ethan caused a pregnant lady to fall down. She went to the hospital and… she miscarried…"

"Ethan caused this?"

"That's what the woman's husband said. Mayor, what do you want me to do here? Do I need to go pick up —"

Blake shook his head side to side as he paced around Sheriff Matthews. "No! No! No! No!"

"But…"

"But nothing!"

"Mayor, I have to do something. That family is expecting…"

Blake stopped in front of the sheriff, leveling the index finger of his right hand inches from Jerry's face.

"You are going to do nothing. I will take care of Ethan."

"Mayor, what do I tell the family? They want answers."

"You won't tell them—and you won't tell anyone else—anything at all."

Sheriff Matthews stared at Mayor Sypolt in shock and confusion.

"You don't have to tell that family anything at all. They're a traveling circus. They'll be on to another town come Monday morning. Out of sight. Out of mind. And while you're at it, don't say a word to any of your deputies. Don't say a word to your wife. Heck, you don't say a word to *my* wife. I'll take care of this."

\#   \#   \#

"Here. Your phone is ringing. It looks like your dad has heard about tonight."

Maggie Still handed her boyfriend his iPhone. Ethan Sypolt took one look, saw the word "Dad" on the screen and laid the phone face down on the dashboard of his Dodge Charger.

"You're gonna get into so much trouble over this…all of us are gonna get in trouble…"

"Hon, don't worry about it. My dad will take care of it."

\#   \#   \#

"Sid, can you just take me home?"

Sid Jones had taken his girlfriend to Riverside Park in the hopes of calming her down after the trauma at the circus. Courtney Vess was usually all smiles and always had her phone in her hand, creating viral videos for her social media. However, since she had filmed the incident at the circus, Courtney hadn't smiled, nor had she picked up her phone.

"Court, I just want to make sure you're okay before you go home. You want to listen to some music?"

"No. I need some peace and quiet…and then I need you to take me home."

"I'll take you home here in just a bit…right after I go take a leak."

Sid turned on the headlights of his Ford F250 and opened the driver's door.

"Why are you turning on the headlights?"

"Babe, there's no one but us out here. I don't want to trip heading down the trail. Don't you be sneaking a peek now!"

Sid felt better when he saw his girlfriend grin for the first time in hours.

"That's better. I'll be right back."

Courtney blushed as her boyfriend closed the truck door and then skipped down the trail before disappearing into the woods. Courtney began to relax a little. *Maybe things weren't as bad as they looked…maybe that lady is okay*... But Courtney's thoughts were interrupted by movement in front of Sid's truck.

A clown stood in the middle of the truck's headlights at the end of the trail. The clown was wearing a dingy yellow costume, with giant red shoes and black gloves. The clown's left hand held a yellow balloon with a smiley face painted in dripping red paint. The clown had a blood-red smile that curved unnaturally upward to right beneath the blackest of eyes. Long, dark, stringy hair partially covered the clown's grease-painted face and draped over his large red shoulder pads.

"Sid..."

The clown raised his right hand and slowly waved at Courtney.

Courtney rolled down the passenger door window and yelled, "Sid! This is not funny! Take me home! Now!!"

The clown lowered his right hand and cocked his head.

"Sid! I'm serious! I am not laughing! Stop this crap now and take me home!"

The clown shrugged his shoulders, walked off the right side of the road and disappeared into the woods.

Courtney leaned out the passenger window and tried to see where the clown was.

"Sid...are you there?"

When she received no answer, Courtney slowly got out of the truck and walked around to the front of the vehicle.

"Sid...where are you?"

"Right here, babe!"

"OH! MY! GOD!!" Courtney screamed and jumped at the sound of her boyfriend's voice behind her.

"*Why are you scaring me?* After everything that we've been through tonight!"

"Babe, I'm sorry...I didn't mean to -"

"And where did you get that creepy clown costume?!"

"What clown costume? What are you talking about?"

Courtney slapped Sid's face, whirled around, and climbed back into the truck.

"Take me home. Now."

Sid stood in stunned silence and watched as his girlfriend closed the passenger door and buckled her seat belt. Not knowing what else to do, Sid climbed into his truck, closed the driver's door, and buckled his seat belt.

"Babe, I am sorry…all I did was sneak up behind you and -"

"What is that smell? Did you step in something?"

Sid sniffed and was overcome by an odor he had only smelled once before when he was a kid and he had discovered a dead raccoon beneath his grandparents' porch.

"I didn't step in anything…"

A new voice: "Oh, yes…you stepped in something…"

Courtney and Sid turned to see a clown sitting in the backseat. Courtney instantly recognized him. The one who had been on the trail.

"Hey, bud! Get your ass out of my truck before -"

The clown covered Sid's mouth with his gloved hand. Sid had to fight the urge to gag as the odor of death and rot filled his nostrils.

"How about a little trick?" The clown's gravely whisper sent chills down Courtney's spine, filling her with a terror she had never known before. Courtney reached for the handle on the passenger door as the clown waved a finger at her.

"No, no, no…the show is just getting started, little lady…"

As Courtney tried to escape, the door locks engaged.

With his left hand still clamped over Sid's mouth, the clown produced a deflated yellow balloon with his right hand. The clown swung the deflated balloon in front of Sid's eyes, as if trying to hypnotize him. Tears began to stream down Sid's face and the clown stopped swinging the balloon. Sid's eyes grew wide when the clown opened his mouth in a wide smile that showcased a cavern of jagged, rotten teeth and an even more intense smell of death and rot.

"Girlie, you might want to get your phone out for this one…"

The clown shoved the deflated balloon up Sid's left nostril. Sid began to buck, but the seat belt and the clown's left hand held him in place.

With a wave of his right hand, the clown produced another deflated yellow balloon and shoved it up Sid's right nostril. Sid's eyes grew impossibly wide as his airways were becoming completely constricted. Sid's ears rang from the sound of his heartbeat and the din of Courtney's horrified screams.

With another wave of his right hand, the clown produced a small air pump. The clown shoved the pump up Sid's left nostril, pulled the trigger repeatedly as Courtney screamed louder. Sid bucked to no avail as the clown alternated the pump from his left and right nostrils, pulling the trigger quicker and quicker.

Sid's bucking slowed as blood began to trickle from his nose and his eyes. Slowly, Sid's throat became engorged. The clown continued pumping air into Sid's nose as his victim's throat began to split right down the middle. Blood gushed all over the front seat of the truck as two inflated yellow balloons broke free from Sid's throat.

"Now… for the encore…"

Courtney lost control of her body and couldn't stop screaming as the clown placed his bloody left hand on her cheek.

"I've had my eye on you, missy…"

The coppery smell of Sid's blood overwhelmed the odor of death and rot as the clown took the index finger of his right hand and traced a crimson trail down Courtney's forehead to her right eye.

"One…"

The clown extended his middle finger alongside his index finger and traced two bloody trails down Courtney's forehead to her closed eyes.

"*Two*…"

Courtney held her breath, anticipating and dreading whatever unspeakable act the clown had in store for her. When nothing came, Courtney slowly opened her eyes to see the clown grinning at her with his mouthful of rotten jagged teeth.

"Nyuk…nyuk…nyuk…"

The clown drove his fingers into Courtney's eye sockets, popping her eyeballs like blood filled grapes. Courtney's body convulsed as the clown continued to push his hand into her skull. Courtney stopped moving when the clown's two fingers protruded from the hair on the back of her head.

#   #   #

"Good morning, dear! You care if I walk with you?"

Gracie Lawson didn't sleep well after the events of the night before at the fair, but she still intended to stick to her routine morning walk. What wasn't routine was her boyfriend showing up in her driveway to take a walk with her.

"Brison, what are you doing here so early?"

Brison Turner climbed out of his GMC pickup truck and walked over to his girlfriend.

"I know last night bothered you…"

"Brison, we just stood there and did nothing while Ethan just…"

"I know, dear. It's okay. Come on. Let's take a walk. That'll make you feel better."

#   #   #

"Do you think she's okay?"

Brison wasn't sure who Gracie was talking about. All he was sure of was that he should've worn something other than boots for a one-mile walk.

"Who?"

"That woman…the clown lady…the one Ethan bumped into."

"Gracie, I'm sure she's fine. Can we head back home? I'm wearing blisters on my feet."

"Sure…I've had enough walking for today. Let's get back to the house and I will make us some…breakfast…"

Brison looked up from his sore feet to see why his girlfriend trailed off.

"Gracie?"

"Do you see that?"

Gracie pointed to the pasture on the right side of the road. A clown stood in the middle of the pasture. The clown wore a baggy black costume with large white buttons down the middle. In his left hand, the clown held a yellow balloon with a smiley face drawn poorly with bright red paint. The red paint matched the clown's blood-red smile and his long, stringy red hair, which almost covered the clown's black eyes.

"Maybe it's someone's jacked-up scarecrow…"

The clown raised his right hand and began to wave at the stunned couple.

"Brison, that's no scarecrow…"

"Come on. Let's get back to the house."

Gracie and Brison began walking back toward the safety of Gracie's home. With each step they took, the clown kept pace in the pasture, never taking his black eyes off the couple.

Gracie and Brison began to jog. The clown kept his eyes on the couple and began to jog, as well.

"Gracie…run!"

As the couple ran toward Gracie's house, the clown picked up the pace and made a beeline toward the panicked pair.

"Gracie, get to the house! I've got this!"

Gracie ran away as Brison stopped in the middle of the road and pulled his iPhone from his back pocket. Brison unlocked his phone and attempted to dial 911, just as the clown barreled into him. Brison hit the ground hard, and his phone fell from his hand.

The clown walked over to Brison's phone, raised his comically large right shoe, and stepped on the device, crushing the phone and Brison's hope for rescue.

As Brison tried to get up off the dirt road, the clown walked over to him and kicked him with the same large shoe that crushed his phone…somehow, the shoe looked even larger than before.

Brison fell back to the ground, clutching his side. Brison tried to catch his breath and the sharp pain in his side when he inhaled let him know that the clown had broken some ribs.

"Why are you doing this? What have—"

The clown kicked Brison in his face, breaking his nose and scattering teeth and blood across the dirt road. Through the searing pain, Brison could see the clown's shoe had indeed grown to at least three feet long.

The clown bent down so he was nose to nose with Brison. The smell of rot and impending death filled Brison's nostrils as the clown opened his mouth in an unnaturally wide grin.

"Ain't this a kick in the head…"

The clown stood up, cocked his head to the left, raised his large shoe off the ground, and kicked Brison once again in the face. Brison's head left his body and sailed into the pasture.

"It's up…and it's good!"

#   #   #

Gracie approached her driveway but came to a sudden stop when she noticed another clown at the other end of the road. This clown was dressed in a black tuxedo. The clown had long black hair that surrounded a face with a blood red smile, red rubber nose and dark eyes. The clown was sitting on a tricycle that had a yellow balloon with a poorly drawn red smiley face attached to the handlebars.

The tiny bell trilled twice. *Ring ring.* As the clown rang the tricycle's bell, Gracie bolted for her front door.

Ring ring.

Gracie ran inside and locked the door behind her. Gracie looked through the front door's peephole, but the clown was nowhere to be seen.

Ring ring.

Gracie turned around and saw the clown's tricycle sitting inside her house at the end of her hallway. Gracie slowly approached the tricycle, wondering how the clown's tiny vehicle got into her home.

Gracie leaned over and touched the tricycle's bell.

Ring—

A hand landed on Gracie's shoulder and a chilling whisper filled her left ear.

"How 'bout we go for a ride, G-belle…"

Startled, Gracie stumbled and fell to the floor. Before she could get back to her feet and run away, the clown landed on top of Gracie. Gracie's heart raced as the clown's face drew closer to hers. The clown opened his mouth in a grin, revealing a set of jagged, rotten teeth. The smell of death overwhelmed Gracie.

"Not so fast, Gracie-belle…the party is just getting started…"

Tears streaked down Gracie's face as the clown caressed her face with the black rubber glove on his right hand. The clown extended his index finger and traced a trail from Gracie's forehead to the tip of her nose. The clown then pinched Gracie's nose.

"Got your nose."

Without any further warning, the clown ripped Gracie's nose from her face.

"AAAAAAHHHHH!!"

Gracie shrieked in pain and shock as the clown held her nose above his head, allowing the blood to drip onto his face. She bucked in terror as the clown dropped her nose into his mouth, looked at her and smiled.

"Num…num…num."

Gracie's tear-filled eyes grew wide as the clown placed his left hand over her mouth. Gracie buckled beneath the clown when she realized she couldn't breathe.

The clown removed the rubber nose from his face and slowly placed it in the bloody, gaping hole in the middle of Gracie's face. The clown laid his right index finger on top of the rubber nose and smiled at Gracie as the life drained from her eyes.

"Boop."

#   #   #

"Dylan, have you heard from Sid?"

Dylan Matthews was trying to make things right with his girlfriend when Ethan Sypolt interrupted their dinner with an impromptu phone call.

"E, I haven't heard from Sid or Brison."

"Dylan, you haven't told anyone about last night…have you?"

"No. I haven't talked to anyone except Caitlynn…and I am trying to fix things with her but you -"

"Did your dad say anything?"

"E, I just told you I haven't talked to anyone…that includes my dad."

"Good. I'm just worried…"

"E, I don't know what happened after we left, but I am not gonna throw you under the bus. Your secret - whatever it is - is safe with me."

\#　　\#　　\#

"Who was that?"

Dylan knew Caitlynn Taylor wasn't fond of his best friend, so he was afraid to tell her that their make-up dinner had just been interrupted by Ethan Sypolt.

"That was Ethan…"

Caitlynn squinted at Dylan and asked, "What did he want?"

"Something must have happened after we left last night."

"What did he do?"

"I don't know, but I told him his secret was safe with me."

"So, you're going to cover up for whatever he did…be his alibi?"

Dylan shook his head and placed his hands on Caitlynn's shoulders.

"It's not like that. He's my best friend. I'm just—" The doorbell chimed. "Were you expecting someone else tonight?"

Caitlynn looked at Dylan and shook her head. "I wasn't even expecting you. Cocoa and I were planning on an evening alone, watching *Kitchen Nightmares.*"

Caitlynn walked over and peered through the peephole of her front door. Standing on her front porch was a clown wearing a dingy, tattered blue outfit. In his left hand, the clown was holding a yellow balloon with a poorly drawn red smiley face. In his right hand, the clown held a bicycle horn.

The clown honked the horn, an odd, blaring sound. Then he cocked his head to the left and waved the horn, as if he knew he was being watched.

Honk-honk!

"What is that noise?" Caitlynn turned and looked at Dylan with look of concern and confusion written all over her face, while Cocoa looked at the front door and growled.

"What is it?" Dylan asked.

"There is a…creepy clown…on the porch…"

Dylan looked through the peephole and saw nothing but an empty porch. "There's no one out there."

Caitlynn looked through the peephole and was shocked to see nothing. "I swear there was a *clown* out—"

Honk!

Caitlynn and Dylan turned to see the source of the sound was a clown standing in the kitchen, holding a bicycle horn in one hand and a large butcher knife in the other.

"Caitlynn, run!"

Caitlynn grabbed Cocoa and started toward the front door.

Honk!

Caitlynn stopped in her tracks and looked at the clown.

"How's this for a kitchen nightmare?" The clown waved the knife as Caitlynn backed toward the front door.

"Little lady, I'm not here for you or your little dog, Toto…" The clown pointed the knife at Dylan. "I'm here to have a little face-to-face with you, boss…"

"Caitlynn, get out of here…go get help."

The clown took a step forward and Caitlynn rushed out the door with Cocoa wrapped tightly in her arms.

"Now…for that face to-face…"

"Bring it on, Bozo. It's not beneath me to whoop a clown's ass."

The clown playfully waved the knife as he stepped toward Dylan, a large grin spreading across his grease-painted face. With unnatural speed, the clown crossed the room and jumped on Dylan, taking him to the ground.

"'Sup?"

"What do you want?!"

"We're having this little face-to-face because I heard you like to cover things up…"

"I don't know what you are talking about, you crazy son of a—"

The clown raised the knife with his right hand. Dylan began to scream as the clown took the point of the knife, placed it under Dylan's chin and began to carve his face from his skull. Dylan wailed and tried to get out from under the clown as his attacker grabbed his skin with his left hand and pulled.

The clown looked at his bloody trophy and smiled, then carefully placed Dylan's face over his own. The fresh blood held Dylan's skin in place over the clown's face as the clown leaned over his victim.

"How's this for a cover-up?"

\#   \#   \#

"Sheriff Matthews! You've got to get out here! Quick! This creepy clown broke into my house and he's in there right now with Dylan!"

Caitlynn had called Dylan's dad as soon as she was able to get herself and Cocoa down the road in her Mustang.

"Caitlynn, calm down. Did you say someone broke into your house? A ...*clown?*"

"Yes, yes! Please hurry!"

\#   \#   \#

Sheriff Jerry Matthews and Deputy Chandler Smith had arrived at Caitlynn's house within minutes of her frantic call. Since then, Caitlynn and Cocoa had been sitting on the tailgate of Dylan's truck, waiting for the officers to investigate what had happened inside.

"Caitlynn?"

"Yes, Sheriff?"

"Where is Dylan?"

Caitlynn looked perplexed at the Sheriff and Deputy.

"What do you mean? He was in there with that clown."

Sheriff Matthews looked at his deputy and pointed to his patrol car. "Chandler, would you head back to the station and let me talk to Caitlynn?"

"Yes, sir. If you need me to help you look for Dylan, let me know."

As Chandler got into his patrol car, Sheriff Matthews approached Caitlynn. "Caitlynn, Dylan is not in there."

"What…"

"Aside from his truck here, there's no evidence of Dylan here at all."

"What about the *clown?*"

Sheriff Matthews shook his head. "No clown. No evidence at all of anyone breaking into your place. You want to tell me what y'all are up to? Is this a stupid Yee-Yee Boys thing?"

"Uh…no…I swear there was a clown…and it was after Dylan…"

#   #   #

"I swear! I haven't seen him!"

"Ethan, if you're lying to me and this is one of your stupid Yee-Yee Boys pranks—"

"Caitlynn, I haven't seen Dylan! I swear on my life!" Ethan looked at his iPhone after Caitlynn disconnected the call.

"What was that about?"

Ethan handed his phone to his girlfriend and shook his head. "Maggie, I don't have a clue…something about a clown attacking Dylan…and now he's missing…Can you believe Caitlynn thought *I* had something to do with it?"

"Did you?"

"Are you serious?"

"The Yee-Yee Boys have done worse…like what you did last night to that poor lady at the circus."

Ethan slammed his hands against the steering wheel.

"That was a total accident!"

"Mom told me today that the lady lost her baby…"

Ethan mumbled, "It was an accident…"

Silence filled the car. Maggie looked out the window across the poorly lit Berryhill Park.

"We should go home. Maybe you could go talk to Sheriff Matthews… or your dad…"

Tap, tap.

Ethan and Maggie jumped at the sight and sound of a flashlight tapping on the driver's side window.

"Who is that?!"

"Maggie, chill. I'm sure it's one of Sheriff Matthews' flunkies."

Ethan reached for the door handle.

Tap, tap.

A second flashlight tapped on the passenger window. Both doors flew open, and Ethan and Maggie were overcome by the two flashlights and the reek of something rotten.

"Hands up…don't move…" The gravelly voice sent shivers down

Maggie's spine.

"Who are you—"

Two clowns appeared from behind the flashlights. The only things that were visible were the clowns' faces: dingy greasepaint; large, blood-red smiles, and eyes that appeared to be completely blacked out.

"We are just some friendly folks here to discuss a few pressing matters…"

The clowns climbed into Ethan's car and simultaneously reclined the driver's and passenger's seats. Before the couple could react, the clowns climbed on top of Ethan and Maggie.

"What are you doing, you sick—"

Before he could finish his thought, Ethan felt the weight on top of his body increase as another clown climbed into the car and crawled onto Ethan. Screams filled Ethan's ears as a fourth clown crept into the car and slithered on top of Maggie.

"Get off of us now, you -"

The breath left Ethan's body as a fifth clown entered the car and pounced on top of the developing clown dog pile. A sixth clown entered the passenger side of the car, adding more weight on top of Maggie.

Maggie's screams ceased and silence filled the car as more clowns poured into both sides of the vehicle. Suddenly, both car doors closed, and the vehicle creaked under the weight of the multitude of passengers within. Slowly, the creaking stopped, and blood seeped from beneath the doors of Ethan's car.

#   #   #

Sheriff Matthews usually looked forward to a Sunday morning as a day of peace and rest, but he had spent the entire night trying to locate his missing son. Now, his awful night had spilled into the next day.

While searching for Dylan, Sheriff Matthews received a call from Deputy Amanda Neal of an abandoned vehicle at Berryhill Park. Upon his arrival, the sheriff discovered the car belonged to Dylan's best friend, Ethan Sypolt. Even more concerning was the fact that there was a large amount of blood inside and beneath the abandoned vehicle. Floating next to the vehicle was a lone yellow balloon with a crudely painted red smiley face.

Sheriff Matthews now found himself back at Mayor Sypolt's front door, hoping the mayor knew where Ethan was…and perhaps where Dylan was.

DING DONG!

Sheriff Matthews stepped back from the front door, waiting. Finally the front door opened, and Mayor Blake Sypolt looked sleepily at Sheriff Matthews.

"Sheriff? What's going on?"

"Mayor, have you seen your son?"

"No…why?"

#   #   #

"You know they're responsible! Those carny folks did something to both our boys! You need to call in backup! Call in the city police…the Arkansas State Troopers!"

Mayor Sypolt had insisted on riding with Sheriff Matthews to the White County Fairgrounds to talk to the Chilcott family about any possible involvement with their missing sons.

"Mayor, we have no proof that the Chilcotts have anything to do with anything. I am just going to talk to them…and you're going to stay in the car."

"Sheriff, your own deputy said that old lady threatened anyone involved in her daughter's…mishap…"

"Stay in the car. I've got this."

Sheriff Matthews put his patrol vehicle in PARK, climbed out of the SUV, and made his way across the parking lot. The fairgrounds were eerily silent, and Sheriff Matthews wasn't quite sure where to go. Suddenly, the sound of a calliope echoed from somewhere inside the big top.

Sheriff Matthews pulled back the tent flap and entered the darkened big top. Sheriff Matthews reached for his flashlight but stopped when the calliope suddenly stopped and a light shone down from the top of the tent, illuminating the middle of the big top.

Dozens of yellow balloons with red smiley faces filled the middle of the big top. A lone clown rose up in the middle of the sea of balloons. The clown was decked out in a bright red outfit that clashed with his pale face and bright yellow hair. The clown's blood-red smile curled up to unnatural proportions as he held up his index finger, almost as if he wanted Sheriff Matthews to wait for a moment.

Sheriff Matthews slowly stepped forward as the clown sank below the sea of yellow balloons.

"Hey!"

Sheriff Matthews pulled his Glock 22 from its holster and aimed at the location where the clown had been. Sheriff Matthews stepped toward the sea of balloons that hovered above the ground right at chest level.

"Hey, yourself, copper…"

The clown rose up from the balloons and Sheriff Matthews could see he was holding something in his right hand. Sheriff Matthews stepped into the sea of balloons toward the clown and immediately noticed the sounds of clinking metal in the balloons all around him.

Something was in the balloons…

Sheriff Matthews looked at the balloons surrounding him and could see something…what appeared to be lots of tiny pieces of metal…gleaming inside each balloon.

"Did you lose something?"

Sheriff Matthews could now see that the clown was holding a limp body by the neck in his right hand.

"Daddy…i got a little boo boo…"

The clown used his right hand to move the head of the lifeless body, animating his bloody ventriloquist doll.

"Dylan?" Sheriff Matthews recognized the clothes on the lifeless body as those of his missing son…but the body…had no face…

"Face it, daddy…we've got problems…"

With his left hand, the clown slapped what was left of Dylan Matthews' visage across his face. Sheriff Matthews raised his Glock and started to step forward.

"Not so fast, copper…"

The clown dropped Dylan's body beneath the balloons and, with a snap of his fingers, produced a hat pin in his hand.

"Another step…and things are about to get poppin' in here…"

Sheriff Matthews took one step, and the clown stuck the hat pin in one of the balloons. When the balloon popped, shards of razor blades were expelled from the balloon into surrounding balloons, setting off a chain reaction of exploding balloons that showered the big top and a stunned Jerry Matthews with shards of razor blades. Silence settled across the big top as a bloody Sheriff Jerry Matthews fell dead to the ground.

#   #   #

Gunshots!

Mayor Sypolt exited Sheriff Matthews' patrol vehicle when he heard what he believed to be rapid gunfire coming from somewhere inside the big top. He started toward the tent and then stopped.

I need to call for backup…I don't even have a gun…

Mayor Sypolt turned to run back to the patrol vehicle when he ran right into Moira Chilcott and the cane she had pressed against his chest.

"Ma'am?"

A cold grin swept across Moira's face.

"Mister Mayor."

Click.

As Moira pressed a small, hidden button at the top of her cane, Mayor Sypolt's eyes grew wide. Pain coursed through his chest as Mayor Sypolt felt a blade puncture his heart.

Blake Sypolt slowly fell to his knees as Moira took a step back and retracted the blade from the mayor's chest. Life seeped from the mayor as blood soaked through his shirt and he fell to his hands and knees.

Mayor Sypolt looked up at Moira with fear in his eyes. "Why…"

Moira walked over to the dying man, placed her right hand under his quivering chin and lifted his head up so she could look Blake Sypolt eye to eye.

"Your blood…took my *heart… our* heart. Now, we have returned the favor. Vengeance is mine…"

Moira released Mayor Sypolt and turned to walk away. As his vision began to blur, Blake Sypolt could see a group of clowns appear from nowhere. The clowns grabbed Blake's arms and legs and began to carry him toward the big top, whispering in unison, *"Vengeance is mine…vengeance is mine… vengeance is mine…"*

"Saith the Lord…"

Moira stopped in her tracks, turned around and held her cane up in the air. The clowns immediately stopped as Moira walked over to Blake Sypolt and once again took his chin in her hand.

"What did you say, Mister Mayor?"

"…Vengeance is mine saith the Lord…"

Moira smiled and slowly shook her head.

"Oh, no, Mister Mayor. The Lord has nothing to do with what has happened here. We did the good Lord's work for him… gave him the weekend off. Vengeance is mine. All mine."

Moira dropped the mayor's lifeless head, stepped back and watched as the clowns carried his body into the big top.

#   #   #

"I thought we were going to get some pizza after church…"

Danielle Wilson tapped her husband on the shoulder and pointed down the road as Louis Wilson drove on.

"I just have to run by the fairgrounds and lock up. The Chilcotts are always gone by high noon. You can set your watch by 'em. This won't take long."

"I didn't realize County Judge Wilson worked on the Lord's day…"

"Awww…I don't consider padlocking an old iron gate 'working.'"

"You do know that circus lady has the hots for you, don't you?"

Louis blushed as his wife laughed.

"Well, that's weird…"

"What is it, Louis?"

"Over there where the big top was… ain't that Sheriff Matthews' ride?"

Louis parked his pickup truck and he and Danielle walked over to the White County Sheriff's Department SUV that was parked in the middle of the empty fairgrounds right where the big top had stood just hours ago.

"Louis…is that a…balloon?"

A yellow balloon with a crudely drawn red smiley face floated slowly into view from the back of the SUV. A paper sign was tied to the end of a string hanging from the bottom of the balloon.

"What does it say?"

Louis walked over and grabbed the sign.

"It says, 'The Bill is Paid.' That's odd…"

"What's odd?"

"Moira Chilcott always pays up front. They didn't owe us anything…"

"Hmmm…maybe the note means *your* bill is paid."

"What did we owe the Chilcotts?"

"I don't know…but thankfully, that bill is paid."

JUSTIFIED

By Bryan Young

WAITING IN THE CEMETERY SEEMS like the only real option. It's business for the dark. And you don't want to get caught on camera anywhere. He's definitely wearing a bodycam. You've seen the footage from it.

Over and over again.

On the news, in the courtroom, in that little room at the police station where they show the family what really happened because they have to.

You know exactly where it is, too, that all-seeing eye, just over his left breast. It watches everything. It records everything. And somehow every time it records some atrocity, it becomes "legally justified."

Like it's magic or something.

That term feels imbued with a new clarity, walking through the graveyard in the dark. You think about things being "legally justified", because if you think about the bodycam anymore, you're going to start thinking about the footage. And if there's anything that makes you more upset than the term *legally justified,* it's the footage from the murderer's perspective. And reliving that nightmare one more time would be enough to make you scream.

The first time you heard the term, the DA pulled you in with the rest of the family before he made his findings public.

"I want you to know that I am very sorry about this," he told everyone there, the small group most affected by such a senseless killing. But if he was sorry, he wouldn't have ruled things the way he did then, would he? "But I wanted to let you all know first, before we held our press conference that I won't be able to press charges."

"Why not?" you asked, full of fire and anger. Mainly because you knew your mother wasn't going to have the strength to ask without her husband there. Or anywhere.

"My hands are very tied in these matters," he explained with the confidence of a wolf and the patience of a saint. "You see, I am not allowed to interpret anything outside the bounds of the law. The law determines what is and isn't justified, no matter how I might feel differently. And I can't say this publicly, but I *do* feel differently in this case. According to the law, however, if there is any reason the officer feels like their life might be in any danger, they are legally justified to use any force they may feel is necessary to quell the threat."

"What does that mean?" you asked. Frustration grows as he talks in circles. Mainly because the reality of what he's saying hasn't sunk in yet.

"It means that in the eyes of the law—because on the tape there is enough indication that there was a situation where his life could have been in danger—any actions he took were legal. No matter how they ended up."

"My father didn't have a gun." You clenched your jaw so tight you bit into the side of your cheek.

As the DA continued, the fresh-copper taste of blood pooled in your mouth. "I understand that. But the way the law was written and designed, it means that you don't actually have to have a gun, but with the information the officer had at the time, he had a reasonable belief there *could* have been a gun. So his threatened safety is the same based on his perception. I'm not allowed to take the fact that there wasn't a gun present into account. The standard, like it or not, is whether or not the officer *felt* there could be a threat."

"That's bullshit." You swished the taste of blood around to the other side of your mouth and wondered why you were even there. It was all ridiculous.

It was all bullshit.

"I'm just the referee. I can take this to court, but the trial would last all of an hour before the defense counsel proved that the officer acted in a legally justified way. I can only take the crimes I have a chance of winning to court. I know it's not justice, and I know it won't be easy to hear, but that was why I wanted to meet with you all beforehand."

Mom thanked him for his time. She was stunned, too. It's fine, she said. It doesn't matter. Your father's at rest now and that's just the way it is.

"Justice never brought back the dead," she told him.

"This guy has done this three other times, though," you told the DA as though it might be news to him.

"I understand, but that's also not part of what I'm legally allowed to take into account. That would be a disciplinary measure inside the department itself."

Heat swelled in your chest, and you wanted to scream. This guy was going to go back out on the street.

At this point, he'd become a serial killer.

And dad was just the latest victim.

So that's why you're in a cemetery.

At first, it was just to visit his grave. Pay your respects. But you noticed the cop car roll through and stop. And your heart skipped a beat when you realized it was him sitting in the driver's side. Looking around like nothing was wrong.

Was he coming to pay his respects, too?

Or did he come to shit on him in death the way he shot him up in life.

Asking around, you a find that the cop spends most of his evenings there in the cemetery. Doesn't have anything to do with paying respects.

Has everything to do with him just finding an out of the way spot where there aren't any supervisors. He's as lazy as he is dangerous.

On one hand, it's probably better that he's not out there killing anyone else. On the other hand, he's just getting away with it all.

And then the gears start to turn.

And going vigilante doesn't sound too bad.

It's just that it has to be done carefully. Right?

You've got to be careful when you're thinking about this sort of thing. And once you start thinking about it, just like a murder on a bodycam, brutal and violent, blood everywhere, it starts to take over your brain.

Then all of a sudden, it's night, you're sitting in a cemetery talking to spirits, and you're thinking about all the ways you're going to make this son of a bitch pay.

Cemeteries are different at night than during the day. And it never feels more acute than when you're thinking about it because you're there. During the day, you feel a little safer. Like nothing can hurt you. Like there is no chance of someone rising from a grave or a ghost chasing you into an early one.

But at night, every creaking branch, every rustle of crisp fall leaves, every frigid autumn gust leaves you wondering if there's someone or something behind you.

Hands creep up your back and tap you on the shoulder. A voice whispers in your ear, too close so you can feel the hot breath, "Why are you here?"

But you don't answer. You can't. You'd just be talking to yourself.

There's no one in the cemetery save for you and a few thousand former people.

And him.

The one who keeps getting away with it.

Well, it's about time you got away with it, right?

The key, really, is to lure him away from the car somehow and get him from behind, right?

His car, just like him, has a camera in the front. Especially when it has the lights on. Both machines of mass destruction. Tools of violence and death.

For folks like you, nothing good ever came from an interaction with a cop or its car. And this one in particular had been given chance after chance to prove he could do better, and he refused. Four people were dead.

Two brutalized. Probably more out there harassed, profiled, or otherwise intimidated. It'd be doing everyone a favor.

You just need to avoid the cameras and lure him out. Easy, right?

It's the dead of night, so that's an easy advantage to take. There's a grave with smooth stones piled atop it. It feels wrong, but you know it's the sort of thing they would understand when you take half a dozen of them and load them into your pockets. This was how David took down Goliath, right?

The rocks would do well enough to start. The knife in your pocket seems like the most sensible way to deal with the rest, but it's not like you're even thinking that far ahead. All that's needed right now is to get him out and about. See how he could be snuck up on.

Thirty paces to the side of his car is a massive tree. Old. You don't know what kind, but it's the same sort that would make dad proud when he'd watch you climb up it as a kid. Like he knew and somehow put it there just for you. And if you could get up into the tree, maybe it would all work.

Circling slowly around the back of the police car, the tree is easy enough to climb. The perch is just above the normal eye-line, and if the cop is as shitty as his reputation suggests, he's not going to look up.

Maybe it's the perfect spot.

Or maybe he'll have an easy fifth victim.

Someone has to do something to prevent that, though. The problem is bad enough that it's worth trying to fix. And thinking of all the days you'll never have with your dad stokes the fires of rage inside your heart's stove.

This is the right thing.

The first rock hits the cop car with a loud ting. The noise itself is startling, you can't even imagine what it would have felt like to the cop. But after a moment, the spotlight on the side of his door brightens and moves around, looking for the source of the disturbance. Right now, in his head, it's probably just a fluke. Maybe a bird flew too low. Or a bat hit the windshield searching for a bug.

He has no idea what it really was.

How could he?

The spotlight scans around and, probably seeing nothing, shuts off again.

The next rock hits lower against the car this time. It hits the door itself rather than the window.

And that's enough to do it.

The door opens and he comes out of the car slowly. He's smaller than you expected. Too short to have killed so many. Somehow, his mustache makes up for it and tells the rest of the story. There's an inadequacy in his step that's confirmed when he draws his gun.

Who could blame him?

A cemetery was a lovely place for another murder. Not that throwing rocks at cop cars should have been grounds for execution.

"Legally justified."

Fuck them all.

With the law the way it is, anything can be grounds for execution if the cop just says they're frightened and threatened enough.

That phrase hangs in your head as the cop slowly walks closer to your position, gun still drawn.

"Come on out," he says. He seems to think that anyone would trust him not to shoot and would really come out, hands up.

So you throw another rock.

It lands way off to his side and when it hits a headstone, he snaps his attention in that direction, leading with the gun as though the rock should die, too.

But he's close to you.

His back is turned.

And he's *so* close.

He backs up slowly, maybe even as though he's putting his back to the trees. He doesn't know where the danger lurks. And he's ready to shoot anything if it suits him.

You've got to be careful with guys like that.

They're liable to shoot anybody.

Today a dad, tomorrow a kid.

The day after that, anyone else who looks at them wrong.

No, if the system wasn't going to offer justice and the other boys in blue were going cover for him and keep putting him on active duty after he murdered someone, it is a responsibility of the aggrieved to handle things.

Right?

You ask yourself that question over and over as the knife comes out of your pocket. It makes no sound as it's opened, turning on the hinge. It was your father's knife. Of course it was. It's the one he taught you how to camp with. How to whittle. How to start a fire.

Now he is going to teach you something altogether different with it.

It was one of the few possessions that felt important enough to keep after everything that happened.

Clicking the blade into place, a breath catches at the top of your chest and there's a nagging worry that he'll be able to hear the breathing.

"Show yourself!" he says again, allaying any concern. He has no idea what's going on or where he is.

And he's right there.

Just below you.

Dropping from the tree, the knife plunges down first as though the entirety of your body is aimed right for the tip of the blade.

As you come down, the blade's sharp tip pierces into the spot where his neck meets his shoulder, just inside his collar.

There's screaming.

It could be anyone's. Yours. His. The spectral cry of your father beyond the grave.

A gun goes off.

The cop's gun.

Then again.

Better make it quick. If you tarry too long, everyone happy to cover up for him will be there and they'll all be trigger happy, too. But they don't understand that their violence begets violence, right?

The knifes makes a jagged splooge of a sound as it comes out of his neck. A spray of blood shines red in the scant reflection of the headlights beyond.

He screams and tries to turn.

But you know if he turns, you're going to end up in view of his camera, and that's the last you need. If they know it's you, they'll think it's some type of revenge rather than justice.

So you take a step around him, hoping to stay his shadow, then stab at the back of his neck again. It's not less than he deserves, and you can't feel bad about it. Caught in the moment, adrenaline coursing through every corner of your body, you wonder if that is what's making you feel like a person not yourself. How could you be willing to do this? But then it dawns on you that there's nothing *wrong* with what you're doing.

An eye for an eye is what they always say, right?

Sure, it makes the world blind, but in the meantime, you need to take out the stick carving out all the other eyeballs in the world. You can prevent someone else's family from going through what yours did. And if the system won't hold him accountable, why shouldn't you?

It's the only thing that that makes sense.

Maybe there's a better way to fix the system, but it's broken now and the only tool you have in your hands is a knife. There aren't any other options.

Before he can turn again, the knife reaches out, almost as if it's possessed on its own, thirsty for his blood. It drags its tip across the front of his throat, separating the skin and revealing the muscle and bone beneath.

He gurgles and reaches up for the knife, but it's gone already.

It glistens high in the air over the back of his head and descends rapidly, a flash against the night.

The dulled tip finds purchase in the small of his neck, right where it meets his back, just above the line of his bulletproof vest.

The knife goes in with a satisfying crack.

The gun goes off again, and the killer struggles to catch his breath, but there's nothing catching it. His lines have been cut.

His body limps forward as the life goes out of him. You aren't sure how you know the ghost escapes his body, but he's no more. It's palpable.

An ascending chill.

You weren't expecting that.

You've never felt a human just cease to exist and something dies inside you as well. It shouldn't have been this easy, but you realize every time he'd taken a life it had been even easier. It's almost as though they just fainted, but there's a coldness there you didn't expect.

Blood spurts everywhere, spattering across you like a horror show.

As if in slow-motion, he falls face down into the grass, the camera on his shoulder aimed straight down at the hell he's been remanded to.

Standing there, breathing heavy—in and out, in and out—the realization comes crashing against you like a wave on rocks. You've done it.

There's no taking it back.

Looking down, there's blood on your hands.

In every sense of the word.

Focusing down to the ground, he lies there in a heap.

Suddenly a hundred questions enter your mind. The first being what to do with the body.

Then you wonder if you should just leave him there. To rot. Maybe the crows will get to him before the other cops do. Maybe that's just wishful thinking.

But leaving him feels like the sensible thing to do, right? They probably have some way to track his movement, even if he doesn't have his phone on him.

Just leave him for someone else to find. But then you wonder if there's any evidence you might leave behind unwittingly, anything that could tie them to the truth what just happened. Because if they could trace it back to you, it wouldn't be hard to figure out a motive.

The DA would press charges in forty seconds flat.

Justice moves swift against those who buck the system.

Looking at the knife, dripping rubies in the dark, you know you can't leave it, much as you might want to. Maybe you never want to use it again. It used to represent something so wholesome, such wonderful memories, and now every time you see it, it would hold nothing but horror.

As you stand there, weighing your options, wondering what to do next, wasting time, he bleeds more and more. The grass soaks up so much of it, like a tipped-over barrel of oil, *glug glug glugging* away until it was empty.

He never had a chance.

Perhaps he had more of a chance than those he attacked. Those he shot at. Those he executed.

At least he died for committing murder, though nothing about being the executioner feels good. All of the fire you thought might be quenched by taking your revenge has only intensified. There's nothing about what you did that will make you whole.

It's not going to bring your father back.

You keep telling yourself that even with the pain you've now taken on, at least it might prevent someone else from losing their father.

Or son.

Or loved one.

You blink and wonder how much time has passed. You're still standing there. Frozen. It could have been an hour or a minute. You just don't know.

Can't know.

Once you come to your senses, you know there's a laundry list of things to do. Especially since his blood isn't just on your hands. It's on your face and your clothes. Laundry in the literal sense. They don't waste time on that sort of thing in forensics. One look at you and they would know what you've done. So the questions are simple: how do you get home, dispose of the evidence, clean yourself up, and not get caught?

The first step is to take one.

Stepping forward, your shoe almost slips on the slick patch of grass that has soaked up all of the cop's dirty blood. Steadying yourself, you take another step.

And then another.

Soon you're off and running like a nervous racehorse after the drop of the gate, running for someone or something, somewhere. You live close enough by, you were just out for a stroll to clear your head.

With all that blood all over you?

"Would you believe I cut myself shaving?" you see yourself saying.

But you wouldn't even believe that. The blood is just *everywhere*.

You have to remind yourself that what you've done is a service. It's true what they say, all cops are bastards, but the one you just killed was—straight-up—an unrepentant murderer. He killed your father and three other people besides. You have to keep reminding yourself of that, because otherwise it won't go away: all the thoughts that you've done something wrong. All the concern that you're in danger.

But you're a wreck.

They'll catch you.

And for a moment you wonder if this is what he felt like the first time *he* killed someone. Did he share your doubts and fears? Did he feel like running? Did he feel like the blood would stain him for the rest of his life?

Not likely.

You know for a fact he didn't.

He sat around and waited to gloat to his buddies.

That's what the papers had said about the first one.

Legally justified my ass.

Maybe you were putting him out of his misery. There's no way he could have become numb to this existential dread unless he was truly a monster.

In either case, you were still doing someone—*everyone*—a favor.

But his killings were "legally justified." And yours wasn't. It was merely *morally* justified, which doesn't matter in a court of law or a system designed to protect guys like him.

At the edge of the cemetery, you come to realize that running doesn't matter. You'll do what you can to escape, but ultimately, you've done the right thing. And if you die for it, at least you'll die for something you believe in.

Looking over your shoulder, you can almost see him behind you. Like a shadow back there, creeping behind you and existing there forever. A haunted, angry phantom.

You have to get away.

It's the least you can do.

Just to spite the bullshit system.

No matter how large that shadow looms behind you, you'll just have to keep running.

You cling dearly to the fact that your outrage is justified and unless they're going to fix the system on their own, more and more like you will do it for them.

That's the least you can do, right? ♜

POCKET FULL OF POSEY

By Alethea Kontis

"ALL THOSE BITCHES NEED TO die."

"Now, now, Rosalyn. These were all the people who were cruel to you in high school?"

"The ten people the planet would be better off without, yes."

"You can't still feel that way. You haven't seen most of them in a decade."

"Google is an amazing tool, Dr. Ford."

The psychiatrist chuckled and set her legal pad on the tasteful mahogany and glass table beside her chair.

I probably bought that table, thought Rosalyn, and that chair.

Dr. Ford crossed her legs, leaned forward, and clasped her hands. Rosalyn braced herself for whatever stupid idea was about to slide off that silver tongue that insurance companies had shelled out so much for on her behalf over the last decade-plus. Silly as those ideas were, though, Rosalyn still took Dr. Ford's advice more often than not. All those mundane sociology experiments were multivitamins for her soul; Rosalyn swallowed them with a large grain of salt (and sometimes a lime chaser). They were her church on Sunday, her good deeds for the week/month/year, and once accomplished she was free to move about the rest of her life with a light heart. Light*er*. Less dark than normal.

Dr. Ford's smile showed off eighty-three percent of her professionally whitened teeth. "You need to go to this reunion."

"I need world peace too, but you don't see that happening."

"The first step to world peace is making peace with yourself."

Rosalyn sighed. It was always a losing battle, not that she played to win. "You want me to walk into the lion's den."

"I want to prove that there is no lion's den. There never was."

Every muscle from the top of Rosalyn's head to the tip of her toes went stiff. What kind of professional talk was that? How could she say that, knowing the Hell Rosalyn had walked through every day at Freedom High?

"I can't. Not alone."

"But you won't be alone..."

Rosalyn raised an eyebrow. She was trying to weasel out of the event, not ask for a date.

"...you have Posey," Dr. Ford finished.

Rosalyn couldn't help but smile at the name, and she pulled Posey out of her purse. Aunt Jo and Uncle Dickie had given her the darling gnome keychain on her fifteenth birthday. Gnomes had always made her smile, that in itself was such a rarity that her father landscaped a garden in which she could display her collection. Posey was one of the few female gnomes. She had a fat daisy on her little red hat, a golden monkey on her shoulder, and a red cap mushroom in her arms. The irony that this symbol of purity and cuteness was ready to poison her enemies at a moment's notice was what Rosalyn loved best.

For Dr. Ford, Posey embodied all the loved ones Rosalyn admired and never wanted to disappoint. Posey was a cute, dangerous, portable conscience that held the keys to Rosalyn's getaway car.

"I. Have. Posey," Rosalyn repeated dutifully.

"You'll be fine," said Dr. Ford.

"I'll be food for the wolves," said Rosalyn.

"There are wolves in the lion's den?"

Rosalyn nodded. "And they all have sharp teeth."

Dr Ford laughed again, from the belly, shoulders shaking; the genuineness of it startled Rosalyn and made her wonder briefly if her shrink was having a seizure.

"What's funny?"

"Oh, Rosalyn. You have what all of us wish we had at our high school reunions: you're beautiful, successful, and not a little bit famous. Anyone who didn't know your name then certainly knows it now."

True enough. If they couldn't afford any of the Rosey-O high-end-nano hair product line, then they'd seen her on the covers of magazines, or the guest appearance on *Whoopi*, or splashed across the rags at the grocery store checkout lines. The scandal had been viral, proving the WorldWideGrapevine could still propagate faster than any biotech.

The hair products had started out as many other things do—a laugh, a lark, payback on the science teacher her freshman year who suggested that ridiculous fair project on hair dye. Add some punk, Manic Panic, nanotech, a few too many Starbucks Vitamin Waters, and far too little sleep. It was inevitable for two genius roommates to come up with a nano-enhanced, programmable hair dye. It was also inevitable for Natasha—high on Water and the rush of completion—to try the test batch too soon. The nanites affixed themselves to every hair follicle on her skin, entering her body, her bloodstream, and then her brain far too quickly.

Natasha had lived long enough to sneeze and ask Rosalyn for a tissue.

Dr. Ford had taken on double duty as grief counselor, the 4.0 was followed immediately by an offer from an overly caffeinated venture capitalist, and the rest was history the lawyers made sure Rosalyn never had to talk about again.

"...must be *someone* you want to see after all these years," Dr. Ford was saying.

"Josie." The word popped out of Rosalyn's mouth without asking permission, which Rosalyn would have denied. After all those years, the two syllables still broke her heart.

"Ah," was Dr. Ford's professional reply. "So here's what I want you to do."

"Beyond walking through the doors?"

"Oh my, yes. I want you to go down this list and say hello to each person on it. You don't have to swap cookie recipes or cry on each other's shoulders; just a polite salutation. That's all."

Rosalyn took The Kill List back from Dr. Ford and gingerly folded it along the deep creases made with rage so long ago. She didn't have to look again at the rounded handwriting in a variety of colored inks; she knew every name by heart. Rosalyn wondered how many other shrinks were returning similar lists to emo kids of the aughties and suggesting they make amends. "You are a cruel woman, Dr. Ford."

"You wouldn't have me any other way."

# # #

Rosalyn slid her sapphire green Jaguar into the farthest parking space from the clubhouse. Her father, who'd spent large amounts of time in Afghanistan before the occupation ended, had taught her to always have an eye on her exit strategy. It was a hard habit to break, and so far, one Dr. Ford hadn't asked her to.

She took three deep breaths, slid on her strappy black Dakota Fanning heels, and adjusted her enormous Lady Gaga sunglasses. A decade ago she'd walked the halls at Freedom High in black lipstick, a fuchsia lace tutu, and rainbow knee socks. Now, she opted for low-key: a simple black dress and one of her least ostentatious necklaces. Ironically, it was a large lacquer cross on a raw silk burgundy choker.

If this did turn into a gang hit, she could at least use it as a weapon in a pinch.

She smoothed down her shoulder-length, straight, brown hair. It was only colored with an out-of-date version of the Rosie-O nanites that only made the ends black, as if they'd been dipped in ink. Thanks to Rosalyn, brown hair was now quite the rarity among humans within her own income bracket. She figured she was going to stick out like a sore thumb anyway; she certainly wasn't going to look like she was trying.

She beeped her car locked and kissed Posey for good luck before dropping her keys into her tiny Birkin clutch. She could do this. She could totally do this. And when it all went down in flames, she always had her exit strategy. Thanks, Daddy.

The first set of glass doors she tried to the clubhouse was locked, and she refused to call it a sign. She marched all the way to the front of the building intently, like she was walking a Paris catwalk.

There was Daisy Scofield, standing behind the welcome table, twenty months pregnant and beaming like sunshine. Anyone else would be high on Starbucks decaccinos, but Daisy Scofield had been beaming like that since she'd popped out of her own mother's womb. She gave Rosalyn a smile that would have knocked Dr. Ford over at twenty paces, and Rosalyn was glad she still had on her sunglasses.

"Rosie Posie Pudding Pie, kissed the girls and made—" Daisy slapped a hand over her traitorous mouth and a cloud went over the sun.

"A girl always wants to be remembered for her accomplishments," Rosalyn said as she scanned the HELLO, MY NAME IS stickers on the table between them. She let the glasses slide down her nose and gave Daisy a lusty wink. "I still make the girls cry."

Daisy giggled behind her hand and then gasped when she saw which sticker Rosalyn had slapped to her chest. "Silly Rosie. Now what do I do if Susan SanGiovanni decides to show up?"

"You didn't hear? Murdered, poor thing. Her husband snapped, killed her and her children in their sleep, and then hung himself. They said it was some sort of Call of Duty PTSD episode or something. I'm wearing the name tag in her honor."

Daisy's cornflower blue eyes brimmed with tears. "Oh my. I didn't know. Bless her heart. Yes, you should wear the name tag. She would have liked that. I'll say a prayer for her."

Rosalyn patted Daisy on the shoulder and continued down the main hall. She hoped Susan SanGiovanni did show up. There was a shortage of good stories in the world.

Rosalyn smirked at the screamingly happy sign some mad scrapbooker with access to Photoshop and too much glue—possibly Daisy—had assembled so that no one mistook what was behind Doors Number One and Two for anything other than the Best Reunion EVAR. Rosalyn wrapped strong fingers with perfectly manicured nails around the handle and pulled.

What was actually behind the doors was a nightmare.

Honestly, Rosalyn was pretty sure she had woken in a cold sweat from a scene just like this. Towers of fruit posed by chocolate fountains and lukewarm egg rolls smiled at her from their warming trays. A line started at the canditini bar and wrapped halfway around the room, and Christina Leffler serenaded the far-too-sober assembly with a stirring rendition of Taylor Swift's *Anti-Hero* like she was performing on New Year's Eve in Times Square.

Rosalyn glanced down to make sure she was still wearing clothes. Check. She was awake. This was for real, all right.

In a class of over five hundred students there were only about fifty people in the room; leave it to the student council members of 2014 to make their own reunion list exclusive. Nitwits.

They were all there, the entire Kill List from A to Z. All shiny and happily ignorant of how much Rosalyn's palms itched for a gun with ten equally shiny bullets.

Number 10: Scott Ziwicki. Scott always stayed in last place in every incarnation of The Kill List because Rosalyn liked the completeness of ending the list with Z. Scott had been one of the first names, though, as he originally coined the "Rosie Posie Pudding Pie" rhyme. The acclaimed lyricist had gone on to pen several horrible novels starring a female protagonist named Rosie Pye. He probably never would have been published had Rosalyn herself not gone on to such fame and infamy.

Number 9: Thuy Vu. Terminally petite Thuy had broken Rosalyn's pencil in the second grade, causing Rosalyn to retaliate and slap the wretched vandal. They were both ushered to the principal's office, one of the only times Rosalyn was ever called into the principal's office. It scarred her for life. After that, she made a point of never getting caught.

Number 8: Brendan Lee. Brendan had been caught multiple times cheating off Rosalyn's tests, but the teacher never moved him. He always wore a sneer every time Rosalyn was around, like he'd just smelled rotten eggs.

Number 7: Nick Smith. Nick's transgression was that he was totally obsessed with Rosalyn. The puppy dog love might have been flattering at one point, until the day he realized he was going nowhere with her and turned everything he knew about her into jabs and jokes.

Number 6: Mrudula Rue. The bitch touched her iPad. *Twice*. Nuff said.

Numbers 5 and 4: Mark and Amanda Owen. The siblings were close enough in age to be in the same grade. Mark was the class clown, which meant nothing that crossed his path was sacred. Amanda always had one ear attached to the phone, and there was usually a boy on the other end. If she wasn't talking to the boy, she was talking about the boy. And she had an unnatural addiction to corn dogs.

Number 3: Aimee Branson. Head cheerleader and Class Secretary. Far too beautiful to give anyone the time of day. She had only ever turned up her pert little nose at Rosalyn. Rosalyn still remembered how perfectly balanced her nostrils were, even when flared.

Number 2: Christina Leffler. Christina always had to be center stage, always had to have the spotlight. She'd gone so far as to record Rosalyn during her audition for the High School play and post it on YouTube. Rosalyn became a laughingstock and Christina got the solo. Christina always got the solos.

Number 1: Arielle Bublé. Back in elementary school, Arielle had been one of her very bestest friends. She and Rosalyn and Josie Camire had been the Three Musketeers. They shared everything from cupcakes to gum. They finished each other's sentences. They knew each other's passwords. They were inseparable. And then one day, out of the blue, Arielle walked up to Josie and Rosalyn and announced that she couldn't be friends with them anymore, because she was going to be friends with Aimee and Christina and Thuy.

Rosalyn was only slightly less devastated that day than she was a week later, when Arielle read Rosalyn's diary out loud in front of the whole cafeteria. The teacher caught her and made her stop, but not before everyone had heard the dramatic scene about Josie and Rosalyn kissing in the closet. Arielle had been in that closet too, but as the reader, had conveniently edited herself out of the scene.

And there she was, on the other side of the dance floor, perfect as a princess in a pink chiffon dress with matching streaks like ribbons in her long champagne blonde hair. She chatted prettily with Thuy and someone on the wait staff. Mark pressed an orange sticky note to the waitress's back. Amanda stood behind him, eating all the crescent rolls. Nick sidled up to the buffet table with her and sexually harassed the ice sculpture.

Rosalyn's heel hit the cheap linoleum of the dance floor and she froze. Her stomach cramped. She wasn't ready. She couldn't do it. Not yet.

Luckily, she didn't have to. A petite ball of squee came barreling toward her, an afro of rainbow curls flashing like a bad acid trip. Rosalyn noted that Aimee Branson had splurged for the glitter upgrade to her hair pyrotechnics. Or her husband had, Rosalyn noted, as the rock on Aimee's left hand dug into Rosalyn's back.

"Oh-em-gee, I was driving myself crazy hoping that you'd come. And I am so glad you did! You have totally made my year! I love you!"

Aimee squeezed tighter—her perky implants were as rock hard as her wedding ring.

"Look!" Aimee affected an even higher pitch as she showed the diamond off and answered Rosalyn's unasked question. "It's Aimee Lee now. Brendan and I got married!"

"Confused" would have been an understatement. Rosalyn and Aimee had not been BFFs. And Brendan? Really? Three and eight on The Kill List now together in wedded bliss. Vomit- worthy, to be sure.

Rosalyn glanced over Aimee's shoulder and through her neon stripper curls to see Brendan, the ruby pinstripe of his suit mirrored in his dark hair and goatee. *Chameleon expansion pack. Nice.* And not a sneer to be found. He was checking out Rosalyn's ass instead. She barely recognized him without his nose crinkled in disgust.

Rosalyn felt lightheaded and looked around for video cameras. Of course, had there been any, Christina would have either been in front of them, or directly behind them. Since she was moving from her last song right into Miley Cyrus's "Flowers," Rosalyn figured she was safe from any sort of spotlight.

Aimee seemed to be waiting for Rosalyn to say something, so she said, "Congratulations!" and hugged them both. She then crossed her arms in front of her, pinching the inside of one elbow to make sure she was still part of reality.

Aimee launched into how many children she had, and what she was doing now. Something with curtains. Between Christina's crooning and the roaring in her ears, Rosalyn couldn't be sure.

Aimee's frequency was like a homing device, and eventually it brought the entire Kill List to the fore. Rosalyn didn't even have to seek them out; they all came to her. Another surprisingly unexpected development.

They each hugged her warmly and started up conversations like there had never been ten years and a moat of hatred between them. They also crowded around her in a complete circle, claiming her as theirs and shielding her from the rest of the room. Rosalyn peeked between them and caught a glimpse or two of someone she might recognize, but every time she did, one of them moved into her line of sight and asked a silly question.

"Did you fly here from somewhere exotic?" asked Thuy. The nanites in her hair cascaded blue Vietnamese characters down the silken ebony length. Rosalyn secretly hoped they said, "Touch my hair and die, asshole."

"Yeah," Rosalyn answered. "Great Falls." Granted, she only kept her condo there for her visits with Dr. Ford.

"What was Whoopi like?" asked Mark. His pink hair matched his shoelaces. Rosalyn wondered if Mark had ever come out of the closet.

"Really funny, actually. My stomach hurt for days afterward from laughing so much."

"What exciting adventures are you off to next? Exploring any new inventions? How's your love life?" Scott was as full of questions as he was of fecal matter. His hair was a dynamic mix of traditional blonde, brown, red, and gray that succeeded in being annoyingly eye-catching.

Rosalyn coyly answered frustration with frustration. "I shouldn't bore you with details."

"That's really a shame about Susan," Amanda said between mouthfuls of crescent roll.

Rosalyn patted her name tag sticker. "I was really broken up about it."

"Did you like my song?" asked Christina.

"You always were a nightingale," lied Rosalyn.

"How come you're not sporting any of the newest Rosie-O product?" asked Mrudula. Her hair slowly faded from blue to red, with her change in mood. "Don't you get all you want? Or was that not a perk of selling the formula?"

The truth wasn't something they wanted to hear. It never had been.

"I much prefer seeing it on other people," said Rosalyn. "All of you wear it so well."

And they did, too. Each one of them, male and female alike, had one or more glitzy, ridiculously expensive, Rosie-O expansion packs. They all bragged about how many they had, as if competing for her affection, and the inventive ways they'd used them on everything from pets to naughty bits.

Rosalyn drank the one or two neon canditinis that were handed to her. She didn't say much, just let them carry on selfishly about their shallow little lives. She laughed, but not with them.

Finally, Arielle put a thin, alabaster arm around Rosalyn. "Oh, how I've missed us," she said to the group.

"Me too," said Rosalyn, meaning something completely different.

As always, Dr. Ford had been right. There was no lion's den, and there were no wolves. There were only fish—large, silly, cheap carnival goldfish. They were born, grew up, married each other, had kids, and never left the pond of Northern Virginia. It may as well have been small town Kentucky for all that gene pool multiplied.

Only people who stepped outside the fishbowl realized how small it was. These popular people weren't fat and bald, like the clichés had her hope for; they were all still just as beautiful as Rosalyn remembered. But they were also sad. This tiny little goldfish bowl was all they would ever know, and all they cared to know. Dead or alive, it didn't really matter in the long run. This small, small world was the fate to which they were doomed.

Rosalyn pitied them. And three seconds after that, she wanted to escape from their suffocating embrace. She knew if she cried "potty," the girls would all come with her; such was the way of the herd. So she faked a vibrating phone and excused herself out to the hallway to return her very important imaginary call. She scooted past Daisy, who had taken a break from her table and was peeking through the doorway at the festivities.

"They haven't changed a bit," Rosalyn assured her.

"Most people never do," Daisy said with a sigh.

Rosalyn wasn't technically lying—she actually had missed a few texts from Kelli Keene, her new bestest-bestest. Kelli made sure, in very few words and no uncertain terms, that Rosalyn knew exactly what she was missing by not hurrying up to join her in the Cayman Islands. Kelli also sent two pictures: one of a strawberry daiquiri with a ridiculous amount of fruit, and one of her getting frisky with a cabana boy.

Rosalyn wasn't jealous. Much. She'd done what she'd needed to do, and she'd be on her way soon enough. She better be. The next message would be a video, featuring more Kelli and fewer clothes. That was typically her M.O.

She made a quick pit stop in the bathroom, closing the door on the outside world and reveling in the quiet. She had a longstanding tradition of hiding in bathrooms: one of the habits that Dr. Ford had made her stop. Rosalyn figured she'd be forgiven just this once. Conquering the Kill List was a big step.

She walked to the sinks, placing her palms down against the cool counter. She looked in the mirror, tore off her stupidly huge sunglasses, and looked again.

She was not one of them. She never had been. Making money and being famous didn't make her one of them. Their pretending that she was and making a big show didn't make her one of them either. Once upon a time, that's all it would have taken, and maybe, in their little fishbowl world, that's still all it took. But not in hers. Rosalyn would walk away from this building and never look back.

She turned the faucet in front of her on full blast and thrust the ends of her hair beneath the water, washing every bit of the nanite blackness down the drain until there was nothing left but brown. Brown old Rosalyn. Pure Rosalyn and nothing else.

She spun around in the mirror and looked over her shoulder, making sure it was all gone, making sure that there wasn't a sign on her back left by Mark. Or a knife left by Arielle. She took a Burt's Bees Shimmer from her purse and applied it with a shaky hand.

"If you've got a stash of that stuff, it's more precious than gold," a voice said from behind her. "I can't find Shimmers anywhere anymore."

Rosalyn adjusted her eyes to focus on Josie. There in the mirror they were together, just like they'd never been apart. Her soft eyes were still green as olive branches, complementing the ice green frosting on the layered ends of her hair that curved around her heart-shaped face. Her Cupid's bow lips curved up into a smile. She was a vision come to life; ten times more beautiful than Rosalyn had ever dreamed.

"Take it." Rosalyn turned and offered Josie the slender yellow tube of Shimmer. Josie did not disappear; she was right there in flesh and blood. But everything was different now. They had both moved on. That close friendship, that bond between them, had only lasted as long as it took for the teal Sharpie in her yearbook to dry. Even standing here in 3-D, Josie was still a memory, a picture in a wallet, a tag on a FaceSpace album.

"Thank you," said Josie, who also seemed to be at a loss for words. The lines of communication went both ways; it hadn't been only her fault that the two of them had grown apart.

Rosalyn wasn't here to build bridges or heal old wounds. She and Josie just hadn't been meant to be. And that was that. Life went on.

Rosalyn cupped Josie's face in her hand and kissed her on the cheek. "You look good," she whispered. Despite the cupid's-bow smile, a fat tear escaped and slid between Rosalyn's fingers. Without another word, Rosalyn left the bathroom slightly proud of herself.

She still had it.

"Leaving so soon?" asked Daisy as Rosalyn passed by her table again.

"I have to meet someone," explained Rosalyn. "I could really only stop in for a minute."

Daisy held up a hand. "No explanation necessary. I'm just glad you came at all. It's really nice to see you, Rosalyn."

Why hadn't she and Daisy been closer? Rosalyn tried to think back, but memory escaped her. Not that it mattered. What mattered to Rosalyn was the here and now. Daisy's optimism, remarkable enough back then, was in this decade rarer and more precious than crude oil.

Rosalyn reached into her bag. "A picture for old time's sake?"

Daisy smiled and snuggled into the crook of Rosalyn's arm as she deftly flipped the camera around to take a selfie. The flash was only slightly brighter than Daisy's smile.

"Gosh, Rosalyn. That flash… I think I'm blind."

"One more time," said Rosalyn. "I think I blinked."

That's right. One more time with the hidden EM pulse for good measure, just to make sure every nanite left on Rosalyn's and Daisy's bodies was rendered completely inert. The Rosie-O product she'd worn in had been old, one of the very first incarnations, from a stash she'd secreted away for a time such as this.

Rosalyn called it Version 4.0.

She air-kissed Daisy and wished her luck with her baby—or however many babies were brewing in that enormous belly. She dropped the "camera" back into her purse and rummaged for her keys, finding them before she reached the exit doors. She popped the red cap of Posey's mushroom up with her thumbnail. She slid the pad of her finger over the tiny button there…and froze.

Josie.

Gods, she'd touched Josie in the bathroom. She'd washed the 4.0 nanites out of her hair by then, but there was no way to be sure Josie didn't get any on her. In fact, she was 100% sure that she couldn't be sure. That was the whole point of having the EM camera. But it was too late to turn back to find her. It had been too late for about a decade now.

Rosalyn pushed the button.

She stood at the doors, staring outward, just long enough to hear a sneeze.

Rosalyn calmly strode the length of the parking lot to her getaway vehicle. In twenty minutes she'd be on a private jet to the Caymans, unburdened and free, and this shiny little fishbowl would be nothing but a headlight in the rearview mirror, another anonymous star in the sky.

She'd miss Dr. Ford. ♜

ANOTHER DAY

By Liz Holliday

I DON'T THINK BILL KNOWS there's anything wrong. This morning he got up and went to the bathroom. As usual, he was startled when he looked in the mirror and saw the blood and bruises covering his face. He probed for tender spots, picked at the scabs, and winced when he made himself bleed. After that he tore off a bit of toilet paper and made the whole mess worse when he tried to clean himself up.

Then he shambled into the front room and slumped in front of the box for a while. Please, I willed him, do something else. Anything else. But he slumped into the armchair just as he always does.

The drink came later, but not much later.

In a while, when he's drunk himself into a stupor and then almost come back out of it, I find myself in the hall, shivering with fear and the cold that comes of tiredness. The place stinks of cider and cigarettes and blood.

Motes of dust dance in the honey-colored light that slants in through the hall window. I've had time, so much time, to notice everything. It was realizing that the patterns of falling dust are not always the same that first gave me hope.

I glance at the bedroom door. It's only a few steps away. I try to go that way, but I cannot make myself move, and then the sound of the television in the front room snags my attention. Horse racing.

"... there's Diamond Girl and she's going away down the home straight, she's two lengths clear, but Ice Dancer's making a late break. She's coming up on the inside but it's too little too late and it's Diamond. Diamond Girl wins by a short head..."

As always, I hesitate, wondering if he backed either, if he won, if he lost, what it will do to his mood.

And then his voice. "Is that you, Cath? Get in here."

And I want to go to the other door, the bedroom door, to get my things and go. Or just to run, like I did last night, after what happened... happened. But my purse is in there, with what little money I have. I can't spend another night on the street.

I want to go into the bedroom. I try again to force myself to do it, but I can't.

But I can't stay in the hall, either. There are certain things I just have to do.

So I go into the front room. A step, two steps, ready to run. But I won't be fast enough. I'm never fast enough.

He lumbers up out of his chair. I'm mesmerized by what I know is going to happen, just as I was mesmerized the first time by fear.

He comes towards me. If I could move... If I could move, even now it might be different.

And then he stops. I catch my breath.

"Cath?" he says. He sounds bewildered. He's never spoken to me before in this way, at this time. Not since this began. Not for a long time before that. For a second, I can see the boy I used to love trapped inside the damaged man in front of me, and that old love fills me up like light.

"Bill," I whisper.

I go to him, and he smiles—that smile!—and I forget to be afraid. "You're hurt," I say, and touch the sore place on his face lightly with my fingertips.

"I don't know—" His breath stinks of cider. I don't care.

"Here—let me." I pull an old tissue out of my cardigan pocket and spit on it, then dab gently at the bloody scabs.

"You came back," he says, and I feel the moment start to slip away.

"I was in the bedroom." It isn't a lie, really. I was everywhere. Nowhere. Waiting.

His eyes go hard and cold, like chips of ice. "You went..." He pauses, as if he's searching for something. "Last night, you went out."

"No no," I say, rushing the words, trying to hold on to what can't be held.

"You were going to go out," he amends.

"That's right," I say, looking down, not meeting his cold eyes because that always got him going. "But I didn't—" Not then, I didn't. Not till afterwards.

"Only because I stopped you," he says, and pushes me away. I stumble back. Now we're in our proper positions again. Something inside me eases. "Found out about your little date, didn't I?"

"I wasn't— there wasn't any date," I say. It's the truth. No date, no fancy man, just me going to my cleaning job.

"Don't lie to me, you bitch!" he shouts. His hand goes to his face, and this time I can see him remembering.

I want to run. I have to run. But I can't move and he's undoing his belt with one hand and now I can move but it's too late. I turn. He grabs my arm and pulls me round. My head slams against the doorframe.

"You like that, bitch? You like how it feels? You see what you did to me?"

I do see. And I remember the weight of the cider bottle in my hand, how its own momentum pulled it down as I hit him once and then again. It shattered the second time. Cider sprayed everywhere—golden, with that sickly sweet-sour smell that has never faded. I remember the bright blood on the brown glass. How it stained the paper label. I'm glad I don't have to do that again, the argument, the fight, the way I dodged at the last moment, and he fell, so that I got my chance to hit him.

That moment of terror and the visceral, murderous joy that bubbled up underneath it when I thought I'd killed him. Then the bitter sense of relief when I realized I hadn't. Not because I was glad he was alive, but because if I'd been charged with his murder, it would have given him a final victory.

All of that is behind me.

But he has his belt off now, the strap end wound around his hand. Light glints on the buckle as it flies through the air. I duck down and round and take the blow on my shoulder. The metal bites through my cardigan and the thin dress underneath. I feel my head snap back and my lips peel away from my teeth as the scream pours out of me, though I'm used to this pain. I know he'll hit me again and again and again, harder each time.

Someone come, I think. Someone stop him. But I know no one will come, and no one does.

He's holding my arm tight, but I wrench myself round. I see the belt coming down, the buckle. His hand's slick with sweat. I jerk free.

Even as I'm running towards the kitchen, I remember all those other times he beat me— how he would be sorry afterwards and beg me not to tell anyone. How he would explain that it wasn't his fault, that I just wound him up, and he couldn't bear to think of me with other men, and if I would just stop, if I didn't have such a mouth on me... if, if, if, then it would all be all right.

And I wonder what will happen if I stop. Just stop. Will he do that? Will we end up curled together in bed, with him swearing it will never happen again and me apologizing for making him hurt me?

But I don't stop. I can't. I'm too scared, or perhaps the pattern is too strong.

I hear him shouting, but his words are so much gabble. It has taken me a long time to work out that he's calling me sweetheart, asking me to come back. Telling me to come back.

I don't. I'm in the kitchen now, wrenching the drawer open. The knife's there, almost as if it's waiting for me. It's a good weight, that knife, solid steel and wood, a wedding present from my mother.

I don't suppose anyone ever told her it's unlucky to give knives as presents.

I hear him come in. "Come on, sweetheart," he says. "You know I didn't mean it. Have a drink with me—let me make it better."

"I should never have come back," I say, and know it for ultimate truth.

"You know we belong together—that's why," he says.

"No," I answer. The word clots like vomit in my throat. That I might belong with him is the most horrific idea I've ever heard. But if I don't, why am I here? Why am I always here? "Don't touch me. Don't come near me."

I wave the knife vaguely in the air. Light glints wickedly on the blade. I'm terrified of it, and he knows it. But I'm not as scared of it as I am of him, and he doesn't know that.

"Come on, sweetheart," he says. "Get a grip. Have a drink and then you can clean yourself up."

Get a grip, I think. Yes, this time maybe I will get a grip.

He comes over, smiling, smug. He knows I haven't got it in me to use the damn knife. But when he reaches for it, I wave it again. I try to do what I've never been able to do before and put some force behind the blow. But it's still just an accident, as always. A line of blood appears on his arm. It's not deep. I'm sure it's not deep. But he squeals.

I stare at him, at the knife, at the blood, appalled. He rounds on me. He doesn't need the belt this time. He just slams his fist into the side of my head. For a moment I don't feel the pain. Then I stumble. He hits me again, and I crash to the ground.

The knife falls from my fingers and skitters across the floor.

This is it, my last chance to change things. I crawl towards it, but I'm slow. It seems that the harder I try, the harder moving becomes. He's on his feet, and though he's nursing his wounded arm he's faster than I am.

But I'm there. I'm *there*.

My hand closes over the knife.

His booted foot comes down on my fingers. I scream. This pain is new and so I welcome it.

"Want this, bitch?" he says as he scoops up the knife.

I can't speak. I know what's coming now. Pee dribbles down my legs.

I feel the cold touch of the blade as it goes in. For a moment it doesn't hurt at all. Then it bites as he drives it home and pulls it out and drives it home again.

I'm dying. I've been dying since the moment I found myself in the hallway. I wish I could have taken the other door.

As everything seeps away from me, I think that maybe I was wrong. Maybe I'll never be able to take the other door.

But maybe next time, or the time after that, I'll be able to pick up the knife.

END

I think Bill knows there's something wrong. This morning he got up and went to the bathroom as usual, but when he looked in the mirror and saw the blood and bruises, he didn't seem surprised. Usually he touches his face, probes for tender places, picks at the scabs, winces when he makes himself bleed— all before tearing off a bit of toilet paper and making the whole mess worse when he tries to clean himself up. Then he shambles into the front room and slumps in front of the box for a while.

The drink comes later, but not much later.

This morning, though... this morning he just looked in the mirror and gave an odd, half-hearted shrug. He pulled a piece of paper off the toilet roll, then let it fall into the sink. I think I heard him swear before he wandered into the front room. Please, I willed him, do something else. Anything else. But he slumped into the armchair, as usual.

Later, when he's drunk himself into a stupor and then almost come back out of it, I find myself in the hall, shivering with fear and the cold that comes of tiredness. The place stinks of cider and cigarettes and blood.

Motes of dust dance in the honey-colored light that slant in through the hall window. I've had time, so much time, to notice everything. It was realizing that the patterns of falling dust are not always the same that first gave me hope.

I glance at the bedroom door. It's only a few steps away. I try to go that way, but I cannot make myself move, and then the sound of the television in the front room snags my attention. Horse racing.

"... there's Diamond Girl and she's going away down the home straight, she's two lengths clear, but Ice Dancer's making a late break. She's coming up on the inside but it's too little too late and it's Diamond. Diamond Girl wins by a short head..."

As always, I hesitate, wondering if he backed either, if he won, if he lost, what it will do to his mood.

And then his voice. "Is that you, Cath? Get in here."

And I want to go to the other door, the bedroom door, to get my things and go. Or just to run, like I did last night, after what happened... happened. But my purse is in there, with what little money I have. I can't spend another night on the street.

I want to go into the bedroom. I try again to force myself to do it, but I can't.

But I can't stay in the hall, either. There are certain things I just have to do.

So I go into the front room. A step, two steps, ready to run. But I won't be fast enough. I'm never fast enough.

He lumbers up out of his chair. I'm mesmerized by what I know is going to happen, just as I was mesmerized the first time by fear.

He comes towards me. If I could move... If I could move, even now it might be different.

And then he stops. I catch my breath.

"Cath?" he says. He sounds bewildered. He's never spoken to me before in this way, at this time. Not since this began. Not for a long time before that. For a second, I can see the boy I used to love trapped inside the damaged man in front of me, and that old love fills me up like light.

"Bill," I whisper.

I go to him, and he smiles— that smile!— and I forget to be afraid. "You're hurt," I say, and touch the sore place on his face lightly with my fingertips.

"I don't know—" His breath stinks of cider. I don't care.

"Here—let me." I pull an old tissue out of my cardigan pocket and spit on it, then dab gently at the bloody scabs.

"You came back," he says, and I feel the moment start to slip away.

"I was in the bedroom." It isn't a lie, really. I was everywhere. Nowhere. Waiting.

His eyes go hard and cold, like chips of ice. "You went..." He pauses, as if he's searching for something. "Last night, you went out."

"No no," I say, rushing the words, trying to hold on to what can't be held.

"You were going to go out," he amends.

"That's right," I say, looking down, not meeting his cold eyes because that always got him going. "But I didn't—" Not then, I didn't. Not till afterwards.

"Only because I stopped you," he says, and pushes me away. I stumble back. Now we're in our proper positions again. Something inside me eases. "Found out about your little date, didn't I?"

"I wasn't—there wasn't any date," I say. It's the truth. No date, no fancy man, just me going to my cleaning job.

"Don't lie to me, you bitch!" he shouts. His hand goes to his face, and this time I can see him remembering.

I want to run. I have to run. But I can't move and he's undoing his belt with one hand and now I can move but it's too late. I turn. He grabs my arm and pulls me round. My head slams against the doorframe.

"You like that, bitch? You like how it feels? You see what you did to me?"

I do see. And I remember the weight of the cider bottle in my hand, how its own momentum pulled it down as I hit him once and then again. It shattered the second time. Cider sprayed everywhere—golden, with that sickly sweet-sour smell that has never faded. I remember the bright blood on the brown glass. How it stained the paper label. I'm glad I don't have to do that again, the argument, the fight, the way I dodged at the last moment and he fell, so that I got my chance to hit him.

That moment of terror and the visceral, murderous joy that bubbled up underneath it when I thought I'd killed him. Then the bitter sense of relief when I realized I hadn't. Not because I was glad he was alive, but because if I'd been charged with his murder it would have given him a final victory.

All of that is behind me.

But he has his belt off now, the strap end wound around his hand. Light glints on the buckle as it flies through the air. I duck down and round and take the blow on my shoulder. The metal bites through my cardigan and the thin dress underneath. I feel my head snap back and my lips peel away from my teeth as the scream pours out of me, though I'm used to this pain. I know he'll hit me again and again and again, harder each time.

Someone come, I think. Someone stop him. But I know no one will come, and no one does.

He's holding my arm tight, but I wrench myself round. I see the belt coming down, the buckle. His hand's slick with sweat. I jerk free.

Even as I'm running towards the kitchen, I remember all those other times he beat me—how he would be sorry afterwards and beg me not to tell anyone. How he would explain that it wasn't his fault, that I just wound him up, and he couldn't bear to think of me with other men, and if I would just stop, if I didn't have such a mouth on me... if, if, if, then it would all be all right.

And I wonder what will happen if I stop. Just stop. Will he do that? Will we end up curled together in bed, with him swearing it will never happen again and me apologizing for making him hurt me?

But I don't stop. I can't. I'm too scared, or perhaps the pattern is too strong.

I hear him shouting, but his words are so much gabble. It has taken me a long time to work out that he's calling me sweetheart, asking me to come back. Telling me to come back.

I don't. I'm in the kitchen now, wrenching the drawer open. The knife's there, almost as if it's waiting for me. It's a good weight, that knife, solid steel and wood, a wedding present from my mother.

I don't suppose anyone ever told her it's unlucky to give knives as presents.

I hear him come in. "Come on, sweetheart," he says. "You know I didn't mean it. Have a drink with me—let me make it better."

"I should never have come back," I say, and know it for ultimate truth.

"You know we belong together—that's why," he says.

"No," I answer. The word clots like vomit in my throat. That I might belong with him is the most horrific idea I've ever heard. But if I don't, why am I here? Why am I always here? "Don't touch me. Don't come near me."

I wave the knife vaguely in the air. Light glints wickedly on the blade. I'm terrified of it, and he knows it. But I'm not as scared of it as I am of him, and he doesn't know that.

"Come on, sweetheart," he says. "Get a grip. Have a drink and then you can clean yourself up."

Get a grip, I think. Yes, this time maybe I will get a grip.

He comes over, smiling, smug. He knows I haven't got it in me to use the damn knife. But when he reaches for it, I wave it again. I try to do what I've never been able to do before and put some force behind the blow. But it's still just an accident, as always. A line of blood appears on his arm. It's not deep. I'm sure it's not deep. But he squeals.

I stare at him, at the knife, at the blood, appalled. He rounds on me. He doesn't need the belt this time. He just slams his fist into the side of my head.

For a moment I don't feel the pain. Then I stumble. He hits me again, and I crash to the ground.

The knife falls from my fingers and skitters across the floor.

This is it, my last chance to change things. I crawl towards it, but I'm slow. It seems that the harder I try, the harder moving becomes. He's on his feet, and though he's nursing his wounded arm he's faster than I am.

But I'm there. I'm *there*.

My hand closes over the knife.

His booted foot comes down on my fingers. I scream. This pain is new and so I welcome it.

"Want this, bitch?" he says as he scoops up the knife.

I can't speak. I know what's coming now. Pee dribbles down my legs.

I feel the cold touch of the blade as it goes in. For a moment it doesn't hurt at all. Then it bites as he drives it home and pulls it out and drives it home again.

I'm dying. I've been dying since the moment I found myself in the hallway. I wish I could have taken the other door.

As everything seeps away from me, I think that maybe I was wrong. Maybe I'll never be able to take the other door.

But maybe next time, or the time after that, I'll be able to pick up the knife.

END

Bill knows there's something wrong. This morning he got up and went to the bathroom as usual, but when he looked in the mirror and saw the blood and bruises, he wasn't surprised. He just pulled a face and shambled off.

I think I heard him mutter my name as he wandered into the front room. Please, I willed him, do something else. Anything else. But he slumped into the armchair, as usual.

The drink came later, but not much later.

In a while, when he'd drunk himself into a stupor and then almost come back out of it, I find myself in the hall, shivering with fear and the cold that comes of tiredness. The place stinks of cider and cigarettes and blood.

Motes of dust dance in the honey-colored light that slant in through the hall window. I've had time, so much time, to notice everything. It was realizing that the patterns of falling dust are not always the same that first gave me hope... ♜

Jeremiah Dylan Cook is a writer who wants to give you nightmares that delight and excite. In addition to Castle Bridge Media, his work has been published by The NoSleep Podcast, Tales to Terrify, Ghost Orchid Press, Scary Dairy Press, Cabbit Crossing Publishing, Timber Ghost Press, The Lovecraft eZine, Hippocampus Press, and others. He's won two writing contests and received the Mario Mezzacappa Memorial Award for Outstanding Achievement in Poetry and Prose while pursuing his bachelor's degree at St. John's University. Jeremiah completed his Master of Fine Arts in Writing Popular Fiction at Seton Hill University and is a member of the Horror Writers Association. You can learn more about his diabolical deeds and eldritch emanations at JeremiahDylanCook.com.

Katya de Becerra is a horror writer from Melbourne. Born in Russia, Katya studied in California, lived in Peru, and then stayed in Australia long enough to become a local. She was going to be an Egyptologist when she grew up, but instead she earned a PhD in Anthropology. Katya's third novel, *When Ghosts Call Us Home,* was nominated for Aurealis and Shadows Awards, received two starred reviews, and was included in several Best of 2023 lists, Kirkus calling it "haunting, intense, and eerily spooky". Katya's other books are YA horror-thrillers *What The Woods Keep* and *Oasis.* Katya regularly publishes short fiction in anthologies and literary magazines. She is also co-editor of the anthology *This Fresh Hell,* which reimagines and subverts horror tropes in new and unexpected ways. Katya is a short version of her real name, which is very long and gets mispronounced a lot. Her fourth novel, *They Watch From Below,* is forthcoming in 2024.

Dotti Enderle is the author of more than 60 books for kids and adults. Her middle-grade horror novel *Wanna Play a Game?* will be out in summer 2024.

Carmen Gray is a Native Texan of Mexican-American heritage. She is a Dual Language teacher in Austin, Texas. Her work has appeared 3 times in different volumes of *Road Kill: Texas Horror by Texas Writers*. She also authored 4 short stories published by Castle Bridge Media and her poetry can be found in a variety of anthologies. She is a freelance writer and editor for Latino and Mueller magazines.

Leanna Renee Hieber is an actress, playwright, ghost tour guide and an award-winning author of Gaslamp Fantasy novels such as the *Spectral City* and *Strangely Beautiful* series. *A Haunted History of Invisible Women: True Stories of America's Ghosts*, non-fiction co-authored with Andrea Janes, explores women's history through ghost stories and was a Bram Stoker Award finalist for Superior Achievement in Non-fiction. She writes and narrates audiobooks of speculative fiction for Everand.com. Her *Strangely Beautiful* saga garnered three Prism Awards and she was a Daphne du Maurier Award finalist for *Darker Still*. Her short works have been featured in numerous notable anthologies, her essays have been featured in magazines like Apex, Psychopomp and The Deadlands and her books have been translated into many languages. Featured in film and television on shows like *Mysteries at the Museum* and *Beyond the Unknown*, discussing Victorian Spiritualism, she is a guide for NYC's Boroughs of the Dead and lectures nationwide on Gothic themes, 19th Century women's history, Spiritualism and the Paranormal. More at leannareneehieber.com.

Liz Holliday has written short stories (her story "And She Laughed…" was shortlisted for the Crime Writers' Association short story award and adapted for the TV show *The Hunger)*, 10 TV novelizations and around 30 books for kids, but she isn't sure she can call herself a writer as she doesn't have a cat. She currently freelances as a question editor for a mobile trivia games company, where her boss says she ought to have 'Professional Pedant' on her business cards. Liz lives in London (England, not Canada) and you can meet her at facebook.com/liz.holliday.39/

Born under the sun sign of Leo, **Serena Jayne** is naturally a cat person. Her short fiction has appeared in *The Arcanist, Daily Science Fiction, Gamut Magazine, Unnerving Magazine, Vastarien: A Literary Journal*, and other publications. Her short story collection, *Necessary Evils*, was published by Unnerving Books. She tweets @SJ_Writer and Instagrams @ jayneserenawriter. serenajayne.com.

Alethea Kontis is a storm chaser, world traveler, and New York Times bestselling author. She has received the Scribe Award, the Garden State Teen Book Award, and is a two-time winner of the Gelett Burgess Children's Book Award. She was twice nominated for both the Andre Norton Nebula and Dragon Award. Alethea also narrates stories for multiple award-winning online magazines, contributes book reviews to NPR, and does freelance work for *Writing the Other.* Born in Vermont, Alethea currently resides on the Space Coast of Florida where she watches K-dramas with her teddy bear, Charlie. Together they are ARMY, VVS, and Black Roses.

Claire Low, also known as Claire Engkaninan Low, is an Australian writer and artist. Her short story 'After I Found Her' was published in 2023 by Clan Destine Press in horror trope-twisting anthology *This Fresh Hell*. A former newspaper journalist and magazine editor, Low is twice shortlisted and highly commended for the Marjorie Graber-McInnis Short Story Prize. As an artist, Low is a six-time prize finalist and one-time award winner (the Reused/Recycled Materials Award, Reimagine 2023). A firm believer in ghosts, she collects gothic dolls, celebrates Halloween all year, and used to force her colleagues to take part in a creepy gift exchange.

Sara Martinez is an author, RPG writer and game designer when she's not chasing her two kids around. She loves to read, write and play games across a variety of genres. Published credits include the short story "Old Wives Tales" in *From the Yonder Vol. IV* from War Monkey Publications and the *Hell on the High Plains* supplement book for Deadlands by Pinnacle Entertainment Group. saramartinezauthor.com/

Will McDermott turned a love of science fiction and games into a writing career. He has published nine novels, more than 25 short stories, and helped create numerous worlds, characters, and stories for card, board, and video games. His fiction is often set in gaming universes, including *Magic: The Gathering, Warhammer 40K, Renegade Legion Universe, iMage Wars*. He is known for bringing larger-than-life characters alive, including *Warhammer's* Kal Jerico and Mad D'onne, Magic's Balthor the Stout and, more recently, *Night Stalker's* Carl Kolchak. Check out willmcdermott.com, w_mcdermott on Instagram or willmcdermott.author on Facebook.

Rob Nisbet has had over 100 stories printed in anthologies and magazines ranging from romance (using his wife's name) to horror. His wife has recently turned to crime. He lives in the sleepy cliff-top town of Peacehaven, near Brighton UK, where he plots his murders and other horrors while walking his ferocious little westie. He has won five international writing competitions including the 2022 Kepler Award for a sci-fi / fantasy short story. He also writes audio drama. He has adapted work by Philip K. Dick for radio and has had several audio scripts produced by Big Finish / BBC for their *Doctor Who* range.

Scott Pearson is a freelance writer and editor working across multiple genres in both traditional and indie publishing. His published works include short stories and novellas in humor, mystery, horror, urban fantasy, and science fiction in various anthologies, such as *Castle of Horror 4, 5, 7, 9,* and *10*. Scott's Star Trek fiction appears in anthologies and the e-book exclusive The More Things Change. For several years he has copyedited the Star Trek novels and edited and written for the Star Trek Adventures roleplaying game. Scott and his daughter, Ella, cohost the very occasional Generations Geek podcast. Scott and his wife, Sandra, live in the wilds of Minnesota. Visit him online at scott-pearson.com and generationsgeek.com. Follow him on Bluesky as @ scottpearson (or the same on Hive, Mastodon, Post, Spoutible, and Tribel) or on Threads as @smichaelpearson (or the same on that place formerly known as Twitter). Please stop Scott from starting an account on any other social media platforms. Oh, no, he just remembered he's also on Instagram.

Michael Joseph Tharnish Roby fancies himself a fantasy, comedy, and horror writer, occasionally juggling all three simultaneously. He started writing for puppet shows in first-grade, and never really stopped, even after Seton Hill University gave him an MFA for doing so. He was previously published in Back Roads Literary Review with the short story *The Decay Diary*, his take on the apocalypse by way of *Alice in Wonderland*. MJTR resides in Des Moines, Iowa, with his wife and too many pets, imagining whatever off-kilter thing he's going to write next. His musings, free short stories, and upcoming publication announcements can be found at mjtroby. wixsite.com/mjtrauthor.

Charles R. Rutledge is the author of *Dracula's Return*, and of three novels in the Griffin & Price supernatural suspense series, written with James A. Moore. His short stories and articles have appeared in over 50 anthologies, including *The Drive-In: Multiplex, Weird Tales: 100 Years of Weird,* and *Clickers Forever.* Charles keeps soil from Transylvania in an envelope on his desk, owns entirely too many editions of Dracula, and is seldom seen in daylight.

Melanie Schubert is a Croatian Australian who lives with anxiety disorder and likes writing about badass anxious characters who do it scared. She is a host and a creator of the writing podcast: Of the Publishing Persuasion, together with her wildly talented and hilarious co-host Angela Montoya (Author of *Sinners Isle 2023*). She has written multiple musical productions for the New Zealand performing arts company Gobsmacked for large-scale stage productions. She lives with her biscuit of a husband and one highly opinionated French Bulldog in Melbourne Australia, but a piece of her heart is always in Japan.

Heath W. Shelby is a horror aficionado…horror movies, video games and reading and writing horror fiction. Heath lives in Searcy, Arkansas with his daughter Caitlynn, her rowdy Boston Terrier Cocoa and his Maltizhu, Leia. Heath is also the father to his son Collin and grandfather to his son's Husky, Uki. Heath spends his free time writing, working as a College Admissions

Advisor, being the play-by-play radio voice for some local high school sports teams, listening to 80s music in his Mustang and hoping his 49ers will win one more Super Bowl within his lifetime. As a writer, Heath's work has so far appeared in *Castle of Horror Anthology Volumes 5, 8* and *10*. Facebook: facebook.com/heathwshelby - Instagram: the_heath_shelby - Twitter: @ heath_shelby

Bryan Young (he/they) works across many different media. His work as a writer and producer has been called "filmmaking gold" by *The New York Times.* He's also published comic books with Slave Labor Graphics and Image Comics. He's been a regular contributor for the Huffington Post, StarWars.com, Star Wars Insider magazine, SYFY, /Film, and was the founder and editor-in-chief of the geek news and review site Big Shiny Robot! In 2014, he wrote the critically acclaimed history book, *A Children's Illustrated History of Presidential Assassination.* He co-authored Robotech: The Macross Saga RPG and has written five books in the BattleTech Universe: *Honor's Gauntlet, A Question of Survival, Fox Tales, Without Question,* and the forthcoming *VoidBreaker.* His latest non-fiction tie-in book, *The Big Bang Theory Book of Lists* is a #1 Bestseller on Amazon. His work has won two Diamond Quill awards and in 2023 he was named Writer of the Year by the League of Utah Writers. He teaches writing for *Writer's Digest, Script Magazine,* and at the University of Utah. Follow him across social media @ swankmotron or visit swankmotron.com.

CASTLE BRIDGE MEDIA RECOMMENDS...

If you liked this book, you might also enjoy reading the following titles from Castle Bridge Media available on Amazon or by order at your favorite book store:

Animal Charmer
By Rain Nox

Austinites
By In Churl Yo

Bloodsucker City
By Jim Towns

The Burning Gem
By Don Sawyer

THE CASTLE OF HORROR ANTHOLOGY SERIES
Volume 1
Volume 2: *Holiday Horrors*
Volume 3: *Scary Summer Stories*
Volume 4: *Women Running From Houses*
Volume 5: *Thinly Veiled: The 70s*
Volume 6: *Femme Fatales**
Volume 7: *Love Gone Wrong*
Volume 8: *Thinly Veiled: The 80s*
Volume 9: *Young Adult*
Volume 10: *Thinly Veiled: Saturday Mournings*
Volume 11: *Revenge*
Edited By Jason Henderson and In Churl Yo
*Edited By P.J. Hoover

Castle of Horror Podcast Book of Great Horror: Our Favorites, Top Tens and Bizarre Pleasures
Edited By Jason Henderson

Cherry Dark
By R.L. Wilburn

Dream State
By Martin Ott

Dominic
By Lee Guzman

FRENCH DECEPTION
A Forgery in Paris
By Janice Nagourney
A Forgery in Lyon
By Janice Nagourney

FuturePast Sci-Fi Anthology
Edited by In Churl Yo

GLAZIER'S GAP
Ghosts of the Forbidden
By Leanna Renee Hieber

Hellfall
By Jay Gould

Isonation
By In Churl Yo

JAYU CITY CHRONICLES
The Hermes Protocol
By Chris M. Arnone
Necropolis Alpha
By Chris M. Arnone

Junk Film: Why Bad Movies Matter
By Katharine Coldiron

MID-LIFE CRISIS THRILLERS
18 Miles From Town
By Jason Henderson
Lost Angel
By Sam Knight
Ties That Kill
By Deven Greene

Nightwalkers: Gothic Horror Movies
By Bruce Lanier Wright

THE PATH
The Blue-Spangled Blue
By David Bowles
The Deepest Green
By David Bowles

SURF MYSTIC
Night of the Book Man
By Peyton Douglas
Dark of the Curl
By Peyton Douglas

Yesterday's Tomorrows: The Golden Age of Science Fiction Movies
By Bruce Lanier Wright

Please remember to leave us your reviews on Amazon and Goodreads!

THANK YOU FOR SUPPORTING INDEPENDENT PUBLISHERS AND AUTHORS!

castlebridgemedia.com

www.ingramcontent.com/pod-product-compliance
Lightning Source LLC
Chambersburg PA
CBHW022127310726
48972CB00007B/2224